School for Lovers
&
Other Tales

Kal Wagenheim

School for Lovers & Other Tales

Copyright © 2014 by Kal Wagenheim

ISBN: 9780996041331

Library of Congress Control Number: 2014943433

Cover design by All Things That Matter Press

Published in 2014 by All Things That Matter Press

To Olga, my dear wife,
also an accomplished scholar,
and
my Mom and Dad (both up in Heaven)

Table of Contents

School for Lovers

A horse-drawn carriage clip-clopped past 91 Spring Street in lower Manhattan. In a darkened bedroom inside the house, hushed voices were heard, some in English, some in Italian. Visitors quietly came and left. Lorenzo Da Ponte, eighty-nine years old, lay in a large bed. His head—crowned by long white hair—was propped up on a pillow. Near death, he appeared peaceful, serene. An ornate clock showed that it was nearly nine p.m. It was the night of August 17, 1838.

A few moments earlier, the Reverend John MacCloskey had received his confession and given him absolution. The priest emerged from the bedroom, left the door ajar, and silently nodded to the people waiting outside. Among them was the elderly man's son, Lorenzo, who had been hiking in the Adirondacks with a friend, when he received an urgent message to return home. By the son's side was his wife.

Three visitors entered: two handsome young women, Anna and Miriam, and Whitman, a tall young man. They approached the bed and looked down at Da Ponte. Tears welled in their eyes.

The elderly Da Ponte, his eyes closed, struggled to speak. He slowly began to recite the mourner's Kaddish, in Hebrew. *"Yisgadal, v'yiskadash sh'me rabbo, b'olmo deevro chiruseh v'yamlich …,"* He was praying for himself.

"He's delirious, babbling again," said another man, who was standing near the bedroom door.

"… malcuseh, b'chayechon uvyo-mechon, uv'chayey d'chol beys yisroel …."

"He told me once," recalled a Mr. Moore, "that as a youth, he studied many languages, even the ancient tongue of the Hebrews."

"… baagolo uvizman koreev …."

"Perhaps he is dreaming of his childhood."

"Yisborach v'yishtabach v'yispoar v'yisromam v'yisnaseh …"

The funeral took place two days later, at noon on August 19, a brilliant summer day, at St. Patrick's Old Cathedral on Eleventh Street in lower Manhattan. Allegri's *Miserere* was performed over Lorenzo Da Ponte's remains. On the coffin was a laurel wreath and before it, on the way from the church to the Roman cemetery at Second Avenue where he was borne and followed by a long train of mourners led by the officiating priests and the attendant physician, was a banner. On its black background was the following inscription in gold letters:

"LAURENTIUS DA PONTE
Italia. Natus.

Littterarum. Reipublicae. et. Musis.
Patriae. et. Concivium. Amantissimus.
Christianae. Fidei. Cultor. Adsiduus.
In. Pace. et. Consolatione. Justorum.
VXII. die. Augusti. MDCCCXXXVIII.
XC. Anno. Aetatis. Suae.
Ampelxu. Domini Ascendit."

At the cemetery, a priest concluded a final prayer: "... the Father, the Son, and the Holy Ghost. Amen." The mourners began to disperse, shaking hands, embracing. Two of the mourners, men in early middle-age, struck up a conversation.

"I was a student of Signor Da Ponte's some years ago."

"So was I. He was a remarkable teacher, wasn't he?"

"Yes he was. Very devoted. Inspiring."

"Of course there were always strange rumors floating about—"

"Such as?"

"Someone said that he was a Jew."

The other laughed. "I heard just the opposite. People used to whisper about him once having been a Catholic priest."

"A priest?"

"It could have all been a misunderstanding. He often spoke about his esteemed uncle and benefactor, a Bishop Da Ponte, in Venice, so perhaps some people thought that he, too, was a man of the church."

"Well, it doesn't really matter now, does it? He's gone."

"Yes," said the other. "One might ask to what extent one man can truly know another. All we can be sure of, I would guess, is that he was a charming old fellow, and that his name was Lorenzo Da Ponte."

Whitman said goodbye to Miriam and Anna who walked away with a young man towards a waiting carriage. Whitman strolled towards the cemetery exit with Mr. Moore.

"Such a fine gentleman," said Whitman.

"Yes, indeed," said Mr. Moore. "Did you know him long?"

"We met five years ago"

* * *

The choppy waters of the East River gleamed in the sun that cool November morning in 1833. As the ferry bobbed along towards Lower Manhattan from the Brooklyn shore, an Italian immigrant sang a boisterous tune and accompanied himself with an accordion.

Non piu andrai, farfallone amoroso,
Notte e giorno d'intorno girando,

Delle belle turbando il riposo,
Narcisetto, Adoncino d'amor...

Several of the passengers—who understood not a word of the foreign ditty, but tapped their toes to its lively rhythm—dropped coins into a tin cup resting on the floor in front of the musician.

Among the crowd on board was a tall, plainly dressed, dreamy-eyed young man of nineteen. In one hand he held a newspaper. In the right-hand pocket of his outer jacket was a pencil and a notebook. As he leaned against the rail, contemplating the water, the land to his west, and the stiff breeze in his face, he listened to his own inner music and composed vivid images in his mind's eye: *An island sixteen miles long, solid-founded; City of hurried and sparkling waters; City of spires and masts; City nested in bays; My city.*

Had he dreamed it all? Thinking back on the past year teaching on Long Island, he recalled writing to a friend: "I am getting to be a miserable kind of dog; I am sick of wearing away by inches, and spending the fairest portion of my little span of life, here in this nest of bears, this forsaken of all God's creation; among clowns and country bumpkins, flat-heads and coarse brown-faced girls, dirty, ill-favored young brats with squalling throats, and crude manners, and bog-trotters, with all the disgusting conceit, of ignorance and vulgarity. Life is a dreary road."

Or had it been a nightmare? Last winter in Southold, a Puritanical rural town, for example. Male teachers often boarded with the families of students and slept in the attic with one or more of the boys. One farmer had reproved him for making a "pet" of his son who returned the affection, but what was the harm in that? "You never paid much attention to girls," his brother George would say. And one Sunday, Reverend Smith preached from the pulpit of the First Presbyterian Church about his "behavior to the children and his goings on." Reports of "bloody bedding" would emerge later. A furious mob had gone to nearby Kettle Hill where hot tar was always available for mending fishing nets. The young teacher hid in an attic, but the mob found him there, cowering beneath a pile of straw summer mattresses. They seized him, plastered tar and feathers on his hair and clothes, and rode him out of town. It took him a month to recover. The school where he taught was renamed The Sodom School. No, it hadn't really happened. It was, indeed, a nightmare. But now all that was behind him.

The ferry reached the Manhattan shore and the passengers disembarked. The young man strode along bustling lower Broadway, clogged with pedestrians, horse-drawn carriages, sidewalk vendors, past a brick wall with a poster that proclaimed: "Andrew Jackson for President." In his reverie, he thought: *The downtown streets, the jobbers' houses of business, the houses of business of the ship-merchants and money-brokers, the river-streets, Trottoirs thronged, vehicles, Broadway, the women, the shops and shows.*

Several minutes later, the young man reached the doorway of a small shop where the sign read:

Da Ponte
Imported Books
336 Broadway

He hesitated, peered inside, then entered. The small shop was cluttered. Old, leather-bound books, with their strong aroma, were stacked everywhere. Italian titles: Dante, Petrarch, Tasso, Metastasio.

Seated, reading and savoring a glass of red wine, nibbling at a plate of bread and cheese, was an elderly man who resembled an Old Testament patriarch. He had a stately presence, a Roman countenance, with long, abundant white hair that fell luxuriantly around his neck. His cheeks were sunken. On the wall directly behind hung a large oil portrait in a gilt frame. A very good likeness, the young visitor thought to himself.

"Mr. Da Ponte? Lorenzo Da Ponte?"

The man rose from his seat. His mannerisms were courtly. He spoke English fluently, but with a trace of a lisp in his speech as if with a foreign accent. He also knew Italian, Greek, Latin, Hebrew, German, and Spanish.

"At your service. I have a complete selection of Italian literature and Columbia University, where I have had the honor to teach, acquired from me more than one hundred volumes for its library."

The old man hesitated, picked up a copy of book, and continued, "Ah, perhaps you would like a copy of my memoirs? They are in Italian, of course. Do you read Italian?"

"No, I—"

"My son Lorenzo is preparing an English translation," said the old man. "There is great interest in the story of my life. The book has received excellent ... no, superb reviews in Italy and in Germany. With lessons you could learn Italian. I have taught hundreds, thousands, of Americans to read and write Italian."

Da Ponte noticed that his young visitor was looking at the oil portrait. "Do you like it? A young man, Morse is his name, had me pose last year. He used to come here all the time to look at my books and chat. Very bright fellow. But now he's off working on mad inventions. Sending messages by electrical impulses, he said. Tried to explain it to me. But I said, 'I'm from the old school. What's wrong with a quill and ink?'" The elderly DaPonte hesitated again, eyeing the young man suspiciously. "You're not by any chance a bill collector, are you?

"No, no. I'm a newspaper reporter. Walter Whitman. I've just begun publishing a weekly paper out in Huntington. The Long Islander. Here's the latest issue. I had hoped to interview you about the new Italian opera house that's opening tonight."

Da Ponte took the paper from young Whitman, glanced at it, and put it aside. "You know opera, Signor Whitman?"

"I've heard so little, but I adore the passion behind it. I don't think there's anything more sensuous, yet more spiritual."

"Good, good. First I must tell you how I came to write the libretto for Figaro, which will be presented tonight ... how I met the immortal Mozart."

"Mozart? What nationality is that? Isn't an Italian opera being performed tonight?"

"You mean to say you don't know Mozart?"

"So little opera comes here to New York. I've only been to the opera twice. Donizetti, and Rossini, I think."

"But Mozart was the greatest of them all, young man. A genius! He was the prize of Emperor Joseph's court."

"Emperor Joseph?"

"Yes, of course," Da Ponte snapped impatiently. "It was more than forty years ago. I was a young man then."

"And you knew the Emperor, too?"

"His Majesty, may he repose in Heaven, Mozart, Salieri, Martini, Haydn, Metastasio, I knew them all when I lived in Vienna." Reaching over for a program, he added, "This is the program for tonight's opera."

Holding the program, the young Whitman read aloud: "The Marriage of Figaro. Music by Wolfgang Amadeus Mozart. Libretto: Lorenzo Da Ponte..."

Bowing, the elderly Da Ponte said, "Your humble servant." Then, turning querulous, he said, "But who, I ask you, remembers the architect of the story, the skilled weaver of the lyrics, the poor librettist? Is that fair? Now, the music, of course, is important, but what about the poetry?"

Whitman reached in his pocket, pulled out his notebook and pencil. He stared intently at the old man with a combination of reverence and curiosity. "Tell me, Signor Da Ponte, how long have you been in America? And what brought you here?"

"That, young man, is a long story. Please sit down. Have some wine. I make it myself. It's quite delicious."

Before Whitman could respond, Da Ponte reached over for another wine glass, filled it, and moved the plate of bread and cheese closer to him. He raised his glass in a brief toast, took a generous sip, and pointed to an ornate, yellowing map of Italy on the wall next to his portrait. He reached over again for a copy of his memoirs, opened the book, and placed it in his lap.

"I was born eighty-four years ago in Ceneda, a small but not obscure city of the Venetian state, in the province of Treviso. Death robbed me of my dear mother when I was five. My father completely neglected my education. Up to my fourteenth year, reading and writing was the extent of my knowledge. I was left completely ignorant in all branches of letters, and while people kept exclaiming, 'Oh, how clever. How talented.' I could inwardly feel only shame at being the least educated of all the young boys in Ceneda. They used to call me, in jest, the clever dunce. I could not tell how deeply all this stung me. One day I chanced to go up to our garret where my father was prone to throw his old papers. I came upon some books that constituted, I believe, the family library including the Buova d'Antona, the Fuggilozio, the Guerin Meschino, Barlaam and Jehosaphat, Cassandra, Bertold, and a few stray volumes of Metastasio. I read them all with incredible avidity; but the author I read twice was Metastasio, the Poet Laureate of Austria, whose verses aroused in my soul the very emotions of music itself. And then, in my fourteenth year …

***

"It was August 19, 1763, the feast of the beheading of St. John the Baptist. A salvo of cannon thundered from Monte di S. Paolo, which rose steeply above the houses; the five bells of the cathedral rang out in response, and the bells of all the principal churches chimed in their turn. The Bishop of Ceneda, Lorenzo Da Ponte, a man of renowned piety, emerged from the Castello di S. Martino and made his stately way along the winding road which leads down to Ceneda. He was preceded by a company of halberdiers in ceremonial dress, drums beating. Next came his household in their best clothes, followed by a large number of clerics. The bishop was accompanied by deputies of the city and by members of the noblest families. In the midst of this grand cortege were the four people: Geremia Conegliano, age forty-one, a Jewish tanner and dealer in leather, and his three sons, Emanuele, age fourteen, Baruch, age eleven, and Anania, age nine, who were to be baptized. Geremia's wife, Rachele Ghella Pincherle, the mother of the three boys, had died nine years earlier. Flanked by their godparents, and the neighbors, they entered the cathedral, which was richly adorned for the occasion. With joyous pomp were received into the Catholic Church.

"The Conegliano family was not unknown in northern Italy. In fact, there was a town of the same name a few miles away from Ceneda. The family had produced a number of scholars, among them Dr. Israel Conegliano, a physician and statesman. He had played such a key role in Venetian-Turkish diplomatic relations late in the previous century that he was rewarded by being made exempt from the severe laws regulating Jewish life in Venice. But Geremia Conegliano belonged to a less distinguished branch of the family; the members were artisans, and lived in near poverty.

Geremia, a widower, had fallen in love with Orsola Pasqua Paietta, a girl of not yet seventeen, who was a Christian. The solution to this dilemma was clear. 'Geremia Conegliano,' said Bishop Da Ponte, following an established custom, 'I baptize thee, and grant thee my surname. From this day forth you are Gasparo DaPonte.' Turning to the three sons, the Bishop smiled. 'Baruch Conegliano, I rename thee Girolamo Da Ponte. Anania Conegliano, I rename thee Luigi Da Ponte.' Then, with a benevolent smile, the Bishop said, 'And the eldest boy, Emanuele Conegliano, I give thee my name, Lorenzo Da Ponte.'

"Mass was celebrated. Bishop Da Ponte, a kindly man, gave a brief but loving address which brought tears to the eyes of his listeners. That night, in the piazza of Ceneda, exploding fireworks lit up the evening sky. The citizens of Ceneda, and the many visitors who had come to share in the festivities, crowded into the piazza to gawk at the spectacular display devised by the famous Professor Gaetano Sarti of Bologna. The brilliant lights were reflected in the faces of the citizenry who gazed skyward. Bishop Da Ponte stood between Geremia Congeliano, now Gasparo Da Ponte, and his young bride-to-be, Orsola. They would be married in two weeks and in the following years she would bear him no less than three more sons and seven daughters. Next to the father were his three sons. Next to Orsola were her parents.

"Turning to Gasparo, Bishop Da Ponte said, 'For too many years you have lived as a widower, and your children have been deprived of a mother. Now that you have embraced the Holy Mother Church, you are free to marry this good Christian girl.' The Bishop placed a fatherly hand on her shoulder.

"Young Emanuele, now renamed Lorenzo, exchanged glances with his future stepmother, who was just three years older than he. She appeared apprehensive. A year earlier, Lorenzo had stood in the synagogue and performed his first act as an adult, reading from the torah for his bar mitzvah ceremony, making him responsible before God for his actions. Now, stirred on the one hand by the desire to embellish my mind with some enlightenment," Da Ponte recalled, "and foreseeing, on the other, what the consequences of such an unbalanced marriage would be, I sought to obtain from the charity of others what I could not hope to gain from paternal solicitude." He shyly approached the Bishop.

"Yes, my son?"

"Your Excellency, my brother and I hope to pursue our education, in literature. Is there a place for us in your seminary?

"Bishop Da Ponte beamed with pleasure and put his arm around the boy, drawing him closer in an affectionate hug. A Venetian patrician, the Bishop spent little money on himself. He paid for much of the cost of rebuilding the cathedral. He constantly visited the sick, the aged and the needy. Each year he provided clothing, and sometimes beds, for several hundred people. He also supported the Ceneda seminary where he strived to recruit the best teachers and students.

The next day, in the seminary, Bishop Da Ponte counted out money as he sat talking with an official. 'We are bringing two young sons of Israel into the flock of The Holy Father. Here are funds to pay for their studies. This is God's work.' Thus, Lorenzo and Girolamo entered the Ceneda seminary, which had been founded in the sixteenth century by Bishop Mocenigo, a member of an illustrious family of Venetian patricians. Young Lorenzo was eager for an education. His father had, for a time, provided him with a tutor, but the man proved inefficient and brutal. Left to his own devices, Lorenzo eagerly read the few books he found among the rubbish in the garret of his home. He dreamt of a life of literature, but other things were in store for him.

"My father, being deceived in the choice of my career, and allowing himself to be guided rather by his circumstances than by his parental duty, was thinking of turning me to the Altar, though that was utterly contrary to my vocation and my character," he told Whitman. "I was therefore trained after the manner of the priests, though inclined by taste and, as it were, made by nature for different pursuits.

"Some weeks later, in an austere room of the seminary, with a large crucifix looking down upon him from the wall, young Lorenzo Da Ponte wrote a letter in awkward, ungrammatical Italian, to Dom Pietro Pietro Bortoluzzi, the priest who was instructing him. 'Esteemed Father, thanks to the lessons I have received, I can now see the eternal truth of the Christian Church. How I lament with bitter shame the blindness of the poor Jews! I have no words to thank God, who has rescued me from the clutches of the Pharaohs. How gracious the Lord has been to me!'"

***

Strolling through the garden of the Seminary, the Da Ponte brothers were chatting with fellow students when they encountered the Bishop. With his usual benevolent smile, the Bishop asked, "And how are my young scholars today?"

In unison, Lorenzo and Girolamo responded, "Very well, thank you, Your Excellency."

"I've received good reports about both of you," the Bishop said. "Lorenzo, they tell me that after just six months you know by heart almost all of Dante's Inferno."

Girolamo interrupted, "It's true, Your Excellency, and all the best sonnets of Petrarch, and the most beautiful works of Ariosto and Tasso. He has a formidable memory. He also writes his own poetry."

"That is wonderful," the Bishop said. "You must show it to me someday."

"In less than two years I had not only translated into verse, *diurna et nocturna manu*, all the ancient poets, but read and reread all those Italians who circulate as writers of real merit," he told Whitman. "And I was not content with reading them. I must needs transfer into Latin the noblest passages of our authors, copying and recopying them again and again, criticizing them, expounding them, learning them by heart, trying my hand repeatedly at every style of meter and composition, striving to imitate the most beautiful thoughts, to use the most graceful phrases, to select the most elegant expressions employed by my usual standard bearers, preferring always and above all others those of my idolized Petrarch, in whose every verse I seemed to find some new treasure at each rereading."

"I have read a little of Petrarch," said Whitman.

"Ah, so you know his poetry?" said Da Ponte.

"Only in English translation. I hope to read it someday in the original Latin, to get the true flavor."

"Good, good. Petrarch was a genius at expressing true emotions. His love sonnets are indescribably beautiful. Well, as I was saying, some poetic talent I had been endowed with by Nature, and my infinite passion for poetry would perhaps have earned for me one day the rank and reputation of a good poet. Had Fortune not interfered continually with my worthy intentions, and drawn me with tyrannical hand into the cruelest and most dangerous whirlpools of life …"

Five years later, on July 7, 1768, the pale corpse of Bishop Lorenzo Da Ponte lay in a coffin in the Ceneda Cathedral, as mourners filed by. Among them was a grief-stricken Lorenzo Da Ponte, now nineteen years old.

The elderly Da Ponte sipped at his wine and told Whitman, "Upon the death of my benefactor, the Bishop, the state of poverty in which my family found itself at that time caused me to renounce the hand of a noble and beautiful girl whom I tenderly loved and induced me to embrace a calling wholly contrary to my temperament, my character, and principles. This opened the door to a thousand dangers and strange vicissitudes, of which the envy, hypocrisy, and malice of my enemies rendered me for more than twenty years a pitiable victim."

"Victim? I don't understand," said Whitman.

Allowing a flicker of a smile, Da Ponte replied, "Permit me, young man, to cover with a veil of mystery this painful moment in my life.

"In the Ceneda Cathedral, as the Bishop Da Ponte's funeral came to a conclusion, Lorenzo was engaged in a heated discussion with his father. 'Father, how can I be a priest? I love the seminary, but I have a sweetheart, Pierina. You know her. I want to marry someday, just like you. I don't want to be a priest!'

"'Son, the Bishop was our protector,' Gasparo Da Ponte replied. 'Now that he is gone, who will pay for your studies? I am poor. As priests, you are taken care of by the Church. You don't know how fortunate you are, with so many people near starvation. Look around you. Is that what you want? Think of your future'"

November 1771. The rear of his head shaved, in the traditional tonsure of the Roman Catholic priesthood, Lorenzo, now twenty-two years old, devoted himself to teaching philosophy and mathematics at the Portogruaro Seminary. He entered the office of Monsignor Gabrielli, Bishop of Concordia, who directed the Seminary. The Monsignor was at his desk. "Your Excellency sent for me?"

"Yes, Lorenzo. You have been here for two years. We are very pleased with your teaching."

"Thank you, Your Excellency. As a biblical scholar once said, *umitalmidai rabadi miculam*, I have learned from my pupils."

"That's Hebrew, isn't it?"

"Yes, Excellency. I studied it assiduously in my youth."

"Ah, yes. Very good. I called you in today because of the recent death of the vice rector. The position, Chair of Rhetoric, requires supervising discipline and teaching Italian to fifty of our best students. The pay is forty ducats a year. Despite your youth, I think you are capable of fulfilling such duties."

"I shall do everything possible to live up to your expectations, Excellency."

"Very well. We shall discuss the details tomorrow afternoon."

"Your Excellency, perhaps this is not the proper moment to ask, but in a few weeks the carnival is being celebrated in Venice. I have never attended. Might I spend a few days there?"

"Yes, of course." Smiling, the Monsignor added, "Be careful, my son. Venice is a city of great culture, but it leads many souls astray. "

A gondola glided along a Venetian canal, between magnificent mansions. Its passenger was a handsome young priest, with dark penetrating eyes. He was completely bedazzled by this, his first visit to such a seductive city.

"Unfortunately, I went to Venice," Da Ponte told Whitman. "I was at the boiling point of youthful spirit. Eager and lively by temperament, and, as everyone said, attractive in person, I allowed myself, through the customs and examples about me, as well as by my own inclinations, to be swept away into a life of voluptuousness and amusement, forgetting or neglecting literature and my studies almost entirely."

"There was a popular saying in Venice, 'A little Mass in the morning, a little gamble in the afternoon, and a little lady in the evening,'" recalled Kelly, the great tenor of his era, in a memoir. "Venice! Dear beautiful Venice. Never shall I forget the sensations of surprise and delight which I experienced when I first caught sight of thee. Thy noble palaces and the magnificent churches with their cloud-capped spires. The Venetians are adorers of music. At La Pieta foundling hospital, there were a thousand girls, one hundred and forty of whom were musicians. The churches were crowded when they gave concerts. While the performance was going on, the most perfect silence was observed. But, at the conclusion of a piece of music, which excited their approbation, the audience expressed it in the most extraordinary manner; they coughed aloud, scraped their feet on the ground, but for some moments, did not utter a word. A practical way of pointing out the beauty of concord in opposition to the horrors of discord. In this city are innumerable pleasures; your youth and good spirits will lay you open to many temptations; but against one thing, and one thing only, I particularly caution you: never utter one word against the laws or customs of Venice. Do not suffer yourself to be betrayed even into a jest on this subject. You never know to whom you speak. In every corner spies are lurking, numbers of whom are employed at a high price to ensnare the unwary and report the language of strangers. But with no protection than a silent tongue, you may do what you like and enjoy everything without molestation. Venice. Dear beautiful Venice; scene of harmony and love where all was gayety and mirth, revelry and pleasure, with what warm feelings do I recall thee to my memory. Day and night were the gondoliers singing barcarolles, or the verses of Tasso and Ariosto to Venetian air. There were barges full of musicians on the Grand Canale serenading their enamoratas; the Piazza of St. Marc brilliantly lighted up; ten thousand masks and ballad singers; the coffee houses filled with beautiful women with their *cicisbeos*, their lovers; or if alone, unmolested, taking their refreshments and enjoying themselves without restraint.

"It was an ancient custom in Venice for personages of a certain vocation to have their portraits painted and hung out the windows of their apartments, to attract notice and visitors. Venice was the paradise of women, and the Venetian woman worthy of a paradise at least of Mahomet's. They were perfect Houri and the Venetian dialect spoken by a lovely woman is the softest and most delicious music in the world to him whom she favors. In short, a Venetian woman, in her zindale dress, well answers young Mirable's description in the play of Inconstant. 'Give me the plump Venetian, who smiles upon me like the glowing sun, and meets my lips like sparkling wine; her person shining as the glass, her spirit like foaming liquor.'"

"The functions in Passion week were carried on with great solemnity," recalled Kelly. "The Doge went in procession to St. Marc, where there were six orchestras erected, and High Mass celebrated. The fair of the Ascension lasted fifteen days. All the theatres were open and at night St. Marc's was brilliantly illuminated. On the Day of the Ascension, the Doge went in grand procession to marry the sea. A singular, magnificent sight. The Doge left Venice in his beautiful *bucantore*, which contained nearly three hundred persons. It was superbly adorned and carried twenty-one oars on each side. There were several bands of music on board. On reaching a certain point, the Doge threw a plain gold ring into the sea saying, 'We marry thee, O Sea in sign of true and perpetual dominion.' He then returned to Venice in the same order; the sea covered with gondolas, barges and boats, and the spectators rending the air with acclamations.

"Venice was always well lighted," Kelly continued. "The shops were kept open until twelve o'clock at night, and most of them not shut at all. The blaze of light which they gave is great, particularly in the Piazza St. Marc and the Freseria, where all the chief milliners and haberdashers live. The taverns were also open the greater part of the night, and supper always ready on the shortest notice. Everyone wore a mask. Nobleman and beggar, artisan and poet, gondolier and visiting royalty, even priests and nuns mingled under the clear winter sky. In the gorgeous rooms of the Ridotto, throngs of masked gamblers crowded around the tables— entire patrimonies were swept away. Gallantry, introduced from Spain a century before, had degenerated into that *cicisbeismo* so vividly depicted by Goldoni in his plays, which found recognition even in some marriage contracts, in which it was stipulated how many *cicisbei* the bride should be permitted to have, and who they were to be, wrote Russo, the historian. Often, the *cicisbeo's* place was usurped by some foppish little abbe, all made up, perfumed and powdered, who, despite the tonsure, danced the minuet, improvised madrigals and toasts, and excelled in all society graces."

* * *

Along a Venice canal, a full-length window of a decaying palace was open. Inside the darkened room, on a large bed, Lorenzo Da Ponte lay naked, passionately entangled with Angiola Tiepolo, a woman in her mid-twenties who was a girl of the poorer branch of the aristocratic Tiepolo family. He was clearly enthralled with her.

"I had conceived a very violent passion for one of the most beautiful, but at the same time, most capricious ladies of that metropolis," he told Whitman. "She occupied all my time in the usual follies and frivolities of love and jealousy, in convivialities, carousals and debaucheries. Angela was tiny, delicate, gentle; a complexion white as the snow with soft and languorous eyes and two charming dimples in her cheeks, like fresh blown roses. She had no great education, but she was gifted with such charm of manner and such vivacity of speech that she not only won her way into one's heart, but fairly bewitched everyone. I fell in love with her. I knew it was wrong."

A young child began to cry. Angiola arose, draped a sheet around her nude body, walked into another room and brought back with her a baby boy, several months old. She lay back down on the bed, next to Da Ponte, and gave the child milk from one breast. Da Ponte lay next to her, at peace, his cheek nuzzled against her other bare breast.

"Not long after I had this little boy," she said, "my husband, who is much older than me, decided to leave and he became a priest." With her free hand, she messed Da Ponte's hair. "Now the Church has returned to me a handsome young lover."

"I don't understand, Angiola. You live in this big palace with your brother. Yet you are poor."

"We are Barnabotti."

"Barnabotti?"

"Long ago we all lived in the parish of St.Barnabas, which is why we are called Barnabotti. The state forbids us to take up employment, but we receive public dole from the state. As families of the nobility it is our birthright."

"The state supports you?"

"Just barely. We are only a little better off than the beggars. That's why my brother Antonio and I go to the Ridotto, to see if we can win a fortune.

"Still flourishing in those days in Venice was the famous gambling house known commonly as the Pubblico Ridotto, or Resort, which was open during Carnival season," he told Whitman. "At the Ridotto, wealthy noblemen alone enjoyed the privilege of playing to unlimited stakes with their own money and the poor, for a certain consideration, with the money of others; with the money, to be exact, of numerous fat-pursed descendants of Abraham."

Three years later, Da Ponte, now 25, appeared at the door of Teresa's bedroom.

"Where were you?"

"With friends at the Cafe de' Letterati."

"Friends?"

"We talk about literature."

"What is her name?"

"You think I am like your brother, gambling and whoring all the time?"

"What is her name?" Teresa flung a bottle of ink at Da Ponte. He raised his hand to shield his face. The bottle crashed against the wall. His face was spattered with ink and his hand drenched in ink and blood. Teresa, suddenly remorseful, rushed over to comfort him.

Later that night, Da Ponte lay in bed asleep, his hand bandaged. Teresa, awake next to him, raised a pair of scissors and carefully clipped off all the hair that curled down about his neck.

The next morning, Da Ponte looked in a mirror and was shocked. A servant entered. "A lady to see you, Master Lorenzo."

Moments later, Da Ponte, hand bandaged, hair roughly shorn, came to the door of the palace where an elegantly dressed woman was waiting. Da Ponte was embarrassed to be seen like this. The woman also seemed uncomfortable.

"Signora—"

"Abbe Da Ponte ... I ... my sons have been expecting you for the past few days for their lessons. When you didn't come, I thought perhaps you were ill."

The woman spotted Teresa, scantily dressed, smirking, several feet behind Da Ponte. The woman stiffened, turned, and walked away.

"So that's my rival," said Teresa.

Da Ponte glared at her angrily. "She paid me handsomely to tutor her sons. Now, she'll dismiss me."

"You'll find another patron." Teresa embraced him and kissed him fiercely on the lips. Da Ponte stood immobile, cold. Teresa pushed him away.

"Go," she said. "Good riddance."

Two years later, in 1776, Da Ponte sat in the library of the Treviso Seminary, writing at a table, books piled high in front of him. His brother Girolamo entered, and peered over his shoulder.

"I'm composing some Latin verses for the students to recite on commencement day."

"And the theme?"

"Happiness. For example: The laws of society distribute wealth unequally. Thus, happiness is more easily attained by some, and less by others."

Girolamo shook his head disapprovingly. "In just two years you've risen from librarian to professor. Why—"

"It's just an exercise," Da Ponte said. "In another poem I support the opposite view: the rich are no happier than the poor. We must stimulate the students to *think*."

"You risk offending certain—"

Da Ponte, annoyed, interrupted. "Only the most dim-witted, evil people could misinterpret this."

In the garden of the Treviso Seminary on August 1, 1776, a graduation ceremony was underway before a large audience, including the Bishop of Treviso and other dignitaries. Judging from the expressions of several priests in the crowd, they were displeased. As Professor Da Ponte looked on proudly, a student read aloud in halting Latin, "*Miraris, Licini, quod nec equo potens. Threicio, Zephyris ocyor, aut Noto.*"

The priests whispered among themselves. "I've heard this Da Ponte is a Jew," said one, "but now I wonder, perhaps he's an atheist."

Another said, "Who gave him permission to publish such trash?"

Still another added, "I'm going to write to the bishop's chancellor in Venice."

On December 14, 1776, a crowd gathered in a room of the Venetian Senate. Da Ponte, looking quite nervous, was present with his brother Girolamo. A distinguished man in his forties approached. Da Ponte whispered to his brother, "It's Senator Memmo."

"Young man," the Senator said, "your poems are most amusing."

"Thank you, Excellency."

. "We're here to lend you a little support. My friend, Signor Pietro Antonio Zaguri, is from one of the great families of Venice." Memmo gestured towards another man, seated nearby, also in his forties, stylish, haughty, androgynous.

Da Ponte bowed slightly in Zaguri's direction. Zaguri acknowledged with a nod and a raised eyebrow.

The procurator, a short, hunch-backed man in his sixties, rose. He held the booklet of poems in one hand, at a distance, as though it were a foul-smelling object. "Your Excellencies, listen to this so-called *teacher*. 'Man cannot reach happiness by following the impulses of his heart. He is prevented from doing so by the laws of society.' This *teacher* challenges the right of a father to refuse his daughter's hand to the man she loves."

There were murmurs from the crowd.

"He questions the right of the state to compel military service. He even says that if a man enjoys gambling and singing, the state has no right to force him to work for his daily bread."

Laughter from the crowd.

"Excellencies," the Procurator continued, "the rumblings of revolution are being heard in France. And what is happening in England's American colonies as I speak? Where would we be if such ideas took root in Venice? This so-called teacher is poisoning the minds of our youth."

It was now Da Ponte's turn to defend himself. He stood up and scornfully said, "Yes, I did write the little poetic skit mentioned by my accuser, but for no other reason than to supply *practice* for my pupils in the art of declamation. In fact, I refute this poem in the opposing thesis."

He held up the pamphlet. "He fails to mention my poem which says that *the rich are not happier than the poor*. Or another, which develops the idea that *a king is not happier than his subjects*. Or still another which affirms that *laws are a necessity, since human frailty requires them*. What most disturbs me is that nowhere does my accuser reflect an appreciation of the *beauty* of these verses, over which I labored so hard. But no matter. As I say in still another of my sonnets, *The learned man is not happier than the ignorant*."

With this comment, several spectators erupted in laughter, which angered the Procurator. Senator Memmo whispered to a fellow senator. "This young man has talent."

"So much the worse," the senator replied. "We must deprive him of the means of becoming dangerous."

Later that day, the sentence was read by a Senate official. As the official's voice droned on, Da Ponte bowed his head, but appeared to be unperturbed. "All copies of the poems are to be confiscated. The Senate orders an investigation of Radicalism in the schools of the Most Serene Venetian Republic. The Abbe, and converted Jew Lorenzo Da Ponte are dismissed."

Laughter and clinking wineglasses were heard at a party in the sumptuous home of Signor Zaguri. Da Ponte, surrounded by male and female admirers, was enjoying his notoriety among the intelligentsia of Venice. His brother Girolamo looked on, concerned.

Senator Memmo told Da Ponte, "You're fortunate. Here in Venice, people have been thrown into prison for lesser offenses."

Caterino Mazzola, a man in this thirties, approached.

Zaguri introduced them. "Da Ponte, meet Caterino Mazzola. He is a poet and librettist, like yourself."

"We have something else in common," Mazzola said. "I was once a student at the seminary."

Zaguri interrupted, "And this is a dear friend of mine, Giacomo Casanova." Casanova was a tall man in his early fifties whose best years were behind him, but he still cut an imposing figure.

Hours later, the party was over, but Da Ponte, Zaguri and Casanova remained, sipping wine. "I spent many a delightful afternoon discussing literature with Zaguri and Casanova," Da Ponte recalled to Whitman.

Zaguri roared with laughter while Da Ponte looked on, spellbound, as Casanova recounted story after story: "But that was nothing. In Paris, I met a young nobleman from Treviso, Count Eduardo Tiretta. The ladies called him Count Six Times, because of his stamina."

"I thought Casanova yielded to no one," said Zaguri.

"He was my better," said Casanova. "Once we met two ladies, a beautiful young virgin and her older aunt, fat, foul-smelling breath, but very rich. We hired a window overlooking the Place de Greve to witness the execution of a young man who had tried to murder Louis the Fifteenth. Actually, he just nicked the King in the arm with a small knife. The window was narrow, so we invited the ladies to stand on a step in front. I stood behind the young woman, and Count Tiretta stood behind Auntie. Hideous screams were heard from below. The poor fellow's flesh was torn with red-hot pincers. Molten lead and boiling oil were poured into his wounds. But Count Six Times had other things on his mind. He opened the front of his trouser, lifted Auntie's skirt from the rear, and mounted her. As the agonized screams continued, I engaged the innocent young woman in conversation to divert her attention from the gymnastics going on beside her."

Zaguri raised in inquisitive eyebrow. "And Auntie?"

"Never batted an eye. Merely appeared a bit … pensive. The execution lasted several hours. While the priests prayed over the poor wretch, four horses tore his body limb from limb."

"And how did you know the young lady was a virgin?" Zaguri asked.

"The next day, when she unwisely bent over to pick a flower," Casanova replied, "my curiosity got the best of me."

Zaguri burst out laughing. He turned to Da Ponte, who was also enjoying himself, but more quietly. "I don't believe half the things he says, but he is *so* amusing, don't you think?"

Da Ponte asked, "Have you been here in Venice very long, Signor Casanova?"

"Two years this time."

"Guess how he earns his living," said Zaguri. "Guess."

In a loud whisper, Casanova said, "The Holy Inquisitors have engaged me as a spy to check on the morals of the citizenry."

"Hah!" said Zaguri.

"Oh, it's arduous work," said Casanova. "I recently sent them a report about an art class where there were *nude models*. I also sent them a list of the chief works of pornography and blasphemy to be found in private collections, after rigorous personal inspections, of course." Zaguri laughed again.

Casanova turned to Da Ponte. "What are your plans?"

"I have few prospects at the moment," said Da Ponte.

"I know the Senate has banned you from teaching," said Zaguri, "but it can be done discreetly. Giorgio Pisani, a nobleman, would like you to tutor his sons."

"Be careful," Casanova warned him. "Pisani is an enemy of the government. Teach his children, but don't get mixed up with him."

Patrons in a cafe were laughing as they read the text of a poem. "I foolishly ignored Casanova's advice," Da Ponte explained to Whitman. "To support Pisani, I wrote a poem mocking three prominent senators. They sought revenge."

Not long afterwards, someone deposited a bulky letter into the mouth of the bronze statue of a lion at San Moise, Venice. That letter soon became crucial evidence in a Venice courtroom. A sign on the door read *Esecutori Contro La Bestemmia*. Several witnesses were there to testify against Da Ponte, who was being tried in absentia.

The court official, holding the letter, droned on in a loud monotone, "This letter accuses the Abbe Lorenzo Da Ponte of horrid and enormous crimes. He has embraced the Christian faith, only to trample on it and ridicule it. He has seduced a married woman and procreated with her in scorn of the sacraments."

A spectator rose angrily from his seat. "Crucifier. Go back to the Ghetto, whence came your despicable ancestors."

"Silence," the official ordered, as he continued reading. "The victim is Angioletta Bellaudi. At age fifteen, she was married to a Signor Bellaudi. The accused, Abbe Lorenzo Da Ponte, had been living for some time as a lodger in the Bellaudi household."

A second spectator whispered to a companion, "She's been behaving like a whore since the age of ten. Her husband had to marry her because he made her pregnant. She'll fondle any young man who sits next to her in church."

Angioletta's sister Caterina was called to testify. "My sister was four months pregnant when the Abbe DaPonte came to live with us. She did take a friendly interest in him. One day, I was shocked to see him put his hand under her skirt while she placed her hand in his breeches. Later, I reproached him, but he denied it. He said, 'May God strike me dead with a thunderbolt while I am celebrating mass.'"

Laura Bellaudi was called to testify. "I am Laura Bellaudi, Angioletta's mother-in-law. I saw the Abbe Da Ponte in his room, without a stitch of clothing, showing himself to Angioletta."

The Vicar of San Luca was called. "Three years ago, the Abbe Da Ponte first celebrated mass in my church. He kept ogling the women, flirting. I was so shocked I told him never to return."

The court official continued to read on. "One day, Da Ponte persuaded Angioletta, then quite pregnant, to elope. Carrying a bag with a few pieces of clothing, she hailed a gondola. She got in, but soon her birth pangs began. She motioned for the gondolier to stop, and got off. She was lying helpless on the ground in an alley-way when Da Ponte found her. Within the hour she gave birth to a baby girl and was taken to the foundling hospital. The Abbe Da Ponte continued to say mass in the San Luca district. He and Angioletta at one time even had rooms in brothels where he organized entertainments. During the next two years, Angioletta claimed she was the Abbe Da Ponte's sister, but she became known in the quarter as 'the priest's whore.' On August 24 this year, Angioletta gave birth to her child by the Abbe Da Ponte. The infant was taken to the foundling hospital."

On September 13, 1799, a horse-drawn coach moved rapidly along a country road. Gazing out the window of the coach was Da Ponte, fleeing from the reaches of the court. In court, the official continued, "The Padre Lorenzo Da Ponte is banished for fifteen years from Venice and all other cities, lands and places of the Serene Republic. If apprehended, he is threatened with seven years in a dungeon."

Two weeks later, in Gorizia, a lavish party was taking place at the mansion of Count Guidobaldo Cobentzl. Da Ponte was chatting with the Count and other guests, when Count Lantieri, a man with a perpetually bored expression, approached them.

"My dear Count Cobentzl," he said, with little enthusiasm, "what a marvelous party."

"Good evening, Count Lantieri. Allow me to introduce the Abbe Lorenzo Da Ponte, a newcomer to Gorizia. As you know, my son Johann is the right-hand man of Chancellor Kaunitz. Two weeks ago, the Abbe appeared at my door and presented me with a poem that describes Empress Maria-Theresa and my son in the most exquisite terms. I've had it printed at my own expense."

"Intriguing," said the Count. "My wife has been looking for an able writer to have a play translated. She's the tall one over there. I've often said she has absolutely no temperament, but she possesses the most beautiful behind I've ever seen."

The Count guided Da Ponte over to his wife. Da Ponte kissed her hand and soon they were chatting.

Dresden. January 1781. Da Ponte, now thirty-two, stood outside the door of Caterino Mazzola, whom he had met some years earlier at Zaguri's house in Venice. They embraced. "Friend Da Ponte, what brings you to Dresden?"

"I spent eight pleasant months in Gorizia, but it was time to move on," said Da Ponte. "I heard of your appointment to the Court Theatre here. I thought that perhaps you might—"

"Of course, you can stay here while we try to find work for you."

"Thank you. What do you hear from Venice?"

"Times are difficult," said Mazzola. "Your former employer, Pisani, has been jailed for revolutionary activities. You were fortunate to escape in time."

A few weeks later, Mazzola sat at his writing desk, when Da Ponte entered, dejected. "The printing of your poems has made you quite popular." said Mazzola. "It seems as though everyone wants to meet Da Ponte. What's the matter?"

"I'm in love."

"But why so sad?" Mazzola asked.

"I love two women."

"And who are these beauties?" Mazzola asked.

"Rosina and Camilla, the daughters of an Italian painter. I ask myself, which one do I love best? I am happy only when I am with them both."

Two nights later Da Ponte was visiting the painter's home and gently flirting with the girls' mother, a vivacious woman in her forties. "Signora," he said, "were you not a married woman, I should never dare come to this house."

The mother whispered in his ear, "He who loves the daughter, should pay court to the mother." She rested her hand on his lips. "Da Ponte, darling, you must put an end to this comedy. My two daughters are madly in love with you and it appears you also are in love with them. A wise mother cannot let things go on like this."

"Signora, I assure you—"

She interrupted him. "The young men who have serious intentions towards my daughters are jealous. My dear Da Ponte, you must make up your mind. I give you until tomorrow, not an hour more." The mother walked away to attend to other guests.

Later that night in Mazzola's home, DaPonte was in despair. "Oh, Rosina ... oh, Camilla, what will become of you, poor things? What will become of me?"

Mazzola burst into laughter. Da Ponte, embarrassed, covered his face. Suddenly, Da Ponte brightened, smiled, and laughed at himself. That night, after packing his few belongings, Da Ponte sat at the desk in his bedroom and wrote a letter:

"Madam,

At quarter past ten I shall be on the diligence to Prague and will continue on to Vienna. I can think of no better relief for the harm I have involuntarily done. May God grant you and your family all possible prosperity.

Your devoted servant,

Lorenzo Da Ponte."

He exited his room, carrying a bag with his clothing. He lay down the bag, and embraced the surprised Mazzola. "Thank you for everything. Please have this letter delivered. I'm going to Vienna."

A few minutes later, Da Ponte was seated in the coach, about to depart, when Mazzola came running, carrying a letter. "Wait, do you know Antonio Salieri?"

"No."

"Salieri is a fellow Venetian like yourself. He has directed the Opera in Vienna for many years. Give him this as soon as you arrive."

April 1782. Da Ponte, at first barely visible through dense dust clouds swirling about in heavy winds, strolled along a street in Vienna, the seat of the Holy Roman Empire. He spotted a familiar face. "Signor Casanova." They embraced and walked arm-in-arm, chatting.

"I'm now the secretary to the Venetian ambassador," said Casanova. "What brings you to Vienna?"

Soon they were seated in an outdoor café and Da Ponte brought him up to date, concluding, "I gave the letter to Salieri a few weeks ago. He said there was nothing at the moment."

"Are you free of engagements next Sunday morning?" Casanova asked.

"And every one thereafter," Da Ponte replied.

"Each Sunday, the Italian literati gather at the home of the poet Metastasio. He has been poet at the Emperor's court the past fifty years. He is very difficult of access, but let me show him one of your poems."

That Sunday, Da Ponte and Casanova entered a large apartment where several men were seated. Metastasio, eighty-four, frail, elegant, sat at the front of the group. Recalling the times as a youth, at home, reading the great poet's works, Da Ponte regarded him and thought to himself, Metastasio, I've worshipped him since I was a young boy.

There was a hush as Metastasio rose before the group. He spoke in a low, gentle voice. People strained to hear him. "Friends, I wish to introduce a new member of our group, Lorenzo Da Ponte. He has written certain verses based on a theme of Ovid and kindly dedicated them to an important German nobleman with whom I am on familiar terms. Permit me to read from his work: *A nymph was Bauci, whose like for beauty was born not in her time and to Philemon, the shepherd, was she as pleasing as that fair swain to her* ...." Hands trembling, the elderly poet gave the text of the poem to Da Ponte. He motioned for him to continue reading.

Da Ponte recalled to Whitman, "When the great Metastasio invited me to read my poem ... I shall never forget that day."

When Da Ponte finished reading, several men applauded and rose to shake his hand. Casanova approached with an ugly fellow in his early sixties. "Abbe Da Ponte, meet Abbe Casti, the renowned poet."

Casti spoke with a strange, hollow voice. "I enjoyed your little poem today."

"I am honored."

"Is it true that you're also writing libretti for opera?" Casti asked.

"I'm trying to find my way. In Dresden, Signor Mazzola taught me —"

Casti cut him off. "Try London, Paris, even St. Petersburg. Here in Vienna, there is nothing for you." He abruptly turned and left.

Casanova whispered in Da Ponte's ear, "Casti is waiting for Metastasio to die. He hopes the Emperor will name him poet laureate. He doesn't want any other Italian poets around."

"But how could he fear me?" said Da Ponte.

"Casti believes that everyone is as much an intriguer as he is," said Casanova. "Do you know Count Rosenberg, the Emperor's adviser on theatrical matters? Casti finds women for him. He's a first-class pimp."

"What a horrible voice."

"His palate is rotting away from the new disease, syphilis."

On his way out, Da Ponte stopped to thank Metastasio. The elderly poet clasped Da Ponte's hand and whispered in his ear, "It is rumored that His Majesty wishes to reopen an Italian Opera in Vienna. This may be an opportune time to call on Signor Salieri."

Antonio Salieri, a short slender man in his mid-thirties, walked briskly across the vast grounds of the palace of Emperor Joseph II. Da Ponte hurried to keep up with him. "Signor Salieri, I have never before spoken to any monarch. How shall I address him?"

"His Majesty speaks Italian *parfaitement,*" said Salieri, "so you can be at ease about that." Salieri abruptly stopped walking. "His Majesty dislikes pomp and ceremony. Do not kneel or seek to kiss his hand. Speak clearly and without cringing. He allows people to contradict him. In fact, he once told me, "I hate flattery."

Minutes later in the palace, Da Ponte, clearly enchanted, was engaged in friendly conversation with Emperor Joseph II, a tall, austere man in his forties, who was simply dressed. "I was passing by the dining room of the French actors' company," said the Emperor, "when one of them called out to me and dared to complain about the quality of the 'so-called Burgundy wine' they were 'forced' to drink. He even suggested that I taste it, which I did. Then I told them I think it excellent, at least quite good enough for me, though perhaps not sufficiently high-flavored for you and your companions. In France, I daresay, you will get much better. I sent the whole lot of them home. Just as well, because I've long wanted to start an Italian opera company here. I've summoned the best voices in all of Europe. Now, we need good libretti. I'm told you are a poet of the first rank. How many plays have you written?"

After a moment's hesitation, Da Ponte shyly replied, "None, sire."

The Emperor took this in stride. "Fine, fine. We shall have a Virgin Muse. Do come and see me again."

As Da Ponte bowed and turned to leave, the Emperor said, "Da Ponte."

"Your Majesty?"

"My late mother was a wonderful woman."

"Yes, Your Majesty."

"But she was from another time. During her reign, your people were treated very harshly."

Da Ponte regarded the Emperor silently, not knowing what to say.

"Even now," said the Emperor. "The Archbishop of Vienna has complained to me about the increasing contacts between Christians and Jews. But, in secular matters, I believe that one must be tolerant. It is my policy to let anyone practice a trade in Vienna, providing he has the required qualifications, and would bring advantages into my states."

"Thank you, Your Majesty. I shall do my best to justify your faith in me." Da Ponte bowed, and left.

Da Ponte strode buoyantly across the palace grounds. Salieri approached, smiling. "The Emperor was very pleased to meet you."

"Really? What did he say?"

"His exact words were, 'He's an amusing and intelligent fellow.'" Da Ponte was clearly delighted. The two men walked briskly along and Salieri continued, "As Poet to the Italian Theater, your salary is twelve hundred florins a year, plus royalties. His Majesty dines at precisely quarter past three. Afterwards he often has a short concert in his apartments where he hears selections from the operas to be performed. He plays the viola and the clavier, and is quite a good bass singer. When the Emperor attends the opera, he is very *ponctuel*. If he is not there at the precise moment when the curtain is to be raised, he has given strict orders that he is never to be waited for."

A Carnival Sunday, 1783. A gay masked ball was in progress at the Hofburg Assembly Room. Da Ponte arrived with Salieri, who introduced him to two dignitaries. "Gentlemen, meet the Abbe Da Ponte, our new poet to the Italian Opera. Abbe, allow me to present Herr Joseph Haydn, the eminent composer, and Baron Raimund Wetzlar, a most generous patron of the arts. Just then, Salieri spied someone else at the entrance; he waved and walked off to greet him.

The three men—Da Ponte, Haydn and Baron Wetzlar—shook hands and began to enter the hall. Blocking their path was a short man, masked, flamboyantly dressed. He handed a pamphlet to Haydn who read the title: *Selections from the great Indian Philosopher Zoroaster, including eight riddles."*

The disguised "philosopher" motioned extravagantly for Haydn to continue reading. Amused, Haydn complied. "If you are poor, but clever, arm yourself with patience, and work. If you do not grow rich, you will at least remain a clever man. If you are an ass, but wealthy, take advantage of your good fortune and be lazy. If you do not become poor, you will at least remain an ass."

Haydn and Wetzlar burst into laughter. Da Ponte, a little slow in understanding, joined in. The disguised "philosopher" snatched the paper from Haydn, handed it to Da Ponte, and mutely gestured, urging him to read on. "'What am I?'" Da Ponte read. "'I have no soul and no body. One cannot see me but can hear me. Only a human being can give me life, as often as he wishes; and my life is only of short duration, for I die almost at the moment in which I am born. For the most part, women produce me gently and amiably; many have modestly confessed their love in this way. Many have also saved their virtue through me.' And the answer to this riddle is ..."

Da Ponte looked to the bottom of the paper, and then with a puzzled expression at those around him. "'A fart.'"

Haydn smiled and exclaimed, "A fart. Why, this can only be my dear Wolfgang."

The "philosopher" Mozart, twenty-seven years old, removed the mask and gleefully embraced Haydn and Baron von Wetzlar, who were laughing heartily. Da Ponte, smiling, was amazed.

"Papa Haydn," said Mozart. "My dear Baron."

"Abbe Da Ponte," said Baron Von Wetzlar, "meet Wolfgang Mozart, composer, musician, and comedian. Wolfgang, the Abbe is the new poet at the Italian Opera."

"I would love to compose an Italian Opera," said Mozart. "I've looked through more than a hundred libretti, but not a single one pleases me."

"I'm busy now writing a new libretto for Signor Salieri," Da Ponte replied. "Perhaps in a few months—"

He was interrupted by Mozart's wife, Constanze, who was in the latter stages of pregnancy. "Woferl, our friends are waiting."

"Abbe Da Ponte, meet my darling Constanze, and," He patted her swollen stomach, "our little heir. You must excuse me, we shall meet again soon, I hope."

Mozart and Constanze hurried across the room to a group of young friends. Soon there was music and raucous laughter as Mozart sat at a piano and played a bawdy tune, joyfully singing the lyrics along with two young men. Da Ponte watched from a distance.

"Before God," said Hayden, "I tell you that Mozart is the greatest composer known to me."

"Is he successful?" Da Ponte asked.

Haydn shook his head. "As a young child he was a prodigy, the toast of all Europe. Now, as a mature artist, he must struggle to survive. It angers me."

Da Ponte wandered over towards Mozart's group as they continued the song. Mozart stopped abruptly. "Our Italian friend will think we Germans are vulgar savages."

"No, no," said Da Ponte, "please continue."

Constanze smiled and asked him, "What would you like to hear?"

Da Ponte hesitated. "Perhaps a love song?"

A young woman in the group whispered into Mozart's ear. He nodded, and turned to Da Ponte. "I composed this to lyrics by one of our poets. I hope you like it." He began to play a beautiful love song, "Au Chloe," while the young woman, a soprano, sang. Mozart, so mischievous moments ago, seemed to be in a heavenly trance as he played. The people around the piano, including Da Ponte, reacted to the tenderness of the music.

Wenn die Lieb aus dienen blauen/
Hellen, offnen Augen sieht/ Un vor
Lust, hinein zu schauen.
When love looks out of your candid, clear,
blue eyes; and longing to gaze into
them, I feel glowing my heart beat fast;

The soprano gazed into Da Ponte's eyes. She was playfully seductive, at times reaching out to him with her arms. Mozart, playing, watched Da Ponte's reaction, smiled.

Und ich halte dich un kusse/ deine
Rosenwangen warm/ Liebes Madchen, un
ich/ schliese Zittern dich/ in meinem
arm! And I take you and kiss your
warm, rosy cheeks, sweet love, and,
trembling, fold you in my arms;
Madchen, Madchen, un ich drucke/
Dich an meinen Busen fest/ Deer im

letzten Augenblicke/ Sterbend nur
dich von sich lasst. Oh dearest,
dearest love, And I press you firmly
to my breast, where I shall hold you
till my last dying breath;
Den berauschen Blick umshcattet/
Eine dustre Wolke mir/ Und ich sitze
dan ermattet/ Aber selig neben dir.
Then a dismal cloud shades my fevered
glance, I sit at your side, weary
but at peace.

There was silence and calm. The friends, and Da Ponte, basked in the afterglow of the music.

Some months later, Da Ponte, now a celebrity, dressed like a dandy, walking stick in hand, strolled along a Vienna street, jovially greeting people.

"After a disastrous opera for Salieri, I had a great success with the Spaniard, Martin y Soler," Da Ponte told Whitman. "Several composers turned to me now, but only two were deserving of my esteem: Martin y Soler, who was the Emperor's favorite, and Mozart. Due to the intrigues of his rivals, Mozart could not exercise his divine genius in Vienna. He was living there like a priceless jewel, buried in the bowels of the earth."

He entered a building at Domgasse and was about to climb the stairs when two men, carrying a piano, perspiring, came staggering down, as Mozart followed. "Careful, careful," said Mozart. "Ah, Signor Da Ponte, welcome. Excuse me for just a moment."

Mozart helped the men guide the piano through the door, onto a horse-drawn cart. They took it away. Mozart and Da Ponte ascended the stairs to the flat. "Each morning I give lessons here at home," Mozart explained. "Every few days we must move the piano to the home of some nobleman, or a hall, where I give a recital. I've one scheduled tonight, and then we must drag it back for tomorrow's lessons. I should have taken up the flute."

The Mozart servant held the door open for them as they entered. Mozart presented Da Ponte to his wife Constanze, while their son, Carl Thomas, a year old, crawled about beneath a billiards table. Constanze picked up the boy and held him in front of Da Ponte, extending the child's hand. "Carl Thomas, meet Signor Da Ponte."

"What a handsome young man," said Da Ponte.

"We lost our first child," said Mozart.

"I heard," Da Ponte said. "That same month I lost my brother Girolamo. A malady of the lungs."

"My own health is not the best," said Mozart. "My doctor has been almost daily at my rooms." He tickled his son. "But now God has given us this little fellow."

Constanze carried the child into another room as Da Ponte looked up at three oil portraits on the wall. "That is my dear father, who lives in Salzburg, a place I detest," said Mozart. "This one is my late mother, may she rest in peace. And this one, believe it or not, is me, when I was just six years old. So, how goes the Italian Opera?"

"Martin y Soler's opera has been a great success," said Da Ponte. "Didn't I see you in the audience one evening?"

"Yes."

"And?"

Mozart hesitated. "It is … very pretty." Da Ponte waited, expectantly, for more praise. "But, I suspect that in ten years nobody will take notice of it." Da Ponte was hurt. There was an awkward silence, and then Mozart continued. "Forgive me. But I think that, with an able poet like yourself, greater things are possible." After another brief, awkward silence, "What do you think of the comedy by the Frenchman Beaumarchais?"

Da Ponte raised an eyebrow. *Le Mariage de Figaro*? I hear that it has caused a sensation in Paris."

Mozart was enthusiastic. "It was banned in Paris for three years. The first night, there was such a crowd that three people were crushed to death."

"Didn't the Emperor forbid a company here in Vienna from presenting the play?" Da Ponte asked.

Mozart picked up the text of the play from a table. "Yes, but he has allowed the text to be printed in German. I like it because it concerns the lives of real people, not gods or mythical figures. Listen. Count Almaviva wants to seduce Susanna, his wife's chambermaid. But Susanna wants to marry Figaro, the count's valet. When Figaro learns of the count's plan, he confronts him." Mozart read from the play text. *No, my lord, you shan't have her. Do nobility, wealth and rank make you so proud? What have you done to deserve such advantages? You took the trouble to be born, nothing more. Otherwise, you are a very ordinary man."*

Da Ponte shook his head. "This is not France. Such talk could be viewed as insolence."

"*They* are the insolent ones," said Mozart. "Four years ago I was living in Salzburg, suffocating as an artist. I humbly asked Archbishop Colloredo for permission to leave his employ so that I could pursue my music here. That great man of God called me a lousy rascal, a vagabond. Count Arco, his chamberlain, kicked me out." Mozart strode angrily around the room. "Kicked me in the ass as though I were a dog. I wanted to kill him!"

Six weeks later, Mozart was seated at the piano in his house, looking at Da Ponte's libretto for *Figaro*.

Da Ponte stood behind him, looking over his shoulder, explaining, "As the curtain rises, we see a room, perhaps with an armchair in the middle. Figaro, the count's valet, is striding across the room, measuring it. Da Ponte recited Figaro's lines. As he did, Mozart tentatively tapped out a few notes on the piano.

"Cinque ... diec i... venti ... trenta ... trentas ...quarantatre. Five, ten, twenty, thirty, thirty-six, forty-three.

"And the girl?" Mozart asked.

"Susanna, his fiancée, perhaps she could be gazing into the mirror," Da Ponte said. "Yes. Trying on a little hat, trimmed with flowers." Da Ponte recited Susanna's lines, in a falsetto, which evoked a smile from Mozart, who tapped out a few notes on the piano.

Ora si ch'io son contenta/ sembra fatto inver per me. Yes, now I'm really happy. You'd think it was made just for me.

"And then?" Mozart asked.

Da Ponte continued with Susanna's lines, while Mozart began playing the piano with slightly greater flourish and confidence.

Guarda un po', caro Figaro/ guarda adesso il mio capello/ Come and see, my darling Figaro, Come and look at my hat.

"Then Figaro responds," said Da Ponte. *Si, mio core, e piu bello/ sembra fatto inver per te/*

Yes, my dear, it's much prettier, you'd think it was made for you!

"Then Susanna and Figaro sing together," said Da Ponte, and here Mozart joined him in a duet.

Ah, il matinno alle nozze vecino/ quante e dolce al mio/tuo tenero sposo/ quelto bel cappellino vezzoso/ che Susanna ella stessa si fe. Oh, on the morning of your wedding, how dear to my/your tender bridegroom. Is this charming little hat that Susanna made all by herself.

"Can we try it again?" said Mozart, his eyes glowing with enthusiasm. "Allow me to just play the music for a moment. I have an idea."

"Yes, by all means," said Da Ponte.

Mozart began to play the melody of the song, at first a bit tentatively, then with growing confidence, and it was lovely. As he played, eyes closed, with great flourishes, Da Ponte regarded him with growing wonder, witnessing the creation of a thing of great beauty.

Some days later, Da Ponte, holding the libretto for *Figaro*, was alone with the Emperor, who paced about his apartment, looking through a sheaf of official papers.

"Your Majesty," he said, "the opera is lacking scores. I thought it would be a propitious time for a work by Mozart."

The Emperor, still staring at the papers, cut him off. "Mozart is a wonder at instrumental music, but he has written very little opera."

"Yes, Sire, but without your Majesty's generosity, I would never have written even one drama in Vienna."

The Emperor stopped, took the libretto from Da Ponte and glanced at it. "This *Mariage de Figaro*, I've just forbidden the German troupe to perform it." He walked over to a table and picked up the text of the Beaumarchais play. Indignant, he said, "Listen to this. Figaro, a common valet, confronts his master, because the Count wants to seduce Figaro's fiancée. Figaro says to the count, *What have you done to deserve such advantages? You took the trouble to be born, nothing more. Otherwise you are a very ordinary man.*'"

Da Ponte turned away and muffled a laugh, since this excerpt, which the Emperor clearly hated, was the very same excerpt that Mozart read to him, and loved.

The Emperor sighed. "The progress of mankind, yes, but all in due time. This play is a call for rebellion."

"Sire," said Da Ponte, "for the opera I've cut anything that might offend good taste. The music is marvelously beautiful. I think you will enjoy it."

The Emperor shrugged and turned back to his paperwork. "I will rely on your judgment. Send the score to the copyist."

It was the night of May 1, 1786. Outside the theatre was a poster: *Marriage of Figaro. Music, W. Mozart. Libretto, L. Da Ponte.*

Inside the packed theatre, it was the third scene of Act II, as an enthralled audience heard the lovely soprano voice of Cherubino, dressed in the trouser role as a young male page, singing an exquisite song of the awakening of innocent love

Voi che sapete/Che cosa e amor/ Donne vedete/ S'io l'ho nel cor. Oh, you who know, what love's all about, tell me, my ladies, what's in my heart.

Emperor Joseph II, accompanied by his entourage, sat in the royal box. As Mozart directed the orchestra, Da Ponte stood anxiously in the wings, overwhelmed by the beauty of the music, silently mouthing his lyrics.

Quello ch'io provo/ Vi ridiro/ E per me nuovo/ Capir nol so. I'll try to describe my feelings for you, but they're so new that I can't understand them.

Sento un affetto/Pien di desir/ Ch'ora e diletto/ Ch'ora e martir. Sometimes I feel/ A strange longing, that brings happiness, or despair.

Gelo, e poi sento/ L'alma avvampar/ E in un momento/ Torno a gelar. I freeze, and then my soul's on fire. And a moment later I'm freezing again.

Ricerco un bene/ Fuori di me/ Non so ch'il tiene/ so cos'e. I'm seeking a pleasure that's beyond me, I don't know where to find it or even what it is.

Sospiro e gemo/ Senza voler/ Palpito e tremo/ Senza saper. I sigh and moan, without meaning to, And I shake and tremble, without knowing why.

Non trovo pace/ Notte ne di/ Ma pur mi piace/ Languir cosi. I can find no peace either night or day. Yet I've come to enjoy my suffering.

Voi che sapete/ Che cosa e amor/Donne, vedete/ S'io l'ho nel cor. Oh, you who know what love's all about, tell me my ladies, what's in my heart.

The audience exploded in applause. Patrons demanded an encore, and still another. Mozart and Da Ponte were called up on stage and stood with the cast, bowing, basking in the glory of the moment. The Emperor applauded vigorously. Seated in a row behind the Emperor were Casti and Salieri, who also applauded, but without fervor.

A few days later, Da Ponte entered the Emperor's quarters. "Your Majesty, three composers have asked me for libretti: Mozart, Salieri and Martin y Soler. I am going to try and please all three."

The Emperor was amused. "Three at once? Sounds impossible."

"Perhaps, Your Majesty, but I shall try all the same."

Da Ponte sat writing in his room, late at night. On his desk were: a bottle of Tokay wine, an inkstand, and a box of Seville snuff. He rang a bell. A young girl entered with refreshments.

Recalling that time many years ago, Da Ponte explained to Whitman, "For two months without pause, I sat at my table for twelve hours every day. In the house where I lodged, a beautiful girl of sixteen was living with her mother. I should have preferred to love her as a daughter, but alas."

Gradually, they became attracted to each other. Da Ponte was busily engaged in writing the lyrics to a song in which Don Giovanni seduces Zerlina. He sang to her, *Orsu, non perdiam tempo/in questo istante/io ti voglio sposar.* Come, let us not lose time; this very moment. I wish to marry you.

And Zerlina replied, *Voi!* You!

The young girl, smiling, brought in a slice of cake and coffee, and served it to Da Ponte as he wrote more lyrics for Don Giovanni:

*Certo, io/quel casinetto e mio/soli
saremo/La ci darem la mano/la mi
dirai di si/vedi non e lontano/
partiam, ben mio, da qui.* There
you'll tell me, "Yes." Certainly, I.
That little house is mine, we shall
be alone, and there my jewel, shall

be married. There we shall give
each other our hands, See it is not
far: Let us leave here, my beloved.

The girl, visible through the door, now sat in the next room, reading a book, while Zerlina replied,

*Vorrei, e non vorrei/ Mi trema un
poco il cor/ Felice, a ver, sarei:/
ma puo burlarmi ancor.* I would like
to, and not like to. My heart
trembles a little. I would be happy,
it's true: But he could still make light of me.

The girl now sat at Da Ponte's side, absolutely still, gazing at him, as he worked. Da Ponte looked up, smiled, as Don Giovanni continued,

Vieni, mio bel diletto!
Come, my lovely delight!
And Zerlina replied:
Ma fa pieta a Masetto.
I feel sorry for Massetto.
And Don Giovanni promised her,
Io cangero tua sorte.
I shall change your fate.
And she began to weaken,
Presto non son piu forte.
Suddenly, I am no longer strong.

Later that evening, the girl, in her nightgown, entered to serve Da Ponte his coffee. She leaned over, revealing her bare breasts. He placed his arm around her waist. Soon she was in his lap. They kissed, as Zerlina and Giovanni sang together, *Andiam, andiam, mio bene, a ristorar le pene d'un innocente amor!* Let us go, let us go, my beloved, to renew the pangs of an innocent love!

Recalling that time, Da Ponte told Whitman, "In sixty-three days the first two operas were finished and almost two-thirds of the last.

It was four months later, September of 1787, when the Mozart household servant opened the door for Da Ponte. Looking haggard, Mozart gazed at the oil portrait of his father. "Forgive me for being so slow with *Don Giovanni*. It has been a terrible summer. The death of my father. You can imagine the state I was in. Now my Constanze hasn't been well."

"How is she?" Da Ponte asked.

"A little better, thank God. Just this week I lost a dear friend, Doctor Barisani. He treated me when I was so ill three years ago. Just twenty-nine years old. Last year, my dearest friend, Count Hatzfield, such a fine violinist, died in Dusseldorf. We were the same age." Mozart stared vacantly out the window. "Since I joined the Masonic Order, it has been quite clear to me: death is the true goal of our existence. I never lie down at night without reflecting that I may not live to see another day."

Mozart turned to an empty bird cage in the apartment. "Do you remember the little starling I bought two years ago? Such a clever little fellow. He could whistle the entire rondo from a concerto I wrote for a friend." He sat at the piano and gently played the theme. "I so loved hearing him in the morning. Last week I buried him in a field." Mozart continued to play on the piano. Da Ponte placed his hand on Mozart's shoulder to comfort him.

Prague: October 1787. Da Ponte, outside the Three Lions Inn, yelled up at a window. "Signor Mozart. Frau Mozart."

Mozart's head appeared a window. He looked cheerful. Constanze's head also popped out. She waved to him. "Signor Da Ponte! When did you arrive?"

"Late last night. I'm staying just opposite." He pointed at the hotel across the road.

"We resume rehearsals tomorrow morning," said Mozart. "How long can you be with us?"

"Just a few days," said Da Ponte. "I must return to Vienna. Rehearsals of my new work for Salieri." He shrugged, apologetically.

"Today we're invited to a party at the country house of the Duscheks," said Mozart. "Everyone will be there."

It was a balmy autumn afternoon. A large party of people had come by carriage to the Duscheks' country house on the outskirts of Prague. Among them were the opera impresarios and members of the cast. Da Ponte had brought with him a certain Signor Casanova. Most of the guests stood outside on the patio a few feet away from the open doors.

Da Ponte was chatting with Baron Bretfeld and Signora Caterina Bondini, one of the cast members, as Mozart, not far off, mingled with friends. "Mozart is a true Viennese, always in good spirits," said the Baron.

"Prague is close to his heart, Baron," said Da Ponte.

"Indeed," the Baron went on, "I believe that Prague esteems him more than Vienna!"

"In Vienna he is a buried jewel," said Da Ponte. "But I have the feeling that the only operas of mine which will survive are the ones he has put to music."

Mozart sneaked up quietly behind Caterina Bondini and rested his chin on her shoulder. In a stage whisper he said playfully, "Signora Bondini, shall we rehearse the scream again?"

She reacted with amusement as he retreated, smiling. She explained to the Baron, "My character, Zerlina, is being abducted by Don Giovanni. She is supposed to scream. At rehearsal yesterday, I tried, and tried, and couldn't get it right. Then the maestro snuck up behind me, pinched me, right on the behind, and I let out such a scream that everyone jumped. 'Perfect,' he said."

Several yards away Casanova, now in his sixties, was chatting with Caterina Micelli, another member of the cast.

"What brings you to Prague, Signor Casanova?"

"I came to oversee the publication of my novel. My dear friend Da Ponte has invited me to attend the opening of 'Don Giovanni.' I decided to stay on a few days."

"The Abbe Da Ponte seems to be a man of distinguished birth," she said. "He spoke of his good uncle, the Bishop."

Casanova chuckled. "Don't be deceived by that. Anyone can see that he belongs to the Jewish race. His parents died when he was quite young, and he was put in the seminary."

"Do you mean he's a baptized Jew?" she asked. "I've also heard rumors that he was once a priest."

"I wouldn't advise anyone to be married by him," said Casanova. "The marriage would be no more valid than if I had performed it."

In the meantime, Da Ponte was now chatting with Teresa Saporiti, another member of the cast, and the host, Herr Duschek. "Signor Casanova seems so distinguished," she said. "He must have held posts at a number of courts."

"He's an adventurer who has spent his days' playing cards, brewing elixirs and fortune-telling," said Da Ponte. "Since I last met him, he's been raised to the aristocracy. But I'm sure he performed the elevation himself."

Caterina Micelli turned to Mozart: "Dear maestro, can you play a tune for us from the new opera?" Others in the group chimed in, "Yes! Yes!" A few men carried a piano and chair from the room indoors out to the patio. Mozart looked to DaPonte, who thought for a moment, then pointed to Felice Ponziano, the bass, a man in his twenties.

"I think you will enjoy this aria," said Da Ponte. "Leporello, the manservant to Don Giovanni, sings to a lady who has been seduced, and discarded, by his master. He wants to console her, but also to explain that she has been one of many conquests." After pause, Da Ponte smiled, and went on, "I received good advice about this, and other parts of the libretto from my dear friend Signor Casanova. They say that when Signor

Casanova was a young man, many years ago, in the cafes of Venice, he would reel off lists of his conquests, which inspired my aria. So I dedicate it to him." Da Ponte bowed in the direction of Casanova, who also bowed.

"You do me great honor, dear Abbe," said Casanova. "But your original text, which I have read, reflects what appears to be abundant personal experience." This, of course, evoked raucous laughter.

Mozart sat at the piano and played, as Leporello launched into the Catalogue aria, flirting playfully with the women in the in the audience, as he sang of Don Giovanni's many conquests:

Madamina, il catalogo e questo/ delle
belle cha amo il padron mio/ un
catalogo egli e che ho
fatt'io/osservate, leggete con me/
In Italia seicento e quaranta/in
Lamagan duecento e trentuna/ cento
in Francia, in/ Turchia novantuna/ma
in Ispagna son gia mille e tre.
Dear madame, this is the catalogue
of the beauties my master has loved;
a catalogue that I have made; observe,
read along with me. In Italy, six
hundred and forty, In Germany, two
hundred thirty one, a hundred in
France, in Turkey, ninety-one, But
in Spain, there are already one
thousand and three!
V'han fra queste contadine/ camariere
cittadine/ v'han contesse, baronesse/
marchesane, principesse' e v'han
donne d'ogni grado/ d'ogni forma,
d'ogni eta. Among them are country
girls, maids and city women. There
are countesses, baronesses, Women of
every rank, shape and age.
Nella bionda egli h'usanza/ di lodar
la gentilleza/ nella bruna, la
costanza/ nella blanca, la dolcezza/
vuol d'inverno la grasotta/vuol
d'estate la magrotta. He often praises
the gentleness of the blondes; the
constancy of the brunette; the

sweetness of the pale one; in winter
he wants a plump one; in summer he
wants a lean one.
E la grande maestosa/ la piccina e
ognore vezzosa/ delle vecchie fa
conquista/ del piacer di porla lista.
The large one is imposing; the small
one always charming; he conquers old
ladies, just for the pleasure of
adding to his list.

As he listened, Da Ponte's mind wandered back several weeks to his room in Vienna. Late one night he was bent over his writing table, composing the libretto, and looked up to kiss the breast of his muse:

Sua pasion predominante/ e la giovin
principiante/ non si piccas se sia
ricca/ se sia brutta, se sia bella/
purche porti la gonnella/ voi sapete
quel che fa. But his overwhelming
passion is the young beginner; He
doesn't care if she is rich; if she
is ugly; if she is lovely; as long
as she wears a skirt; you know what
he does.

The song over, "Leporello" clowning, chased after a young woman who ran off into the garden, giggling and screaming, fending him off, as everyone around laughed and applauded.

Prague: October 29, 1787. The orchestra played the overture of *Don Giovanni* as Mozart directed. The National Theatre was packed with a brilliant audience, including Signor Casanova, who regarded the proceedings with amusement.

As the overture continued, Da Ponte gazed pensively out the window of his carriage, on a country road, the start of a long journey back to Vienna. With regret, he was missing the opening of the opera, but duty called.

Vienna: July 29, 1788. Da Ponte entered the rehearsal hall in Vienna and found several men and women looking distraught.

"What has happened?" he asked.

One tearful woman explained, "The Emperor has ordered Count Rosenberg to close down the Italian Opera at the end of this season."

Da Ponte rushed over to the palace, and gained admission to the Emperor's study. The monarch looked haggard, exhausted; he was battling a lung infection and malaria.

"Sire," said Da Ponte, "it is a pleasure to see you after so long a time."

"I've been out in the field," the Emperor said wearily. "How goes the opera company?"

"Sire, it could not go worse," said Da Ponte.

"Why?"

"We are all overwhelmed with despair at having to leave our adored patron in September."

"The war tax has caused great discontent," said the Emperor. "I've had to increase our army by one hundred fifteen thousand men. The Italian opera costs me eighty thousand florins a year."

Da Ponte pulled out a folded piece of paper.

"What is this?" the Emperor asked.

"A petition, sire."

The Emperor was adamant. "I've made my decision."

"Sire," said Da Ponte, "I ask only for use of your theater and I will give your majesty and Vienna the same spectacles three times a week."

The Emperor was now amused. "You? Are you so rich?"

"No, Sire. These are the names of ladies and gentlemen who have agreed to reserve a box, as is the custom in London. In less than we week we've obtained subscriptions for a hundred thousand florins. This gives us a surplus of twenty thousand."

The Emperor glanced at the paper and appeared pleased. He went to his desk, dipped a pen in ink, and scribbled something on the paper. "Tell Rosenberg that I grant you permission to use the theatre."

In a suburb of Vienna, Mozart sat at his piano, playing. Outside the glass doors, in the garden, Constanze was seated, cutting quill pens for the copyist. Their son, now four years old, played in the garden, singing. Da Ponte entered and greeted Constanze. He messed the hair of the child, then entered the house. "We've moved out here; it's less expensive," said Mozart, who looked quite depressed. My concerts seem to have gone out of fashion. My teaching work has virtually disappeared."

Da Ponte sought to reassure him. "Better days are ahead. The Emperor wants us to prepare a new opera in time for carnival. He's even suggested a theme."

"The Emperor?"

They walked out into the garden as Da Ponte explained. "He says it's based on a true story he heard. I see it in modern dress. I call it *Cosi Fan Tutte, They're all Alike*. The subtitle: *School for Lovers*. The place: a cafe in Naples. Two young soldiers are engaged to two sisters. Don Alfonso, the owner of the cafe, makes the soldiers a wager that their fiancées will be unfaithful. They must pretend that they've been called away to war. Then they return in disguise, and each tries to seduce the other's woman."

"And the outcome?" Mozart asked.

"Utter confusion. The sisters do fall in love with the other men, but, the two men are also attracted to them. I leave it up to the audience to guess who marries who."

Mozart smiled. "I like it."

"His Majesty told me to collaborate with Salieri on this opera."

Mozart's smile disappeared. "Salieri?"

"I had to obey." said Da Ponte. "I gave the libretto to Salieri. But he said he was unable to do it. I was relieved. It was you all along that I had in mind."

Mozart was again smiling. "This gives me all the more reason to create something wonderful."

"The story reminds me," said Da Ponte. "Years ago, in Dresden, I met an Italian couple who had two beautiful daughters. I loved them both. Where is it ordained that a man, or a woman, is capable of loving just one other soul on this earth?"

Mozart looked over towards Constanze, who was on the far side of the garden. "When I was nineteen, I met Constanze's older sister, Aloysia. I adored her. But she married Lange, the actor. I was heartbroken. Even now she is not a matter of indifference to me. When I moved to Vienna and took lodgings with her family, Constanze was all grown up. I fell in love with her. If I had met the two sisters at the same time, I don't know what I'd have done."

"I've found the ideal mezzo for the role of the older sister," Da Ponte said.

"Ah yes?"

"Adriana Ferraresi del Bene. She sang the lead in my last opera. I've made it a rule not to flirt with actresses. But this time I lack the strength to resist. What eyes. What a charming mouth."

"Ah, the mouth." said Mozart, suddenly understanding. "This must mean that she can sing."

"She has an enchanting voice," said Da Ponte. "Her husband is the son of the papal consul to Venice. We are quite friendly. I tell you, I am madly in love with her. She has inspired some of my best poetry."

January 21, 1790. In the Vienna Theatre, Adriana del Bene and the entire cast were preparing for rehearsal when Mozart entered with Joseph Haydn. Da Ponte greeted them. Mozart picked up the baton and faced the orchestra. "Good morning," he said. "*Cosi fan tutte* will open five days from now, the eve of my thirty-fourth birthday. The best gift you can give me is to play with your customary love and devotion."

The musicians applauded. Mozart looked over to Da Ponte and nodded. "Let's try Act One, Scene Two," said Da Ponte. "A garden by the seashore. The two sisters, Fiordiligi and Dorabella, gaze at miniature portraits of their beloved fiancés and sing their praises."

The two sopranos, Adriana, as Fiordiligi, and Louisa as Dorabella, began their duet, with Fiordiligi leading off.

Ah, guarda, sorella/ se bocca piu
bella/ se aspetto piu nobile/ si puo
ritrovar. Ah, tell me, my sister, If
you could ever find a sweeter mouth,
Or a nobler face.
And Dorabella came in:
Osserva tu un poco/ che fuocco ha
ne' sguardi!/ se fiamma, se dardi/
non sembran scoccar. And just look
at That fiery glance! Doesn't it
seem like it's shooting off darts
and flames?
Fiordiligi/Adriana gazed with mock, comic passion at Da Ponte, as she continued:
Si vede un sembiante/ Guerriero ed
amante. He's got the face of a
fighter and a lover.
In response, Da Ponte blew her a kiss, as Dorabella continued:
Si vede una faccia/ che alletta e
minaccia. He's got a look that
fascinates and scares me, too.
It was now the opening night at the Vienna Theatre, and the two women were singing before a full house, including the Emperor, as Mozart conducted, and Da Ponte stood in the wings:
Io sono felice!/ se questo mio core/
mai cangia desio/ amore mi faccia/
vivendo penar! Oh, how happy I am!
If my feelings for him should ever
change, May love make me Live in
misery!

The duet ended, to great applause. A radiant Fiordiligi lead the cast off stage where she was embraced by Da Ponte. She rushed back on stage as the spectators yelled, "Bravo," and threw flowers.

February 19, 1790. Da Ponte sat in the antechamber of the Royal Palace along with several other grief-stricken subjects of the Empire. A mournful Count Rosenberg exited the Emperor's bedroom and told Da Ponte, "His Majesty is dying. For hours he has been dictating letters of farewell."

"May I see him," Da Ponte asked. "Just for a moment?"

Rosenberg ushered Da Ponte in. The Emperor, ashen-faced, lay in bed, propped up with a pillow. He motioned weakly to Da Ponte to come closer. With a trembling hand, he gave Da Ponte a folded note. "Da Ponte, if you ever go to Paris, show this to my sister Marie-Antoinette. She loved your *Marriage of Figaro.*"

Da Ponte was overcome. "Your Majesty, I ...." Rosenberg guided him away.

A few months later, Da Ponte, highly agitated, entered Salieri's office. "What is this? I've being dismissed? It cannot be. My family in Ceneda depends on me—"

Salieri, with a grave expression, interrupted, "Emperor Leopold shows little of his brother's enthusiasm for the opera. He's making a clean sweep. Haven't you heard? He's even fired Count Rosenberg. No one is safe."

"But—"

"All those letters, pressing so hard to keep a job for your lady friend. Someone showed them to the Emperor. I'm told he yelled, 'To the Devil with this disturber of the peace.' Now he wants you out of Vienna altogether."

Angered, Da Ponte replied, "I begged Count Rosenberg to keep those letters confidential. Who showed him my letters?"

"I needn't tell you that you have several enemies in the court," said Salieri, who leaned close to him, and added, in a loud whisper, "As a Jew, you should know better than to make such a pest of yourself."

That night in his living quarters, Da Ponte paced back and forth. Adriana, seated, listened, but was also somewhat self-absorbed.

"I couldn't be leaving Vienna with greater glory. Do you know how many operas I've written in the past eleven years? At least fifteen."

"Lorenzo—" she said.

"And the opera house," he said. "Were it not for my shrewdness and devotion, it would have been closed long ago."

"Lorenzo—"

"Now," he went on, "I'm the victim of hatred, of envy, abandoned by my friends."

"Lorenzo, dear—"

"Scorned, slandered, humiliated by idlers, by hypocrites."

"Lorenzo," she said, "always it seems that everyone is plotting against you. I'm going to Venice with my husband."

"For three years I've been a slave to you, sacrificing my own welfare to keep your position at the opera. Now that I've fallen from favor—"

"There's someone else," she said.

"More treachery? Who is he?"

"No matter," she said. "It's over. The opera, our lives in Vienna. Everything." Da Ponte sat down next to her, deflated, staring vacantly at the wall. Adriana put her arm around his shoulder. "Where will you go?" she asked.

"Perhaps Trieste," he said. "From there, I can try to persuade the Emperor to allow me to return. I'd like to visit my family, but after all these years I'm still not allowed to enter Venice. Could your husband intercede in my behalf?"

"I'll see what can be done," she said. She held him in her arms. They remained pensive.

A few weeks later, Da Ponte sat at the table of a sunny outdoor café in Trieste, writing a letter:

Dear Mozart,

My financial situation is desperate. I'm reduced to selling my clothes in order to buy food. I've lost my patron, my mistress, and most of my friends. Why don't we try our luck in London? I've been given permission to return briefly to Vienna and shall visit you in a few days.

Huddled against the gray winter weather of Vienna, Da Ponte walked towards Mozart's apartment. He knocked at the door and a sad-faced Schemmer, the servant, opened, revealing an apartment that was barely furnished.

"Good morning. Is Signor Mozart here?"

Blinking back tears, Schwemmer said, "You have not heard? It was in all the newspapers. Herr Mozart passed away a week ago."

Stunned, Da Ponte replied, "I have just arrived from Trieste."

"We are all in a state of shock," said Schwemmer. "After the funeral, Frau Mozart went with the children to stay with her family. I am here all alone."

On a table near the door, Da Ponte spotted a death mask of Mozart. He picked it up, stared at it, horrified. "What is this?"

"The night Herr Mozart passed away," said Schwemmer, "Count Deym made two plaster masks: one for himself, and this one for Frau Mozart. But she could not bear to look at it."

"Did he suffer a long illness?" Da Ponte asked.

"Herr Mozart took to his bed in late November, but a week later he appeared to recover," said Schwemmer. "He fell sick again in early December. We were with him night and day during his agony, Frau

Mozart, Herr Sussmayr, Frau Mozart's sister Sophie. Until the very end, he was working with Herr Sussmayr on a Requiem. When he fell unconscious for the last time, Frau Mozart fell to her knees, imploring the Almighty for His aid. She could not tear herself away from Herr Mozart, however much we begged her. He passed away just before one in the morning on the fifth. The day after that dreadful night, crowds of people passed by the window and wept and wailed for him. Such a loss."

The servant suddenly remembered something. "Ah! Before his illness struck, Herr Mozart wrote you a letter. I came upon it yesterday as I was cleaning." He disappeared for a moment and returned with a sealed letter.

As he took the letter, Da Ponte asked, "And where was Herr Mozart buried?"

"In the churchyard of St. Mark's, just outside town," said Schwemmer. "You will see the freshly dug earth."

"No gravestone?"

"It is the custom now, ever since the Imperial Decree. Many people are buried in a common grave."

The carriage arrived at the cemetery. The day was grim and wintry. Da Ponte walked upon the muddy ground to a large area of freshly shoveled earth. He opened the letter, and a cold breeze shook the paper as he read it.

My dear Da Ponte, in response to your letter, I would love to join you and go to London. But how can I? First, I was hard at work on The Magic Flute, which was presented recently at Schikaneder's theatre. I hope you can see it. Salieri and Caterina Cavalieri came to the opening night. You can't believe how nice both of them were; they said it was a grand opera, worthy of being performed for the greatest monarchs. Now a stranger has commissioned me to compose a Requiem Mass. I see him continually before me. He entreats me and urges me and impatiently asks for my work. I continue to compose because that fatigues me less than resting. Anyway, I have nothing more to fear. I know well that I am on the boundary line of life and death. I shall die without having known any of the delights my talent would have brought me. And yet life is so full of beauty, and just at present my career shows auspicious prospects. Alas! Nobody on earth is master of his fate; it will be as Providence decrees.

Da Ponte folded the letter, placed it in his pocket, returned to the carriage, and departed along the mud-rutted road.

Trieste, several months later. Da Ponte was chatting with Mister Grahl at a gathering in the Grahl home. "Like you, Signor Da Ponte," said Mister Grahl, "we are newcomers to Trieste. I had businesses in London for a number of years."

"But Signor Grahl, you don't speak with an English accent."

"You might say we're a cosmopolitan family," Grahl replied. "I was born in Dresden. My wife is French. But we spent many years in England." Grahl motioned across the room to a young woman in her early twenties whose face was covered with a veil. "Our daughter, Nancy, spent the first sixteen years of her life in London. She's an accomplished linguist: English, French, German, even a little Italian. She is of marrying age and we are eager to find an appropriate suitor. You are a man of the world, widely traveled. Have you any suggestions?"

Da Ponte fixed his gaze upon the mysterious veiled young lady. "I know a wealthy Italian gentleman in Venice, a Signor Galliano, who is unmarried. I could write to him."

"I would be most obliged," said Mister Grahl. He then excused himself to attend to another guest.

Da Ponte, intrigued by the faceless woman, approached her. "Mademoiselle, the style in which you are wearing your veil is not in fashion."

"Why?" she asked. "What is the present fashion?"

"Like this Signorina," he said, as he delicately raised the veil and draped it over her head, revealing a very attractive face. Nancy, not amused, walked away in a huff.

Da Ponte approached the father once more. "Signor Grahl, thank you kindly for your hospitality. I must go now, but I shall most certainly write to my friend in Venice. I suggest that we enclose a small portrait of Nancy."

"Yes, of course."

While we await his reply," said Da Ponte, "I wonder if I might call again. I would very much like to improve my English, and my French. In turn, I could teach Nancy Italian."

"An excellent idea," said Mister Grahl. "Why not come tomorrow for lunch?"

A few weeks later, Da Ponte gazed lovingly at young Nancy. They were holding dictionaries, and exchanging language lessons, laughing.

"I did not think it was possible for me ever to fall in love again," he told Whitman. "But my heart was not made to exist without love. However much women may have deceived me, I cannot remember ever having passed six months without loving someone, and loving, may I make the boast, with a perfect love."

One day, Da Ponte came calling, and the father welcomed him. Nancy was also there, in the background, smiling at him. "Mister Grahl," said Da Ponte, "my friend in Venice has replied to my letter. Shall I translate it for you?"

Mister Grahl nodded, and Da Ponte proceeded to read it aloud.

Dear friend, If the girl looks like her picture, she is very beautiful. Reports as to her breeding, character and training could not be more favorable. They tell me her father is quite wealthy. I have plenty myself, but as a precaution in the interests of possible children, I should like to know what dowry he would settle on her upon our marriage?

Mister Grahl snatched the letter from Da Ponte's hand, tore it to shreds, and cast it into the fire. "Ah! So Signore Galliano is after my money and not my daughter." He remained silent a few moments, then turned towards Da Ponte. "I'm not blind. The past few weeks I've seen the great affection between you two."

Da Ponte gave out a nervous laugh.

Mister Grahl turned to his daughter. "And you, Nancy, what do you say?" Nancy lowered her eyes, then looked lovingly at Da Ponte. Her father reached out for Da Ponte's hand and Nancy's and joined them together. They gazed at each other lovingly.

"My entire fortune consisted of five piastres," Da Ponte told Whitman. "I had no employment and no hope of any. But I loved, and was loved in return, and this was enough to give me courage for anything."

"Signor Da Ponte," Mister Grahl asked him, "are you a religious man?"

Da Ponte was somewhat taken aback by the question. "I … not particularly, but I am a God-fearing man."

"I wish to ask a great favor of you."

"Of course," said Da Ponte.

"I myself am not very religious. But my parents, Nancy's grandparents, who passed away a few years ago, were quite religious. They often expressed to me how wonderful it would be if Nancy were to be married in a synagogue."

Da Ponte was stunned. "You are of the Jewish faith?"

"Yes," said Mister Grahl. "Is this of great importance?"

"No … no!"

"It will not offend you?"

"On the contrary. I will be pleased to do so, if it will make you happy."

"Thank you. Thank you. I assure you the ceremony will be carried out with great discretion."

In a small synagogue in Trieste, Da Ponte and Nancy stood together, and gazed lovingly at each other, as the rabbi performed the ceremony in Hebrew. Only Nancy's parents and a handful of immediate friends were present. Da Ponte was undergoing emotions that no one around him understood.

August 12, 1792. Da Ponte and Nancy boarded a carriage, driven by a young man, as the Grahl family bid them an emotional farewell. Da Ponte turned to Mr. Grahl. "We'll go first to Prague and then on to Paris." Da Ponte patted his pocket. "I hope the letter from Emperor Joseph will help me start a new life there."

Some days later, Da Ponte and Nancy were seated in the carriage, holding hands, blissfully happy, as they traveled through the countryside. "Wasn't Prague beautiful?" she said. "Imagine, three of your Mozart operas being performed the same week. You should be very proud."

"Now I want to stop at Dux to see my old friend Casanova," he said. "It's very close by. For the last several years he's been librarian to Count Waldstein."

When they arrived at the Dux castle they were greeted by Casanova, now in his late sixties, and a looking a bit the worse for wear. But he was delighted when guests arrived to break the monotony of life at Dux. His hand-kissing gallantry charmed Nancy. A servant led her into the house, to rest, as Da Ponte and Casanova proceeded to stroll through the gardens.

"She's lovely," said Casanova, "but I can't believe you're married."

Caught off balance, Da Ponte asked, "Who told you?"

Casanova grinned and pulled a letter from his pocket. "The news preceded you. Our old friend Pietro Zaguri has written from Venice."

Da Ponte reached out to seize the letter, but Casanova, enjoying himself, dangled it out of reach. He then read from it. *"A propos of Da Ponte, do you know that he has married a young Jewess named Nancy, to the unspeakable astonishment of a man I know, who could not imagine what it was all about, for he saw her married to an ordained priest, in a Jewish synagogue!"* Casanova stared at him. "I still can't believe you're married."

Da Ponte grabbed the letter, looked it over and handed it back. He shrugged his shoulders and smiled. "I am no longer my own master. Providence orders all my movements. I am giving myself up entirely to the search for happiness."

"But," asked Casanova, "what does happiness have to do with being married?"

"Listen, Casanova, have you ever been in love? Truly in love?

Casanova sighed. "You misjudge me, my friend. Of course I have loved. It was many years ago. I envy you your love, and your youth."

"You've lived a good life," said Da Ponte. "It certainly hasn't been uneventful."

"I shouldn't complain," said Casanova. "Count Waldstein has been generous, allowing me to be his librarian these past few years. I'm grateful to have a place to live, but nothing is right here. The macaroni, they serve too cold. The soup? Too hot. Dogs bark and keep me awake all night." Casanova looked suddenly older, weary. "The village priests bore me with their pious talk. Even the Count doesn't say good morning to me before greeting the others. Or, he will lend someone a book from the library, without consulting *me*, the librarian. The Count's steward has put my portrait on the door of the lavatory with an insolent inscription written on it. The servants laugh at me; at my old-fashioned clothes, which is all I know to wear. At my verses, my stories. At me, Casanova, the friend of kings and princes. Once, I was every woman's dream, every man's envy."

Casanova led Da Ponte inside, into the library, where a long table was covered with what appeared to be thousands of pages of hand-written manuscript.

"What is all this?" Da Ponte asked.

"I'm writing the story of my life," said Casanova, suddenly looking more animated. "It will be a sensation. I already have two thousand pages and need at least that many more to complete the tale."

Nancy stood at the door. "May I come in?"

Casanova brightened, turned youthful and gallant. "Madam Da Ponte. How enchanting you look." They went outdoors to the patio to enjoy a splendid lunch. It was a beautiful August day, with flowers in full bloom. Casanova was in great form. Nancy was fascinated by his stories, captivated by his charm. Da Ponte clearly enjoyed seeing how the old man was rejuvenated by his young wife's presence.

Later in the afternoon, as shadows deepened, it was time for them to depart. As Nancy entered the carriage, Casanova kissed her hand. Da Ponte was about to enter when Casanova grasped his hand. "Take some advice from one who is older and wiser. If you want to make your fortune, go to London, not Paris. But when you are in London, be careful never to go to the Italian Cafe, and never, *never*, sign your name to anything." They embraced and Da Ponte entered the carriage.

Casanova waved goodbye as they departed from Dux. Nancy looked back, smiled and waved. "What an extraordinary man." she said. "So elegant."

As the carriage wended its way along the picturesque country road towards Paris, Da Ponte regaled his bride with tales of his friend Casanova. "I could go on for days and days about his fabulous exploits all over Europe; his grand hoax on the Marchioness d'Urfe, a rich and gullible old woman. He actually persuaded her that he could return her youth. He disguised a beautiful courtesan as an old woman and then

Kal Wagenheim

'transformed' her back into a young woman before the Marchioness' eyes. I like neither his principles nor his conduct, but it is impossible not to love him."

One evening, Da Ponte and Nancy arrived at a country inn near Spires. They were eating supper when they overheard the innkeeper conversing with a patron at an adjacent table. "Have you heard? The French revolutionaries have imprisoned King Louis and Queen Marie Antoinette! Their army has advanced on German territory as far as Mainz."

Da Ponte pulled from his pocket the letter from Emperor Joseph to Marie Antoinette. He unfolded it, looked at it, then crumpled it into a ball. "Paris is out of the question. Casanova said to try London."

"Just as well, darling," said Nancy. "My sister Louisa and her husband Charles are there. Perhaps they can help us."

London: A few weeks later. Da Ponte wrote to his friend at Dux:

My dear Casanova, thanks to your advice, we are safe and sound in London. We have taken a room at 16 Sherard Street, Golden Square. Before I forget, please, when you write, do not address me as 'Abbe'. That is hardly a proper title for one who now has a wife! My Nancy sends you her fond regards. She loves me and I love her. We would be in paradise were it not for the wretched state of our purse.

Da Ponte and Nancy were at home playing chess one evening. He was glum, but she was cheerful. "Checkmate," she said. "Now you owe me one million pounds, or one million kisses. Which shall it be?"

"Nancy, darling," he said, "we have sold or pawned everything. We are so poor, there is sometimes only bread for breakfast, bread for lunch, and sometimes not even bread for supper. When I think of the comfortable life you had with your family—"

Nancy reached over and squeezed his hand. "Don't despair, darling. I'm sure our fortunes will change."

A few years later, Da Ponte was at home, writing a letter. In another part of the apartment, Nancy sat with their two small daughters, Louisa, age five, and Frances, a year old, and a servant girl.

Dear Casanova,

We are well here in London. You won't believe it, but I've settled down at last, as a real family man. If God grants us a little boy, I shall name him after you.

46

As Da Ponte wrote, several thousand pages of hand-written manuscript lay scattered on a long table in the library at Dux. Casanova, the author, was nowhere to be seen. A pen rested next to one page, only partially filled with shaky handwriting.

I continue writing libretti for the opera, Da Ponte continued in his letter. *We've rented the cafe at the theatre, and my darling Nancy runs that. I think she earns more than I do!*

There was a small the graveyard near Dux, offering a pleasant view of a church and a footpath beside a lake. By a freshly dug grave was a large iron crucifix. Engraved on it was: "G. CASANOVA 1725-1798."

Our two little girls, Louisa and Frances, are well, Da Ponte went on. *I hope that someday we can take them to visit you.*

Patrons streamed out of a London theatre, in a gay mood. At the entrance was a large colorful poster: *La Scola de Maritati. Music by Vincente Martin y Soler. Libretto by Lorenzo Da Ponte.* Arm in arm, Da Ponte and Nancy exited the theatre and entered a nearby cafe. The sign outside read: *CAFÉ ITALIANO.* In the crowded restaurant. A table had been reserved for them.

The ghost of Casanova waved an admonishing finger. "In London, be careful never to go to the Café Italiano." But Da Ponte did not hear him. Drinks were served and Da Ponte and Nancy lifted their glasses in a toast. A man at an adjacent table, holding a pamphlet in his hand, spoke loudly to his companions: "Just listen to this. I picked it up outside the theater. *A Short Notice on the Opera Buffa by the title La scuola de maritati, written by the celebrated Lorenzo Da Ponte, who after having been a Jew, Christian, priest and poet in Italy, found himself to be a layman, husband and ass in London.*" This evoked riotous laughter from the man's companions.

Da Ponte rose, reached over to the next table, seized the pamphlet, tore it to pieces, and threw it in the face of the surprised man who had been reading it. He took Nancy by the arm and strode out of the cafe. As they walked along, Nancy gave him a questioning look. "Darling, what did he mean?"

Da Ponte was agitated, angry. "Nothing, my sweet. Just some idiot who is jealous of my work."

Late that night, in the darkened bedroom, Da Ponte lay awake staring at the ceiling, still agitated. Nancy was concerned. "Darling, what is it?"

"Nothing. It is nothing."

She reached out, caressed his head, gently. "You can tell me."

He remained silent. "You can tell me anything," she said. "I love you."

"It's a long story," said Da Ponte. "My dear mother passed away when I was five. When I was fourteen, my father sought to remarry. She was a Christian woman." There in the dark, as Nancy caressed his hair,

Da Ponte told her the whole story, the truth. "So then I came to Trieste, which is where I found you."

"So," she asked, "you're real name is Emanuele Conegliano?"

"Yes."

"And you were born a Jew, like me?"

"Yes."

"And then you became a Catholic priest?"

"Yes."

Nancy giggled. "What is so funny?" he asked.

"It's a wonderful story," she said.

"You're not upset?"

She kissed him. "No. It's like a fairy tale."

They lay there in silence. She cuddled up against him. "You won't tell anyone?"

She took his hand, pressed his fingers against her lips. "It is our secret, forever."

They lay silent in bed for a moment. "Darling," she began.

"Yes?"

"It makes no difference to me," she said. "But, have you ever thought of going back to your original religion?"

After pondering his wife's suggestion for a moment, he replied, "Isn't life hard enough, without being a Jew?"

Nancy giggled. It was infectious. Da Ponte giggled. They hugged and kissed.

Time passed and one day Da Ponte was walking dejectedly along a narrow London street, muttering to himself, "Do not despair. Do not despair. Do not despair."

Shouts were heard. A huge ox rushed down the street, directly towards him, and followed by barking dogs and a throng of people. Da Ponte leaped inside an open doorway. It was a bookstore. He looked around while the proprietor observed him. Da Ponte spotted a well-worn volume on the shelf, removed it, and opened the book. Ah, Virgil, he said to himself, and he read a brief excerpt. There is no need to despair! He turned to the proprietor. "Sir, do you have any Italian books?"

"Too many," the man said.

"I've often thought of dealing in Italian books," Da Ponte said.

"You'll do me a favor in taking them off my hands," said the proprietor. "Come." They proceeded to the back of the store, and he gestured at a rear alcove packed with books. "I can use the space. Give me thirty guineas cash and the whole stock is yours."

Later that day, Da Ponte burst into the house and embraced Nancy. "Guess what?"

Laughing, she asked, "You won the lottery?"

"Almost as good," he said. "I … we … are now the owners of more than six hundred books of Italian literature."

"Books?"

"After three years of writing brilliant libretti," he said, "the ungrateful director dismissed me today."

"Dismissed you? But what—"

"He involved me in some complicated financial matters, didn't want to trouble you," he told her. "Now things have gone sour. He showed me the door. I was walking home, without a job, and God answered me. He sent me an ox."

Now Nancy was truly puzzled. "An ox?"

"Yes, an ox escaped from the abattoir. To avoid it, I ducked into a shop. The man had a large stock of Italian books."

Nancy smiled. She loved him dearly and was accustomed to his harebrained schemes. "Oh, I see. It's perfectly clear now."

He was exultant. "I already have some buyers who will guarantee me a handsome profit. I don't need Mister Taylor and the opera company anymore."

"But how did you pay for them?" she asked.

"A certain usurer of my acquaintance advanced me the thirty guineas," he explained. "By next week I'll have enough to pay him back and still have hundreds of books left over. Pure profit. They must be worth ten times what I paid."

"But darling—"

"There's a life of Michelangelo, a life of Tasso by Serassi, a life of Cellini, another of Petrarch … so many treasures. I'm going to open a small shop of my own. I'll write to Italy and obtain the latest works. Perhaps we can print some of my own poetry."

Two years later. There was a loud knocking on the door. Da Ponte, half asleep, opened and was surprised to see a police officer.

"Lorenzo Da Ponte?"

"Yes?"

"I have an order for your arrest."

"There must be some mistake. I have a wife and children to care for. And tomorrow we're celebrating my fifty-fifth birthday."

"You are to come with me."

A few nights later the apartment was virtually empty of furniture. Nancy and Da Ponte sat at the dinner table with their children. Now there were four: Louisa, eleven; Frances, five; Joseph, four; and Lorenzo, just a few months old, who was in his mother's lap. They could no longer afford the servant girl.

"It's bedtime, children," said Nancy. The three eldest children rose, kissed their parents and left the dining room. Louisa, the eldest, carried little Lorenzo.

"Six times I've been taken to prison in the past month," he said, "and six times I've had to rely on friends for bail. Nearly all our furniture has been sold to line the pockets of lawyers and judges."

"Lorenzo, darling," she said, "I've put aside a few thousand pounds from the cafe. Our entire life savings. Soon they'll be coming after that, too. My family is well established in America."

"America," he said. "What will I do in America? And what about the bookstore?"

Nancy was now losing patience. "Ah, yes, the bookstore. An ox comes running down the street. You jump inside a bookstore, and you buy up all the Italian books. What if it had been a butcher shop, or a dealer in ladies' corsets?"

"Fate drove me into that shop," he said.

"Did fate compel you to endorse those notes for Mister Taylor?" she asked. "Darling, you're too trusting in money matters."

"How could I know that I would become liable for his debts? How could I know that, as a Member of Parliament, he could refuse to pay? Now the lawyers and money-lenders come after me for his debts. My life has turned into a nightmare."

The ghost of Casanova admonished him, "In London, never, *never* sign your name to anything." But he neither saw nor heard a thing.

"For the longest time my sister has been asking us to visit them in America," she said, caressing his face. "I know this is difficult, darling. But I can go on ahead with the children, just to see, or at least until things improve here."

Eight months later: April 1805. Da Ponte was one of three passengers aboard the cargo ship Columbia, as it crossed the Atlantic. A man reached out to shake his hand. "Richard Edwards, I'm heading back home to Philadelphia."

"Da Ponte, Lorenzo Da Ponte," he replied. "A pleasure to meet you. Edwards? I'll call you Eduardo."

"Edwards is my last name," the man replied, "but if you like calling me Eduardo, that's fine."

As the hours passed, they became acquainted. "Eight months ago," Da Ponte explained, "Eight months ago, I gave my wife permission to stay in America for a year. But when I found myself without her, and my dear bambini ... so I go to join them in Philadelphia."

A few days later, Da Ponte told his new friend, "Eduardo, since we'll be together for such a long time, why don't we play a game of cards?" Edwards shrugged and smiled. Da Ponte shuffled the deck.

Fifty-seven days later the ship docked at Philadelphia. As cargo was being unloaded, Da Ponte rushed up to Edwards, who had already cleared Customs. "Eduardo, the Customs people tell me they'll allow me to bring in my trunk full of books duty free. But they say I must pay thirty-two dollars for the other things: the fiddle, tea-urn, my carpet—"

"And?"

"I lost all my money to you in the card games. If you would be kind enough to lend me the money, I'll pay you as soon as I'm reunited with my family." Edwards shook his head, reached into his pocket and gave the money to Da Ponte who hurried off to the Customs area. Minutes later, Da Ponte again ran breathlessly up to Edwards, who was about to depart. "Eduardo, Eduardo."

"Yes?"

"My wife, my bambini. I just learned they've moved to New York. Can you lend me another four dollars for the stage?" Edwards shook his head, smiled, reached into his pocket and gave him the money. Da Ponte nearly smothered him with a strong embrace.

Twenty-one hours later, at sunrise, Da Ponte stepped off a stage in New York City. He walked through the strange streets, gawking at the different surroundings. He stopped a pedestrian, and showed him a piece of paper. The man pointed. Moments later, Da Ponte was knocking at the door of a house. It opened, and there stood Nancy and the children. A tearful reunion, filled with hugs and kisses.

Da Ponte's age-gnarled hand held a nearly empty glass of red wine. The late afternoon sun streamed in through the front window. Whitman asked him, "How long have you been in America, Signor Da Ponte?"

"Let's see. I was fifty-six when I arrived. I'm now eighty-four."

"My God," said Whitman, "twenty-eight years. That's longer than I've been alive."

"I became an American citizen five years ago," said Da Ponte. "Such a wonderful place. But I miss my old country, my friends, my family."

"When you first arrived, what could a man your age do?"

"I had to support my family," said Da Ponte. "Later that year, when the yellow fever broke out, we moved across the harbor to Elizabeth Town, in New Jersey. My father-in-law helped me to open a grocer's shop."

Whitman smiled, with disbelief. "You? A grocer?"

In a modest country store, Da Ponte stood behind the counter as rustic customers came and went. "We thrived at first," he recalled, "but sometimes I sold to rascals who had no intention of paying. I was often obliged to accept as payment lame horses, broken carts, disjointed chairs, old shoes, rancid butter, watery cider, rotten eggs."

One afternoon, Da Ponte, now seventy years old, entered M. Riley's bookstore on Broadway in lower Manhattan. "Good afternoon, sir. Do you by chance carry Italian language books?"

"I have a few," replied Mr. Riley, "but no one ever asks for them."

While they chatted, another gentleman who had been browsing, approached.

"Why is it, I wonder," Da Ponte continued, "are books of Italian literature so little studied in a country as enlightened as America?"

"Oh sir, modern Italy is not, unfortunately, the Italy of ancient times," the man said.

Da Ponte smiled. "So you know our illustrious men of letters? Who are your favorites?"

"Dante, Petrarch, Boccaccio, Ariosto, Tasso ... I can't recall the others," the man replied.

Da Ponte gently took the man's hand. "If you allow me, I could name dozens of great Italian writers."

"But we don't know them here in America."

"Do you suppose a teacher of Italian would find encouragement here in New York?"

"I do believe so," said the man, who handed Da Ponte his card. "Dr. Clement Moore. I'm with the Columbia Theological Seminary. My father is President of the College."

"Lorenzo Da Ponte, at your service."

That evening, Dr. Moore was dining at home with his wife. A servant poured coffee. "I met the most remarkable man at Riley's bookstore this afternoon," he said. "An elderly Italian gentleman. Speaks English fluently. He was able to recite entire passages of Tasso by heart. I remarked that some day I hope to translate the poems of Metastasio. He told me that years ago, in Vienna, he had known Metastasio. Astounding."

"And what does this gentleman do here in America?" Mrs. Moore asked.

"I believe he wants to start a school."

"We must ask him and his wife to dinner," she said. "We can invite the Livingstons, the Duers, the Ogilbies, the Onderdoncks, and your father, of course."

A few nights later, the Da Pontes were guests of honor at a glittering dinner party in the Moore home. The others were fascinated by the courtly Italian and his charming wife, who spoke several languages. Da Ponte was seated next to Bishop Moore who commented, "My son tells me you've been engaged in teaching. Do you enjoy it?"

"It is very stimulating," said Da Ponte. "As a biblical scholar once said, "Umitalmidai rabadi miculam. I've learned from my pupils."

The Bishop was delighted. "So you know the sacred tongue of the Hebrews. I myself have been studying Hebrew and Greek for some years, but I'm far from fluent."

Before Da Ponte could reply, Nancy Da Ponte, still beautiful in her fifties, explained, "My husband studied Hebrew assiduously in his youth. Didn't you, dear?"

Later in the evening, a male guest approached Da Ponte. "I'm told you knew the great Mozart. When Caroline and I traveled in Europe, we learned that Mozart was held in very high regard. But his operas aren't known here."

"Mozart, Salieri, Haydn, I knew them all when I was in Vienna," said Da Ponte. "Mozart was my favorite. But he was was like a buried jewel before I helped persuade the Emperor to allow production of our *Marriage of Figaro*."

Nancy Da Ponte was also the focus of great interest. One lady guest said to another, "Mrs. Da Ponte has promised to give my cook the recipe for her spaghetti Bolognese." And the second lady said, "Nancy, my husband and I plan to sail to Europe next year. Do you suppose you could teach us a bit of French?"

A few weeks later, a sign outside the Da Ponte home at 54 Chapel Street in Manhattan read: *Da Ponte School for Young Ladies and Gentlemen. Language and Cultural Lessons.* Inside, Nancy Da Ponte skillfully fashioned brightly colored artificial flowers. Nancy Da Ponte was demonstrating this art to a group of young ladies. In an adjacent room, daughters Fanny and Matilda were helping to teach Italian to another small group of young women. And in still another room, students, mostly female, listened with rapt attention as Da Ponte, holding a book aloft, passionately addressed them. "What ecstasy would someone feel who had been blind from birth and who suddenly opened his eyes and saw the sunrise, the sky studded with stars, a meadow covered with grass and flowers? Study our great writers. I promise that you will feel the same delight, the same sense of the miraculous."

One evening a steaming bowl of pasta was the centerpiece of the long dining room table in the Da Ponte home. There was the hum of lively talk. The Da Ponte family members and a few young men, including Dr. Clemente Moore, were enjoying dishes of beef, vegetables, loaves of bread, red wine. Nancy Da Ponte, serene and beautiful, ladled out soup from a large tureen. Da Ponte gazed lovingly at Nancy and the children as they chatted with guests. Dr. Moore raised his wine glass in tribute. "Mrs. Da Ponte, I so much enjoy coming here. To dine on your delicious food, and hear *la lingua Toscana*, is like being magically transported to the Piazza Vecchia or the Via Condotta."

"Thank you, Dr. Moore." Nancy replied. "By the way, everyone in New York is talking about your Christmas poem."

"It's just a trifle, for children."

"But it's charming. Please let us hear it."

"Very well," he said, "but your youngsters must help me. Ready?" Dr. Moore looked around the table, urging the children to join in. "T'was the night before Christmas, and all through the house ..." The Da Ponte children cheerfully chimed in. "Not a creature was stirring, not even a mouse."

The years passed, and the time came when Da Ponte would sit alone at that dinner table, in silence.

Back to the present, in the bookstore, Da Ponte looked sadly up at the wall where there were ornately framed family portraits. "A few years ago, our dear son Joseph was taken away from us. Just twenty-one. Still a child. Then our eldest daughter Louisa, the ornament of the family ... just twenty-eight. Why could not He take me and spare them?"

Whitman leaned forward to comfort him.

"But the rudest blow of all came last year," said Da Ponte. "My darling Nancy, my devoted wife for forty years ... twenty years younger than me, yet God took her."

"But surely you are not all alone now?" said Whitman.

"I live with my son Lorenzo," the old man said. "He is a professor of Italian and Greek. I am so proud of him. His wife continues to run the boarding house. Several months ago I opened this little shop. Sometimes the most beautiful faces peek in here. They mistake my shop for the one next door where pastries are sold."

"You've done so much in your life," said Whitman.

"If, when I was young, I had read the story of a man to whom things had happened which have happened to me, how many mistakes I should have been able to avoid," said Da Ponte. "They have cost me so many tears. I've outlived my enemies and almost all of those whom I dearly love. Now, my time has passed. After so many years of hard labor, months have gone by since I had a single pupil."

Two beautiful women, in their late twenties, entered the bookstore silently, out of sight of DaPonte. They bore a striking resemblance to Camilla and Rosini, the two sisters that Da Ponte loved equally years ago. A reincarnation forty years later, each put a finger to her mouth, signaling that Whitman should not announce their presence.

Da Ponte continued his lament. "I, the creator of the Italian language in America! The poet of Emperor Joseph. The inspiration of Salieri, of Martin, of Mozart! I am a forgotten man."

Just then, one of the young women gently placed her hands over Da Ponte's eyes. The other giggled.

"Ah, what's this," said the old man, startled.

"*Buona sera, caro maestro,*" the young ladies said.

Da Ponte rose, magically rejuvenated, with a gallant flourish. "Ah! The loveliest flowers from my Tuscan garden. Mister Whitman, I want you to meet two of my finest pupils from a few years ago who remain ever loyal to me. Miriam and Anna Bancroft. Ladies, this is Walter Whitman, a brilliant journalist. He has been interviewing me about the Opera House."

Miriam and Anna shook hands with Whitman, who commented, "He's told me such fascinating stories."

"It's strange," said Da Ponte. "I remember years past as though it were yesterday. And yesterday, I barely remember."

Miriam said to Whitman, "He really is a marvelous teacher."

"Mrs. Da Ponte was such a lovely woman," said Anna. "He misses her terribly. Sometimes he gets a bit out of sorts. I think he just wants a little attention."

Anna kissed Da Ponte on one cheek and Miriam kissed him on the other. The old man brightened and looked at Whitman. "Aren't women wonderful?" They all laughed.

"Maestro," said Anna, "we'll be taking you to the theatre in our carriage tonight. Imagine, after all these years, your Italian opera in New York."

"Yes, yes, I'll be ready."

"Will you be attending, Mister Whitman?" Miriam asked.

"I would love to. But I'm not dressed properly."

Miriam eyed him for a moment. "My brother Neil was called away to Boston on business. We can dress you up quite nicely in one of his suits."

"Thank you, but—"

"Of course you'll come," said Anna. "How can you write about the new opera house if you don't get a first-hand look?"

Da Ponte turned to Whitman, and smiled. "Aren't women wonderful?" They all laughed again.

As the young ladies walked towards the door Miriam said, "I'll have someone deliver the suit within the hour. Until tonight."

After the young ladies departed Whitman said, "You still haven't told me about the new opera theater."

"For years I've dreamed of an Italian opera house here in America," said Da Ponte. "After my beloved Nancy died, I devoted all my remaining energies to this dream."

A number of well-dressed couples were gathered in the New York mansion of Mr. Dominick Lynch, a wealthy wine importer. They sipped champagne and nibbled on hors d'ouvres, as Da Ponte and Signor

Rivafinoli circulated among them. A soprano, accompanied by a pianist, sang a lovely Mozart aria. As she finished, there was polite applause.

"Is there anything lovelier than bel canto?" said Mr. Lynch. "Friends, I've invited you here tonight because there's excitement in the air. Let's hear from our distinguished former Mayor, Philip Hone."

Mayor Hone, a portly man, rose from his seat, to applause. "As you know, I'm a man of few words." There was laughter. "I'll be brief tonight. Our fair city is America's unrivaled center of commerce. But, I regret to say, in matters cultural, there's room for improvement. New Orleans has a year-round opera company. But not New York. We're about to correct that lamentable situation. Mister Lorenzo Da Ponte, an Italian gentleman who has lived in our midst for some years now, has an idea that deserves our support. Without further ado, let me present Mister Da Ponte."

Several of the guests applauded as Da Ponte faced the crowd. "Thank you distinguished Mayor. Good evening dear ladies and gentlemen. Many years ago, in Vienna, when his Majesty, Joseph the Second wanted to close the Italian Opera, I appealed to the public for support. Leading citizens like yourselves, people of culture, responded generously. The same idea can work here in New York, which deserves to hear the glories of Italian opera."

A practical man in the crowd asked, "How much will this new theater cost?"

"Approximately one hundred and fifty thousand dollars," said Da Ponte.

There were gasps and murmurs. Da Ponte turned to a man beside him. "This is my associate, Signor Rivafinoli."

Rivafinoli unfurled various colored sketches of the theater and explained the plan. "It will be a magnificent edifice. The facade will be neo-classical in style. The interior a delight to the eye."

Da Ponte interjected, "It will contain the first gas chandelier ever seen in a theatre, hanging from a dome frescoed with images of the Muses."

"The paintings on the wall will be made by artists specially imported from Europe," said Rivafinoli.

Da Ponte broke in, "The acoustics will be excellent. The stage will be vast. This theatre will rival, surpass, the finest in Europe."

A man asked, "But how will the money be raised?"

Rivafinoli explained, "We've designed a tier of exclusive boxes, each with capacity for eighteen persons."

"The cost for each box is six thousand dollars," said Da Ponte. "There are only twenty of these exclusive boxes in the entire theater."

"That will add up to one hundred twenty thousand dollars," said Signor Rivafinoli. "We can raise the remaining thirty thousand easily, with ticket sales."

Da Ponte looked around the room. "Now, who would like one of these elegant boxes? Remember, there are only twenty in all of New York."

People were hesitant. Some wives nudged their husbands, who reluctantly raised their hands. Soon hands were shooting up all over the room. Da Ponte looked around, pleased. "Thirty-six, thirty-seven, thirty-eight, thirty-nine. We have a total of thirty-nine bids, and only twenty boxes available."

Signor Rivafinoli whispered in his ear.

"My associate has an excellent idea," said Da Ponte. "We'll have a drawing."

There was a buzz of excitement. Mister Lynch provided a large punch bowl. Signor Rivafinoli began dropping pieces of paper in the bowl. "We've placed thirty-nine numbered slips in the bowl," said Da Ponte. "Those who pick numbers one through twenty win."

"Make that forty," said one man.

"Forty-one," said another.

These were wealthy and competitive people. There were expressions of delight, groans of disappointment, as people picked winning and losing numbers. Da Ponte circulated around the room, greeting the men, kissing the hands of the ladies, who were charmed.

On opening night, patrons began pouring into the new theatre at the corner of Church and Leonard Streets. A poster outside read: *The Marriage of Figaro. Music by Wolfgang Mozart. Libretto by Lorenzo Da Ponte.* A carriage arrived. Da Ponte, the two young ladies, and Whitman stepped out.

Inside the gorgeous lobby of the new Italian Opera House, New York's first opera theater, patrons gazed upward at the dazzling chandelier. Da Ponte, Whitman, Miriam and Anna walked through the lobby. Every few steps an elegantly dressed person shook Da Ponte's hand. The old man pointed to various persons, nodding or waving to them. "There's James Fenimore Cooper," he said to Whitman. "I'm told his novels are masterful. And there is Joseph Bonaparte, the former King of Spain and brother of Napoleon. He has taken a box for the entire season. He bought fourteen copies of my memoirs for his friends. Such a fine, cultured man."

On the fringe of the crowd, Da Ponte caught fleeting glimpses of the ghosts of Mozart, Salieri, Casanova, Emperor Joseph. He was momentarily startled, but quickly recovered.

As the audience filed in from the lobby. People admired the beautiful interior and ran their hands along the upholstered seats. Whitman took out his notebook and hastily scribbled in it: *What a magnificent spectacle to see so many human beings — such elegant and beautiful women — such evidence of wealth and refinement in costume and behavior!*

Mayor Hone stood up on stage, as the spectators settled in their seats. "What a glorious night. I want to introduce a gentleman whose energy and love for the arts is largely responsible for making this all a reality. Mister Lorenzo Da Ponte."

Da Ponte stood up in his front orchestra seat and turned to face the crowd. He was moved by the tribute. It was a triumphant moment for him. At last, after all these years of wandering in exile, he was being recognized.

"Thank you, ladies and gentlemen," he began. "Every day that passes, the three operas of Mozart are more highly esteemed. They cry out in triumph, 'We are eternal.' The words of these operas were written by me. To Mozart, that immortal genius, I gladly yield all the glory which is due him. For myself, may I hope that some small ray of this glory may fall on me."

As the audience applauded, Da Ponte took his seat between the two Bancroft sisters. The lights dimmed. The director strode in to more applause. He bowed, and turned to lead the orchestra. The opening chords sounded to the overture of *Marriage of Figaro*.

Whitman, dazzled, thought to himself, A new world — a liquid world — rushes like a torrent through you. This is art!

Anna Bancroft leaned over and whispered to Da Ponte. "Do you think Americans will understand the Italian opera?"

"Beauty is beauty," he replied. "A rose, a sunset. People respond. It is universal."

"When did you last see *Figaro* performed?" she asked.

"Long before you were born, my child. More than forty-five years ago, in Vienna."

Whitman leaned towards him. "And what is the theme of the opera?"

"It is about love and forgiveness," said Da Ponte. "Yes, love and forgiveness."

"I so wish I understood Italian," he said.

"Listen with your heart. You will understand." Da Ponte's eyes glistened as the music swelled. Mozart and he were immortal. Suddenly, he was startled to see Mozart directing the orchestra. From a box on the side, Casanova looked at Da Ponte, and raised an eyebrow. In another box was a smiling Salieri. In the central loge box, was Emperor Joseph II, solemn and attentive. Next to him were Haydn and Metastasio. In another box, Da Ponte's wife Nancy, young again, blew him a kiss. He lifted his fingers to his mouth and kissed her in return. Whitman noticed and looked over. The seat that Nancy occupied was empty.

Act IV of *Figaro* featured a lush garden at night with two arbors to the right and left. Da Ponte was startled to see that the exquisite aria, *Deh, vieni, non tardar*, was sung by Adriana del Bene, his lover of years ago, young again. In the aria, she beckons to her lover.

> *Deh, vieni, non tardar a gioia bella/*
> *viene ove amore per goder t'appella/*
> *finche non splende in ciel notturna*
> *face/finche l'aria e ancor/ bruna e*
> *il mondo tace.* Come now, my darling,
> don't delay, Come and answer the call
> of love. Before heaven's torch shines
> bright in the sky while the night is
> still dark and the world is at rest.

As this languid aria was sung, Da Ponte silently mouthed his lyrics, as he did decades before in Vienna. Miriam and Anna Bancroft, seated on either side of Da Ponte, reached out and took Da Ponte's hand. Whitman glanced over at Miriam Bancroft, seated next to him. He tentatively reached out with his hand towards her hand, which was on the adjacent armrest. Their fingertips touched gently. She turned, and responded with an angelic smile. Whitman closed his eyes, listening to the music, and composing in his mind:

I hear the sound I love, the sound of the human voice. Her voice is the purest soprano, and of as silvery clearness as ever came from the human throat, she convulses me like the climax of my love grip. Sweet singers of old lands, soprani, tenori, bassi! To you a new bard caroling in the West, Obeisant sends his love.

> *Que mormora il ruscel/qui scherza*
> *l'aura/ Che col dolce susurro/ il*
> *cor ristaura.* Here the brook is
> babbling, and the breezes are playing.
> And their sweet sounds refresh my heart.

All four were seated abreast. Mozart's librettist was linked with Walt Whitman; two poets of love from different worlds, different epochs.

> *Qui ridono i fioretti/ e l'erba e*
> *fresca/ ai piaceri d'amor qui/ tutto*
> *adesca.* Here the flowers are
> laughing and the grass is cool: Here
> everything welcomes the pleasures of love.

Da Ponte looked around. He and his companions remained in 1830s dress, but the rest of the audience was now in modern garb; it was now the twenty-first century and they were seated in the Metropolitan Opera House at Lincoln Center.

Vieni, ben mio/ tra queste piante
ascose/ ti vo' la fronte/ incoronar
di rose. Come now, my dear one and
among these sheltered trees I'll
crown your brow with roses.

The aria ended, prompting a prolonged burst of applause and "bravos".

Lorenzo Da Ponte, eighty-nine, died on August 17, 1838 at his home, 91 Spring Street, corner of Broadway, New York City. He was buried in the Old Catholic Cemetery of Saint Patrick's Old Cathedral on Eleventh Street near Second Avenue on the Lower East Side. The cemetery was dismantled in 1913. Like his immortal collaborator Mozart, the whereabouts of Da Ponte's remains are unknown.

Tragedy in Lafayette Square

Washington D.C. Spring 1857.

On a raised stage, bedecked with American flags billowing in the breeze, the United States Marine Band played a rousing march. A festive outdoor concert was being celebrated on the banks of the Potomac.

On the lawn, a well-dressed crowd of dignitaries sat on wooden chairs facing the stage. Among them was the recently inaugurated fifteenth President of the United States, James Buchanan, a man in his mid-sixties. Seated in the audience, just a few places distant from President Buchanan, was Dan Sickles, thirty-eight, intense, dark hair, moustache. Next to him was his beautiful young wife Teresa, twenty-one, with long dark hair. And a few feet away sat Barton Key, a man in his late thirties with a sad, handsome face, sandy hair, and moustache.

As the music concluded, the audience broke into applause. A bubbly master of ceremonies stood next to the band, raised his hands for silence, and addressed the crowd. He gestured in the direction of President Buchanan. "We are honored to have among us our new President, the Honorable James Buchanan." Again, the crowd burst into applause as President Buchanan stood, waved, and sat back down.

"And now Mister President, honored guests, a special treat," the master of ceremonies continued. "More than four decades ago, at a critical moment for our nation—the night of September 13, 1814—the British were bombarding Fort McHenry. Aboard an American ship in sight of Baltimore was a distinguished lawyer and poet. His name? Francis Scott Key. The next morning, at sunrise, when Mister Key saw that our flag remained aloft the fort, he was inspired to pen the lyrics to a song that stirs patriotism in all our hearts. Many citizens say it should be our national song. I refer to *The Star-Spangled Banner*." There was enthusiastic applause.

"With us today," he continued, "is the son of Francis Scott Key. Following in the footsteps of his late father, he is also a lawyer and attorney for the District of Columbia. Barton Key, please stand."

Barton Key rose to more applause. Dan and Teresa applauded along with the rest.

The master of ceremonies continued, "Now, it gives me great pleasure to present once again the United States Marine Band, and the distinguished baritone John Elkins."

Elkins, a tall, strapping man, appeared on the stage. The band began to play and Elkins sang in a strong baritone voice, "Oh, say can you see, by the dawn's early light …"

As Elkins sang, Dan's gaze wandered off to his left. He spotted an attractive woman, Madame X, in her thirties, several seats away. She gave him a slight smile and raised an eyebrow. Dan raised an eyebrow in return. Madame X blew him a discreet kiss. Dan winked at her, then turned to make sure his wife Teresa hadn't seen him.

As the song continued, Dan recalled the night not long ago in the parlor of an elegant brothel in Washington DC. Well-dressed men—members of Congress and other luminaries—were drinking, chatting, hugging and kissing attractive young women, who were garishly made-up and seductively dressed. Madame X welcomed him with a smile and open arms. They appeared to be old friends. Later, in the bedroom of the brothel, Dan and Madame lay in bed, making love.

Elkins concluded, singing with a flourish, "...and the la-a-nd of the free, and the h-o-ome of the brave." The crowd rose and let loose a burst of applause. As the spectators dispersed, Dan guided Teresa over to Key, who was with his sister Alice, an attractive woman in her mid-thirties, and her husband, George Pendleton, in his early forties.

In the background, Madame X observed them, waited, again with a slight smile. Dan spotted her with a sidelong glance, then turned his attention to Key. "Mister Key, I'm Dan Sickles, the new House member from New York." They shook hands.

"My wife Teresa," said Dan.

"A pleasure," said Key. "This is my dear sister Alice and her husband, Congressman George Pendleton of Ohio."

"We've just moved into our home on Lafayette Square," said Dan. "We're having a game of whist on Thursday night."

Dan, momentarily distracted, looked over Key's shoulder, and saw Madame X walking away. She stopped, turned, smiled, then continued on her way.

"For men only," Dan went on. "The ladies, of course, are also invited, and can grace the parlor."

That Thursday night in the Sickles home, four men sat around a table playing cards, smoking cigars, and sipping at whiskey glasses: Dan, Key, Pendleton and George Wooldridge, a family friend in his mid-forties. A cane leaned against Wooldridge's chair. Resting next to Dan's feet was Dandy, Dan's greyhound. Dan reached over to pet the dog.

"How long have you been in government, Bart?" Dan asked.

"President Pierce appointed me shortly after he took office," said Key.

"What are your plans now?"

"Not sure," said Key. "If Mister Buchanan has someone else in mind for the post—"

"I'm quite close to the President," said Dan. "If you'd like to stay on, I can put in a good word."

"Thank you, Dan," said Key. "I very much appreciate that."

In the parlor of the house, Teresa was entertaining Alice Pendleton and Mrs. Wooldridge. They were sipping tea and munching on cookies.

"I understand that your brother is a widower," said Mrs. Wooldridge.

"Ellen passed away three years ago," said Alice. "Left him with four children."

"The poor man," said Teresa.

"He loved her very dearly," said Alice. "I don't think he has recovered still." Teresa seemed quite affected, saddened.

The card game was over. The guests stood by the door, preparing to leave. Wooldridge hobbled along with his cane.

"Teresa, let me show you around town tomorrow," said Alice.

"I would love that."

"Dan," said Key, "do you like to ride?"

"Yes. So does Teresa. We often ride up at home."

"Well," said Key, "we must do that soon."

The next day, Teresa was strolling along a Washington street with Alice Pendleton. They approached an elegant restaurant, *Charles Gautier.*

"Gautier's is absolutely the best French restaurant in all of Washington," said Alice. "When you entertain at home, they can cook for the largest parties at a few hours' notice." They looked inside the front door and saw an elderly woman, Madame Gautier, seated in a chair, near the confectionary counter. "Madame Gautier," Alice continued, "knows the social status of every customer. Down to the last penny."

They continued walking and Alice pointed to another store. "Francois is the finest hairdresser in town. He speaks Parisian French." And another. "Madame DeLaRue sells absolutely the best hats and gloves." They continued walking and saw three men standing on a corner engaged in a lively discussion. "People in Washington inhale politics with the air they breathe. They talk and think of but little else."

They turned a corner and saw Amelia Bloomer, a woman in her forties, clad in billowing trousers, unheard of in those days, standing on a wooden platform. She was speaking to a small group of women while a few men looked on disdainfully.

"That's Amelia Bloomer and her tiny band of faithful," said Alice.

"Who?"

"Amelia Bloomer. The radical."

In a loud voice, Amelia said, "Women have as good and rightful a claim to vote as their brothers …"

Teresa regarded the scene with great curiosity. Alice amused, shook her head, and smiled. A man in the crowd heckled Bloomer, "Back to the kitchen." Bloomer smiled at the heckler and responded, "Queen Victoria of Britain reigns over an empire of a hundred and fifty million souls. If she is not out of her sphere, why should any woman in this republic be denied her place among a nation of sovereigns?"

The heckler yelled, "I won't have my wife going out to vote and being exposed to all kinds of riff-raff in the streets."

With a mischievous smile, Bloomer replied, "If the streets are such bad places, surely men should also stay indoors. Any place that is too corrupt for women is too corrupt for men."

This prompted some laughter in the small crowd. The heckler, unconvinced, waved at her dismissively. A young woman approached and tried to hand one of the pamphlets to Teresa who smiled nervously, shook her head, no, and kept walking.

Amused, Alice said, "She wants us to vote in elections. What do you think of that?"

"I ... really don't know much about politics," said Teresa.

Alice said, "Men make such a mess of things, might not be a bad idea." She then let out a loud laugh, prompting Teresa to giggle.

Alice and Teresa continued walking and looked down one side street leading to a field with cows and pigs roaming about. "As you can see," said Alice, "this is not New York. After dark, crime is rampant. Men go armed in the streets." Alice pointed towards another side street and assumed a distasteful expression. "Houses of ill fame. They serve only the very best class of patron: men in high office, officers of the Army and Navy, governors, lawyers, doctors—"

"Married men?" Teresa asked.

Alice laughed. "My dear, they all stray once in a while. But they come back, which is the most important thing." Teresa was silent. This had clearly struck a nerve. "I'm not suggesting that your Dan—"

Teresa interrupted her. "Thank heavens there is very little, if any, jealousy in my composition. I don't think I could be very jealous of a person I have never seen or known."

Just then, Madame X came walking out of the street with the "houses of ill fame." She was elegantly, if not flamboyantly, dressed. Madame X nodded to Teresa, smiled, and continued walking.

A few mornings later, Dan and Teresa were having breakfast at the dining room table. The servant, Bridget Duffy, entered with tea, poured it for them both, and left. Dan glanced at the daily newspaper as he ate. Teresa looked happy, enthusiastic. "Alice Pendleton took me all around town yesterday," said Teresa.

Dan kept looking at his paper. "Uh-huh."

"She showed me all the fine shops, restaurants, and a hairdresser," said Teresa.

"Mmmm." said Dan.

"Then we saw Amelia Bloomer making a speech," said Teresa. "Alice says she's a radical."

"Mmmm."

"Amelia Bloomer wants women to vote," said Teresa. "Just like men."

Dan looked up from his paper. "Really?"

Smiling, Teresa replied, "Alice said, 'men make such a mess of things, it might not be a bad idea.'"

Dan stared at her, quite serious. The smile disappeared from Teresa's face. "Is that what you think?" he asked.

"No, Dan, she was just joking—"

"It's not funny," said Dan.

"I guess not."

"Politics is serious business, Terry—"

"I know, Dan. I didn't mean—"

"We'd be in a real mess if we let the ladies run things," he said. Dan went back to reading his paper. Teresa remained silent, sad.

A year passed. It was a sunny afternoon in the spring of 1858. Barton Key, smartly dressed with a white riding cap, rode up on his iron-gray horse to the front of the Sickles Mansion. Teresa, in her riding habit and astride her own horse, waited for him.

"Good afternoon. Where's Dan?"

"He left this morning for New York," she said. "An important trial case." She seemed a bit troubled.

"He goes to New York often, doesn't he?"

"Yes."

Key smiled at her. "Shall we take our usual ride?" Teresa smiled, and nodded. They departed for a canter and chatted as they roamed through the countryside, clearly enjoying each other's company, talking and laughing. As they rode along a trail, clouds gathered. There was a rumble of thunder and rain began to fall. Soon they were drenched and their horses struggled and slipped in the mud. The Greystone Tavern loomed up ahead. Key pointed to it, Teresa nodded, and they headed for it.

Key and Teresa, soaking wet, entered the tavern. The loungers in the bar stared at them. Among them was Samuel Beekman, a man in his thirties.

Key spoke to the landlady. "A room for the lady, please. And send up some tea and toast."

"Yes, sir."

"May I warm myself in your kitchen?" he asked.

"Of course, sir," she said.

Key turned to Teresa and spoke to her softly. "Take off those wet clothes and tuck yourself into bed while they dry. I'll call for you in two hours." The landlady led Teresa upstairs while the men at the bar, especially young Beekman, observed the scene. Key called up to the landlady, "When you're done up there, please bring me a hot whiskey punch." Key draped his wet coat over a chair, then took a seat near the kitchen range. He stared out the window as the rain continued to fall.

Two hours later sunshine poured in through the window of the tavern. Key headed up the stairs. He tapped gently at the door. There was no response. Inside the room, Teresa lay in bed, asleep. Key tapped again, a bit harder. Teresa stirred, stretched groggily. "Yes?"

"Wake up, sleeping beauty," said Key.

Teresa smiled, slipped out from under the covers, and reached for her clothing. In a few moments, Key and Teresa, fully dressed, walked through the bar area towards the exit to remount their horses. As Key passed the men still seated at the bar, he spotted Beekman. Their eyes locked for a moment. Beekman looked at him and snickered. "Good afternoon, Mister Key." Key nodded, looked away.

Key and Teresa cantered home in silence through the sunny woods, the trees glistening with raindrops. "Who was that man at the bar?" she asked.

"Beekman," he replied. "A clerk at the Interior Department."

"Is he a friend?" she asked.

"Hardly. We had a run-in one day over some government matter."

They continued riding for a moment. "I think you should tell Dan about this," said Key.

"Yes, I shall."

A few days later, Dan and Teresa were having breakfast at home. Dan was, as usual, immersed in the daily newspaper. "Dan, the other afternoon while you were away, Barton Key and I were out riding and it rained. We had to stop at a tavern and dry our clothes."

"Lucky you found shelter," he said, as he continued to read. "Might've caught a beastly cold."

Later that day, George Wooldridge, walking slowly with the aid of his cane, came to the Sickles home. He entered the library, shook Dan's hand, and sat down. He pulled a letter from his breast pocket. "Dan, this is a very delicate matter." Dan leaned forward, concerned. "There's a clerk in the Interior Department, Beekman," Wooldridge continued. "Sent me this note. He was in a tavern two weeks ago and he saw Barton Key with your Teresa."

Dan interrupted him. "Oh, that? Teresa told me all about it long ago."

Wooldridge handed the letter to Dan, who glanced at it. "I don't believe it myself, Dan. But Teresa is being slandered. If this story gets around, it won't do you any good either."

The next day, a frightened Beekman was shown into the parlor of the Sickles home by the servant. Dan, with a stern expression, entered the room, holding the letter. He sat facing Beekman and stared at him intimidatingly. "You told Mr. Wooldridge in this letter that you saw my wife and Mr. Key riding together. They stopped at a tavern, took a room, and came out two hours later."

"Yes—"

Dan interrupted him. "Later, when you spoke with him, you said Mrs. Sickles removed her habit, and no doubt there had been intimacy between them."

"No, I never said that I only meant—"

"What did you mean?"

"I—"

"So why did you write this letter to Mr. Wooldridge?"

"I … did notice what seemed to be a flirtation going on."

"A flirtation?"

"Perhaps I was mistaken," Beekman responded.

Sickles rose and glared at him. "Next time, remember. Words have consequences."

"Yes, sir, thank you." Beekman left in a hurry.

Later that day, Key, icily furious, entered the Sickles home library and found Dan seated at a desk. "Wooldridge told me about the letter," Key said. "I wrote to Mr. Beekman. I told him anyone who makes such ridiculous, disgusting slander will have to meet me at the point of a pistol." Key pulled a letter from his pocket, and handed it to Dan. "Beekman denies everything. Says it was all a misunderstanding."

"I know," said Dan. "I invited him here yesterday."

Key was surprised. "Here?"

"Yes. And he apologized."

"Dan, I have four children myself, the oldest is eleven," said Key. "I feel only a paternal affection for Teresa."

"I know you're a man of honor, Bart. But for her sake, I had to run this damned gossip to earth."

Dan forced a smile, reached out and gave Key a strong handshake. Key was gracious but pale.

After Key left, Wooldridge dropped by. "George," said Dan, "I'm going to New York later this week. Would you look in on Teresa, just to see if she needs anything?"

Three days later, Wooldridge was in his carriage with Mrs. Wooldridge. They passed the Sickles home. "Let's drop by and see Teresa

Sickles for a moment," he said. He called out to the driver. "Henry, stop here, please." Wooldridge stepped out of his carriage and helped his wife out. He took his cane and hobbled to the front door. He tried the door and found it was open. They entered and Wooldridge looked around. "Hello? Anybody here?" Hearing laughter, he walked over toward the library and, without knocking, opened the door. Wooldridge was surprised to see Teresa and Barton, in riding habits, sitting beside a round table. Key was sipping champagne. There was a half-empty bottle on the table. Teresa, holding a large wooden spoon was stirring a salad in a large bowl. They looked a bit embarrassed. Key rose.

"Mr. Wooldridge. Mrs. Wooldridge," said Key. "Come in. Mister Key, do you know Mrs. Wooldridge?"

Key bowed. "A pleasure." Mrs. Wooldridge nodded stiffly.

"We've just come back from riding and we were famished," said Teresa. "Please join us."

Wooldridge was uncomfortable. "No thanks, I've just come to collect some papers for the Congressman."

"Would you like a glass of wine?" said Teresa.

"Thank you, but we have an engagement elsewhere," said Wooldridge. "He walked over to Dan's desk and shuffled a few papers. "I don't see them. He must've taken them to New York." They left. Teresa and Key exchanged anxious glances.

Moments later, as they returned to the carriage, Mrs. Wooldridge frowned shook her head.

The night of April 8, 1858. At a gala masquerade ball in a Washington mansion, the guests were dressed as English knights, Italian peasants, gypsy women, Greek goddesses, Turkish sultans, Druid priestess. As guests entered, an usher announced them. "The honorable James Buchanan, President of the United States." President Buchanan entered, in a business suit, smiling, and waving to everyone.

The usher spoke again, "The wife of Congressman Dan Sickles, Mrs. Teresa Sickles." Teresa, dressed as Little Red Riding Hood, entered alone. She looked around and spotted Barton Key, who waved to her. He was dressed as an English hunter: white satin breeches, cherry-velvet jacket, a jaunty cap, and lemon-colored high-top boots. Hanging from his chest was a silver bugle. Next to Key stood his sister Alice. A golden eagle with wings outstretched covered the corsage on her white satin dress. A tri-color slash with the words "E Pluribus Unum" in silver letters hung from her left shoulder. On her head she wore a crown with three stars.

Key approached with Alice. "Hello, Mrs. Sickles"

Teresa smiled. "Hello, Mister Key."

Alice and Teresa kissed. "What a lovely costume," said Alice.

"It's Little Red Riding Hood," said Teresa.

Alice showed off her costume. "I've come in honor of my father, as The Star-Spangled Banner."

"It's beautiful," said Teresa.

"Say, hasn't anyone noticed me?" said Key. He reached for his bugle and blew a loud note, prompting the women to laugh.

"And where is Dan?" said Alice.

"He was called away to New York," said Teresa. "He'll be gone for a few days."

"My George is off somewhere, too," said Alice.

"I was going to stay home," said Teresa, "but Dan insisted that I attend."

"I'm delighted you did," said Key. "We'll keep you company, won't we Alice?"

Later, Key and Teresa were dancing together, enjoying each other's company. She talked to him with great enthusiasm. He listened, interested. The hours passed. A large clock showed that it was past two in the morning. As the crowd thinned and people were leaving, Key looked into Teresa's eyes. "I'll escort you home."

"Where's Alice?" she asked.

"She left earlier, with friends."

"It's all right, I can—"

He smiled. "Little Red Riding Hood should never be out alone." They laughed. He offered Teresa his arm. She took it and they headed for the door.

Later, in the back of the moving carriage, Key and Teresa sat side by side, silently, each looking out a window. After a moment, Teresa looked at Key. "Bart?"

"Yes?"

"Forgive me for asking," said Teresa, "but how long were you married?"

"Eight years."

"And when did Mrs. Key pass away?"

"Three years, three months, and fifteen days ago."

"You must miss her a great deal," said Teresa.

"I adored her," said Key. "But what can one do? God decided to take her."

Teresa was silent. Key looked over, noticed tears glistening in her eyes. "What is it?"

"I am jealous," said Teresa.

"Why?"

"Because no one has ever loved me so." Key reached over and took her hand. She turned to him. They kissed. At first gently, then passionately.

Later, the carriage pulled up to the front of the Sickles home and Key escorted Teresa to the door. They paused for a moment. She opened it, entered and began to close the door. He reached out and gently stopped the door from closing. They stared at each other for a moment. She reached her hand out to him and he entered with her.

Inside the darkened study, costumes lay on the floor: Little Red Riding Hood and the English hunter. On a large red sofa, Key and Teresa were in a passionate embrace.

Several months later. Teresa exited the house and entered the horse-drawn carriage.

"Good afternoon, John," she said to the coachman.

"Afternoon, ma'am."

"To the cemetery, please."

"The cemetery?"

"Yes, please."

The coachman shrugged, pulled at the reins, and they departed. When the carriage arrived at the entrance of the Congressional Cemetery, Teresa got out and said, "I'll return in an hour or so." Cooney waited a moment, climbed down from the carriage, tied the reins to a post, and sneaked along the parallel path, following Teresa from a distance. Up ahead, he spotted Key, waiting astride his horse. As Teresa approached, Key dismounted. They walked off behind a mausoleum. Cooney, a knowing look on his face, returned to the carriage, lit a cigarette, and relaxed in his seat.

Behind the mausoleum, Key and Teresa embraced and kissed. "I've found a place for us," Key told her. Teresa looked at him, questioning. "A house on Fifteenth Street, just a short walk from your home. We'll have it all to ourselves." They kissed again.

A few days later, Key strolled along Lafayette Square and looked over at the Sickles mansion. He pulled out a white handkerchief, and twirled it about. He stopped in the shadow of a tree, removed a pair of small French opera glasses from his breast pocket. Through the glasses he could see into an upper window in the Sickles mansion. Key continued walking, pulled out the handkerchief and twirled it about again. He stopped, under another tree, and looked through the opera glasses. This time, Teresa was looking out the window. She waved, then disappeared.

Later, young black children were playing along Fifteenth Street, part of a poor, racially mixed neighborhood. Number 383 was a rundown, two-story house with shuttered windows and a wood fence around the lot. A gray wisp of wood smoke floated upward from the chimney. Teresa picked her way through the muddy alley and darted in at the rear gate.

In a room on the second floor, the feeble winter sunlight peeked through the closed shutters. A fire burned in the small hearth. The furnishings were sparse: a bureau, a rumpled bedstead, and a basin with a pitcher.

Through the connecting door and scattered about an adjoining room was a comb, a pair of gloves, cigarettes, and a man's winter shawl. Teresa undressed, taking off her black velvet cloak, plaid silk dress and undergarments. She lay naked in the bed, her dark hair undone and draped across the pillow. Shivering, she covered herself with a sheet. Key entered the room and also undressed. Teresa lifted the sheet and Key lay down next to her.

Several nights later on the stage of a crowded theatre, an Italian coloratura sang a melodious opera aria. Dan and Teresa sat side by side in a box. Teresa noticed Key arrive alone and sat in another box. He scanned the audience and spotted her. For the next few moments while the love song continued, Teresa and Key stole furtive glances at each other. Key smiled, blew her a kiss. Teresa looked warily at Dan, next to her, who was focused on the singer.

A few nights later, Teresa and Dan were home at the dining room table. Teresa went over a list and then handed it to Dan. "Here's the guest list for next Thursday's dinner, Dan." He ran his eyes over the names, paused at the initials P.B.K. He said, "Don't you think we're overdoing Barton Key, Terry?"

Teresa was flustered. "But Dan, Barton has had you to lunch at the club several times. Besides, he lives with the Pendletons."

He tossed the list back to her, apparently indifferent. "Do as you choose." Teresa continued writing out monogrammed invitations, but her hand trembled and she appeared tense.

On the afternoon of Wednesday, February 23, 1859, Teresa exited the front door of the Sickles home with her five-year-old daughter Laura. She looked across the street and spotted Key, who pulled a handkerchief from his pocket and waved it. By chance, Beekman was walking about half a block away and spotted them. Teresa entered her home and moments later she exited, but this time without little Laura. Teresa began to walk towards 15th Street. Beekman followed at a distance. Beekman watched as Teresa walked through an alley to the rear entrance of the house. He remained there, suspicious.

Later, Teresa and Key lay in bed together, after having made love. Silently, she lay on her side, looking away from him. She was depressed. Key reached over and put his hand on her bare shoulder.

"Are you all right?"

"I'm going straight to hell," she said.

He laughed and hugged her. "Don't be silly."

"I'm not joking. This is a sin!"

He hugged her tighter. "I love you. Don't you love me?"

"Yes ... but—"

"Then how can it be a sin?"

They lay silent for a moment. "From what you've told me," said Key, "Dan doesn't really love you."

"I guess he loves me ... in his way."

"And you, do you still love him?"

"I've known him as long as I can remember."

Twenty years earlier, a younger Dan, in his twenties, and little Teresa, just eight years old, romped about in a park. They were laughing, as he ran after her.

"We were happy once."

Dan caught her as she fell down on the grass. He tickled her, and little Teresa laughed with delight.

Key hugged her, kissed her bare shoulder. "I want to be with you all the time."

"He's Laura's father."

"Somehow, we'll find a way."

"I'm no good," she said. "I'm a sinful, selfish woman."

Key hugged her, tried to comfort her.

"We must stop seeing each other."

"Is that what you want?"

Tearfully, Teresa responded "No." She turned, and embraced him. "But we can't go on like this. Sneaking around. Lying. I can't bear it."

They lay together, silent, sad.

Later, Beekman watched as Teresa exited the house, looked around, and walked towards her home. Moments later, Key exited the house, looked around, and also walked away. Beekman smiled.

The night of Thursday, February 24, 1859, a few dozen guests were attending a dinner at the Sickles home. Dan and Teresa greeted the guests at the door. John Ward, the New York Times reporter, arrived. Dan extended his hand in a warm welcome.

"John, so glad you could come. Teresa, this is John Ward, a reporter for The New York Times, and a good friend."

"A pleasure, ma'am," said Ward. Teresa extended her hand.

Just then, Key arrived, alone. He shook Dan's hand and bowed to Teresa. She managed a forced smile, but appeared uncomfortable in his presence. Around the room a few guests observed this and began to buzz with gossip. The word had gotten out. Ward, the reporter, noticed Teresa's discomfort.

Later that night on a silver tray resting on a table near the entrance door were several letters, including a yellow envelope. Dan and Teresa bade goodnight to the last of the guests. Dan reached down to the tray and picked up the letters. Teresa, exhausted, headed upstairs to bed.

"I'll be up soon," said Dan. "I want to look through the mail." He entered the study and poked up the fire. He sat and opened the yellow envelope. His face registered shock and grief, as he read its contents:

Dear Sir, with deep regret I enclose these few lines, but an indispensable duty compels me so to do. There is a fellow—he is not a gentleman, by any means—by the name of Philip Barton Key. He rents the house of a Negro man by the name of Jonathan Gray, situated on Fifteenth Street, between K and L Streets, for no other purpose than to meet your wife. And sir, I do assure you he has as much the use of your wife as you have. I leave the rest for you to imagine.

Dan crumpled the note and tossed it on the desk. With tears in his eyes, he recalled a time twenty years earlier.

***

Twenty years earlier, New York City, 1839. A horse-drawn carriage clip-clopped along a cobblestone street in lower Manhattan and passed a street sign that read, "Broadway." Walking briskly was Mister Sickles, a wealthy, self-important businessman in his fifties. Hurrying to keep up with his father was a young Dan Sickles, just nineteen. They turned at the corner of Spring Street, and entered a private home.

In the dimly lit parlor of the Da Ponte home, tastefully furnished in European style, Dan and his father shared a sofa, facing Professor Da Ponte, a man in his thirties. A servant entered, bearing a tray with coffee.

With a bemused smile Mr. Sickles said, "Professor Da Ponte, my Dan doesn't care to follow me in the family business. He wants to be a typesetter."

"It's an honorable trade, Mister Sickles," said Da Ponte.

"But I insist that Dan also attend college," said Mr. Sickles. "I was wondering, while he works and pursues his studies, may he board here with your family?"

"We'd be delighted to have him," said Da Ponte.

Professor Da Ponte and Mister Sickles rose and shook hands.

That evening the Da Ponte family was seated at the dinner table that was bedecked with steaming Italian dishes and glasses of red wine. Professor Da Ponte entered with Dan, who looked around, shyly.

"Meet our newest guest, Daniel Sickles," said Professor Da Ponte, as he guided Dan around the table. He started with his wife, an attractive woman in her thirties. "My wife Emily." He stopped by his parents, a woman in her fifties, and a man in his seventies. "My dear mother and my father, Lorenzo Da Ponte Senior." The elder Da Pontes nodded and smiled. "Perhaps you have heard of my father. He wrote the libretti for some of the great Mozart's operas."

Dan smiled and nodded. He was somewhat awed by this imposing family. Professor Da Ponte guided Dan over to another couple, a man in his forties, and a woman in her thirties, who was holding their three-year-old daughter.

"These dear friends also share our roof and table," said Professor Da Ponte. "Signor Antonio Bagioli, the opera entrepreneur, his Signora Maria and their precious daughter Teresa."

Little Teresa smiled at Dan and reached out her arms to him.

"Look," said Signor Bagioli, "she is a real coquette."

Signora Bagioli put little Teresa in Dan's arms. He was surprised. Everyone at the table laughed. Dan looked down at Teresa, and she looked into his eyes and smiled. Dan smiled broadly. He felt welcome.

***

On Friday, February 25, 1859, Dan, his eyes bloodshot red, sat slumped in a chair of his office at the Capitol. His friend, George Wooldridge, concerned, hobbled in on a cane and sat down near him. Dan pulled the crumpled letter from his pocket and unfolded it.

"George," said Dan, "last night I received this." Holding back tears he handed the letter to Wooldridge. "It says Barton meets a lady at a house on Fifteenth Street. Can you see if it's Teresa?" Dan put his hand to his head and sobbed. Ashamed by his sudden outburst, he jumped up from his chair and exited the office.

Later that cold, rainy day, Wooldridge emerged from a carriage across the street from the house on Fifteenth Street. Standing beneath his umbrella he watched the house. A young black man walked by. Wooldridge pointed to the house and engaged him in conversation.

Two hours later, Wooldridge waited in a corridor outside the House Chamber. Dan exited from the Chamber and anxiously approached him. They spoke briefly and the anguish showed on Dan's face. Wooldridge tried to calm him. Dan walked away.

Dan staggered home through the cold, rainy streets. He ignored others who greeted him and regarded him with concern.

Soaked from the rain, Dan entered the house, walked right past Bridget Duffy, the servant, who noticed his wild, distracted look. Dan sat alone at the dining room table. A stony silence. Dan did not touch his food. Bridget entered and said, "Mrs. Sickles has a headache. She remains in bed." Dan, tears gleaming in his eyes, got up angrily. "Have my dinner sent upstairs."

Dan entered the bedroom and called out sharply, "Terry."

Teresa, apprehensive, came out of the dressing room.

"Where were you Wednesday afternoon?"

Teresa, blanched, swayed a bit, and sat down in a chair. "I … I think I was shopping, Dan."

Dan came closer to her, clenching and unclenching his fists. "Weren't you at a house on Fifteenth Street with Barton Key?"

Teresa's head drooped. Dan stooped down and shouted, "Tell me."

Dan grabbed Teresa, pulled her from the chair and shook her violently. "Were you?" Dan grabbed her left hand and wrenched the wedding ring from her finger. Teresa collapsed back into the chair. Bridget knocked at the door. They fell silent. Bridget brought in Dan's dinner tray and rested it on a table. She stirred the burning wood in the fireplace and then exited as she glanced sadly at Teresa.

Downstairs the alarmed servants heard Dan shouting, Teresa sobbing. Suddenly all was quiet. Upstairs in the bedroom, Teresa sat at her escritoire holding a pen, her face streaked with tears. Dan opened the bedroom door wide, then stood beside her. He was straining hard to control his emotions, but looked as though he was about to explode. "Now write. Write down in your own words what happened. Everything!"

The pen dropped from Teresa's hand. "Dan I can't."

Dan picked up the pen, put it in her hand, and closed her fingers over it. "You must. You owe it to me. God knows what may come of this."

Slowly, hand quaking, Teresa began to write. Two lines and she was unable to continue. "I don't know what—"

Dan, pacing about in a cold fury, stopped and asked her. "Tell me about the house on Fifteenth Street."

"What is there to tell?"

"Everything. I want to know everything!"

"There was nothing to eat or drink there. The room is warmed by a wood fire—"

"Write that down," said Dan. "How many times were you in the house on Fifteenth Street with Mister Key?"

"How many times? I don't know."

"Whose house is it?"

"I believe the house belongs to a colored man."

"When did you first go there?"

"The latter part of January."

"By yourself?"

"Mister Key generally went first," Teresa replied. "We've walked there together—"

"How many times?"

"Perhaps four times. I don't think it was more."

"Write that down."

She hesitated. "I said write it down!" She began to write. She finished, her hand trembling. "And when you were with Mister Key?"

"I usually stayed an hour or more."

"And what did you do?"

She was silent. He leaned close to her, menacingly.

"There was a bed in the second story."

Dan, his voice growing louder, asked, "What did you do?"

"I … did what is usual for a wicked woman to do."

Dan tried to contain his anger. "Write that down." She wrote.

"And when did your affair with Key begin?"

"The intimacy, of an improper kind, commenced in that house this winter."

"Write that down." Tears streaming down her cheeks, she wrote. "And that was the very beginning?"

"Mister Key has kissed me in this house a number of times."

"Here? In our home?"

"Last spring, in April or May."

"Kissed?" said Dan. "Nothing more?"

"We … had connection in this house."

Trembling, Dan asked, "In this house? Where?"

"In the parlor … on the sofa. You were sometimes out of town, and sometimes in the Capitol."

"Write." Still crying, she wrote, as Dan paced about. "And Mister Key came to this house, even after I told you, more than once, not to invite him?"

"Yes."

"Write that down." She wrote. "And then?"

"I didn't think it safe to meet him here because the servants might suspect something."

"The servants."

"Mister Key then told me he had hired the house as a place where he and I could meet. I agreed to it."

"Write." She wrote, as he hovered over her. "How did you arrange your meetings?"

"When we met in the street and at parties. I never would speak to him when you were at home. I knew you didn't like me to speak to him."

"Write." She wrote, as he paced, tears now welling in his eyes. "And when was the last time you saw Mister Key?"

"I think it was Wednesday last."

"Wednesday, the twenty-third?"

"Yes."

"Write that down." She wrote. "What happened on Wednesday, the twenty-third?"

"I went to Fifteenth Street alone. Laura was at Mrs. Hoover's."

"You left Laura at Mrs. Hoover's?"

"No."

"How did she get there?" asked Dan. "All by herself?"

"No. Mr. Key left her there at my request."

Containing his anger, Dan said, "I see. He escorted our daughter. Write that down."

"Dan—"

"Write!" She wrote. "At least you had the decency not to take Laura with you to that house."

"Dan, I would never—"

Interrupting her, he asked, "And then what happened?"

"Immediately after Mister Key left Laura at Mrs. Hoover's, he met me at Fifteenth Street."

"And?"

"I undressed myself. Mister Key undressed also. We went to bed together."

"Write that down." She wrote. "Now, I want you to write the following." He proceeded to dictate slowly, as she wrote. "This is a true statement written by myself, without any inducement held out by Mister Sickles of forgiveness or reward, and without any menace from him. This I have written with my bedroom door open and my maid and child in the adjoining room, at half past eight o'clock in the evening. Teresa Bagioli"

Teresa finished writing, put down the pen and looked at Dan, her eyes swimming in tears. She was exhausted—physically and emotionally.

Dan walked over to the nursery door and leaned in. "Bridget? When you've finished putting Laura to bed, please come in here."

Bridget entered looking apprehensive. Dan covered the main part of the confession with a large blotter. "I want you to witness this signature." Dan handed the pen to Teresa. "Please write down the following: Written and signed in presence of Bridget Duffy. February 26, 1859. She wrote, then Dan took the pen from Teresa's hand. "Thank you." He gave the pen to Bridget. "Would you please sign this?" Bridget, in embarrassed silence, signed the document as Dan paced the floor, fingers pressed to his temples. Bridget left the room, quietly, sadly.

Suddenly, like a dam bursting, Dan began to moan. "Laura. My little Laura." Dan strode into the nursery, picked up the drowsy Laura from her bed, and carried her into his bed.

The clock showed midnight. Teresa lay on the floor in the bedroom, her head resting on a chair, tears streaming down her cheeks. She remembered seven years ago, the year 1852.

Teresa, then sixteen, heard the bell at the front door of the Da Ponte home in Manhattan, and opened it. Dan, then thirty-three, stood there, smiling. They looked at each other, unsure, curious.

"Teresa?"

"Dan?"

"My God," he said, "you're all grown up."

"It's been nearly eight years."

"And beautiful."

She smiled, radiantly. "How are you, Dan? You've been upstate all this time?"

"I was doing fine with my law practice," he replied, "but I've moved back to the city. I'm going into politics."

"So we'll be seeing more of you now."

"Most definitely."

They smiled warmly at each other.

Now, back in the present, a tearful Dan, in bed, held his daughter Laura in his arms. He remembered six years ago, in his father's home.

Mister Sickles, seated at his desk in the library, stared in disbelief at the younger Dan, seated opposite him, and asked, "You want to do what?"

"I want to marry Teresa Bagioli."

"But she's just a child. Half your age!"

"We love each other."

"Love." Mister Sickles said, in a half mocking tone. "Can't you wait until she's a bit older?"

"We want to get married now."

Mister Sickles rose, stared out the window. After a pause he asked, "Is she pregnant?"

Dan, a bit ashamed, nodded.

His father, still staring out the window, muttered, "My God."

"But father, we do love each other."

Mister Sickles turned, approached his son, and leaned over him. "You're running for Congress in a few months."

"Don't you think the voters would prefer a married man?" Dan asked. "A family man?"

Mister Sickles stared at his son, frustrated, unable to come up with a rejoinder. He shook his head, clearly displeased.

Not long afterwards at the church altar, Dan and Teresa stood solemnly facing each other as The Minister had them repeat the vows. "Do you Daniel Sickles take Teresa?

Bagioli ...." As the Minister continued, Mister and Mrs. Bagioli, and Mister and Mrs. Sickles sat beside each other in the front pew. They strained to appear pleased, but were clearly not overjoyed.

Sunday, February 27, 1859. Barton Key rose from the chair in the barbershop at Willard's Hotel and examined himself in the mirror after the shave. He was dressed in gray-striped trousers, matching vest, white shirt, brown tweed jacket, brown overcoat.

"Mild day for February," the barber commented.

"Yes, think I'll take a stroll," said Key, and he left the shop.

Later, in the Sickles home, the wall clock showed 10:30 a.m. Bridget Duffy returned from church and saw Dan, grim-faced, descend the stairs and enter the library. She began to cry. George Wooldridge arrived and found Dan in the library, eyes bloodshot and red, pacing back and forth, at times pressing his hands to his temple. He approached Dan, reached out to pat his shoulder, but stopped just short of touching him.

A few hours later it was an unseasonably warm Sunday afternoon. Several people, including Barton Key, strolled along in Lafayette Square, near The White House. A young couple approached. They had just come from church and the man held a bible in his hands. Key greeted them.

"Good day, Mister Key," the man said. "Have you been ill?"

"I've not been feeling very well," Key replied. "I've a mind to go west and hunt buffalo. It would either cure me or kill me, and I don't care much which."

The couple departed. Suddenly, the Sickles' greyhound, Dandy, ran across the street and playfully jumped up at Key who took out his handkerchief and whirled it three or four times, pretending he was playing with the dog. As the dog ran off, Key continued to wave the handkerchief, and looked up towards Teresa's window.

In the Sickles home, Bridget entered the nursery where little Laura was asleep. She looked out the window of the corner room and saw Key in Lafayette Square, waving the handkerchief, as the dog ran off.

In the library, Dan, seated, stared at the wall, as he spoke to Wooldridge. "George, I'm dishonored. What shall I do?"

"Send Mrs. Sickles to her mother in New York," Woolridge advised. "It's near the end of the session and her going will excite no remark. It will be half a year before the House meets again. You should take a trip to Europe, arrange a separation."

Key continued walking in Lafayette Square, whirling his handkerchief as he strolled along, while inside the library, Wooldridge looked out the window and spotted him. He turned to Dan. "I just saw Key."

Dan rushed to the window and looked out. "That scoundrel! He's making signals. God!"

"Easy," Wooldridge said. "Only we know of this."

"No. The whole town, the whole world, knows it."

"Calm down."

"No, no, my friend," Dan said. "All Washington is talking about it."

Wooldridge shrugged. "If that be so, as a man of honor—"

Dan seemed frantic, disoriented. "Where is he now?"

Wooldridge, still looking out the window, replied. "I don't see him."

"Let's go over to the Clubhouse," Dan said. "He may have a room there."

Wooldridge rose and moved towards the door. Dan said, "Go on ahead." As Wooldridge exited the house, Dan opened the door to the basement and ran down the stairs. He hastily rummaged around in the where he stored his saddles and guns. He grabbed a large-bore, single-shot Derringer. He also picked up a muzzle-loading Colt revolver, fired by means of separate caps affixed to the butt of each chamber. Dan rushed back up the stairs and slammed the door as he left.

February 27, 1859, 2 p.m. Barton Key walked east along Pennsylvania Avenue approaching the southeast corner of Lafayette Square. Coming from the opposite direction, Wooldridge met him at the corner of Pennsylvania and Madison.

"Good afternoon, Wooldridge," Key said. "What a fine day we have."

"Did you come from the Clubhouse?" Wooldridge asked him.

"Yes."

"Do you know if Mister Stuart is in his room?"

"Yes," Key replied. "He's quite unwell."

"I'm going up to see him. Good day."

As Wooldridge turned towards the Clubhouse, Dan, carrying a Derringer, walked rapidly towards them from the north side of the square. From twenty feet away, he shouted, "Key, you scoundrel. You've dishonored my house." Now ten feet away, Dan faced Key, who stood near the corner lamppost. Key thrust his hand inside his coat and pulled out the pair of small French opera glasses.

Dan fired. The shot tore a hole in Key's jacket and grazed his right side.

Key shouted, "Murder."

Dan raised his arm to fire again. Key jumped at him, seizing Dan by the collar of his coat.

The two men grappled. Key tried to strike him with the opera glasses. Dan's Derringer fell to the sidewalk. Dan stepped back, but Key grabbed him from behind with both arms around his waist.Dan squirmed out of Key's grasp, swung around towards him, reached into his overcoat pocket, and pulled out a second gun, the Colt revolver.

Key backed away, pleading, "Don't. Don't shoot!"

Dan followed him as Key retreated up the middle of the street towards the Clubhouse. Desperate, Key tossed the opera glasses at Dan. The glasses seemed to float in the air, hit Dan on the lower leg, and fell to the ground. Dan, within ten feet of Key, fired. The bullet struck Key in the right thigh, just below the groin.

Key gasped, "I'm shot." He staggered towards the sidewalk, pleading, "Don't! Don't kill me."

"You've dishonored my house," Dan said. "You must die."

Key leaned against a tree, trying to hold onto it. He slumped to the ground, lying on his right side, one hand over his groin. Again, he pleaded, "Don't..." Key tried to prop himself up on his elbow.

Dan came closer and pulled the trigger. It snapped, misfiring.

"Murder," Key yelled. "Murder. Don't shoot."

Dan re-cocked his weapon, puts it close to the left side of Key's chest and fired. Key seemed to wilt and fell back, mortally wounded. Dan put his gun to Key's head and pulled the trigger again, but it misfired.

Thomas Martin came out of the clubhouse, and rushed up. Dan, enraged, tried again. He pulled the trigger and once more it misfired.

"Mister Sickles," Martin yelled. "For God's sake."

"He violated my bed."

Francis Doyle, who also came out of the clubhouse, put his hand on Dan's shoulder. Dan jerked his arm away and drew back several steps. Wooldridge, who had watched the whole scene from a few paces away, came over, took Dan by the arm, and led him away towards the corner of H Street and Madison. As Dan quietly walked away, he put the gun in his pocket.

Key was still alive, barely breathing. Doyle and Martin picked him up and carried him into The Clubhouse. They placed Key on the floor inside one of the rooms off the front hall. Doyle overturned a chair and rested Key's head and shoulders on the rung of the chair. Martin put his hand on Key's heart and felt for a pulse. "What happened?" he asked.

Key stared blankly at him, not understanding.

"Do you have a final word for your children?" Martin asked.

Key continued staring at him. Doctor Coolidge, a surgeon, rushed in. He opened Key's shirt and trousers to examine the wounds and shook his head sadly.

Minutes later, Dan pushed his way back into the Sickles house, while a large crowd gathered outside. Inside, a few friends had arrived. There was also a police officer.

Dan threw himself onto a sofa and began to sob. Wooldridge entered holding the opera glasses that he had retrieved from the street. Wooldridge gave the glasses to Dan, who asked, "Is Key dead?"

"Yes."

Dan muttered, "One wretch less in the world." Dan rose and headed for the stairs. The police officer stopped him.

"I just want to get some papers," Dan said.

"Your wife is up there alone," the officer said. "We don't want you harming her."

Dan waved him away. "I have no such intention." He climbed the stairs and entered the front bedroom and closed the door.

Teresa, still in her dressing gown, her black hair wild about her, turned from the window to look at Dan, her dark eyes wondering. Dan, holding the opera glasses in his fist, stared at her. "I've killed him." He turned and left, slamming the door behind him, and lumbered back down the stairs. All heard Teresa's anguished scream.

The next day a newspaper vendor stood next to a tall stack of Washington newspapers and waved one aloft, showing the headline: TRAGEDY IN LAFAYETTE SQUARE. He shouted, "Extra! Extra! Tragedy in Lafayette Square! Tragedy in Lafayette Square! Customers approached and gave him coins and walked off.

March 1, 1859, 2 p.m. Inside the Key home, Barton lay "life-like" in a mahogany coffin with silver trimmings that were covered with black cloth. He was dressed in a black coat and pants and a white vest. His hands, covered with white kid gloves, held a bouquet. Flowers were strewn inside the casket. On its lid was a plaque bearing the inscription: PHILIP BARTON KEY. DIED FEBRUARY 27, 1859. AGE, 39. As mourners filed by, Key's sister Alice and her husband George stood there, thanking them.

Meanwhile, Dan, his face covered in lather, was seated in a chair, being shaved by a barber in his comfortable jail cell. It was an arched room about twenty feet square with whitewashed walls, a fireplace, desk, two bureaus, chairs and stools. Books and writing materials cluttered the shelves. A box of flowers rested on the window sill. Photos of his daughter Laura were on the wall above the desk. His greyhound, Dandy, rested at Dan's feet, waving its tail. The barber finished and left. Dan lit a cigar.

Dan's father, looking quite upset, was allowed to enter the cell. "You hot-headed fool. That's no way to settle things."

Dan looked away, saying nothing. "No woman's worth it," his father continued. "No matter how you come out of this, you've killed your career—White House and everything else."

"Don't you think I know that?" Dan replied. "And if I had to, I would do it again. We couldn't live together on the same planet."

The father looked at his son's haggard face and his expression softened. He pulled out his checkbook. "Well, we must get the best men for your defense."

In a darkened bedroom of her parents' New York home, Teresa, grief-stricken, lay in a fetal position, staring at the wall, her eyes glistening with tears. Her mother, Mrs. Bagioli, came in, sat on the bed next to her, and caressed her hair. "Teresa."

Teresa did not answer.

"Reverend Haley is here to see you."

Teresa stirred. "Who?"

"The pastor of the Unitarian Church. He's come from Washington and wants to see you."

I can't see anyone."

Mrs. Bagioli continued caressing her hair. "He says it's important. Come." She helped her daughter rise from the bed.

Teresa, drained and weak, and Mrs. Bagioli entered the parlor. Waiting for them was the Reverend William Haley, a short, slender man dressed in black. He sat opposite Teresa's father, who held little Laura, on his lap. He looked at her, sympathy in his eyes.

"I come from your husband's side, in his prison cell," he said.

Tears welled in Teresa's eyes, but she did not speak.

"Come little Laura," said Mister Bagioli. "Let's play outside." He lifted the little girl up in his arms and left the room.

Now Reverend Haley addressed himself to Mrs. Bagioli. "Dan says he is willing to allow Teresa to keep custody of their daughter." Mrs. Bagioli nodded. "Providing she remains here in New York with you." Mrs. Bagioli nodded again. Reverend Haley reached into his pocket and pulled out a small object. He looked to Teresa. "The wedding ring he took from your finger." He held it out to her. She stared at it, without moving. "I persuaded him to return it to you." Reverend Haley placed it in her hand. As tears welled in her eyes, Teresa hesitated, then slipped the ring back on her finger.

***

President Buchanan was seated at his desk in the White House when an aide entered. "Mister President, Congressman George Pendleton of Ohio is here to see you. He's with his wife, Alice."

"Show them in," Buchanan replied.

The aide had a worried look. "She's the sister of Barton Key."

"Yes, I know."

Pendleton and Alice entered. Buchanan rose from his desk, and shook Pendleton's hand.

"Hello, George."

"Mister President."

Buchanan turned to Alice and took both of her hands in his. "My sincere condolences. Your brother was a fine man."

Buchanan guided them to a nearby sofa and sat in a chair opposite them.

"Mister President," Pendleton said, "the government has named Robert Ould, my brother-in-law's former assistant, to prosecute the case."

"That's what I'm told."

"Mister Ould is an able man, but the defense has an entire battery of experts. Can't something be done to help Mister Ould?"

"The government's resources are limited."

"But Mister President—"

"I'm terribly sorry," Buchanan interrupted. "But I can't be accused of interfering."

"It wouldn't be interfering, Mister President," Alice said. "All we ask is that you provide some support for Mister Ould."

"I simply cannot."

With tears brimming in her eyes, Alice said "But my brother was murdered in cold blood, in plain daylight."

"I'm terribly sorry."

Now her voice took on a bitter tone. "Everyone knows that Mister Sickles is your friend. What kind of fair trial will that be?"

Her husband tried to calm her. He looked at the President apologetically. "Is there any objection if our family should find an assistant for Mister Ould?"

"I suppose not."

"Would the government be able to help with the expenses incurred by the assistant?"

"I'm afraid we are unable to do so."

The aide peeked in, coming to the rescue. "Mister President, your appointment with the French ambassador. He's waiting outside."

Buchanan rose from his chair. "Terribly sorry."

Day One: April 4, 1859

A raw spring morning. A few hundred men and a few women crowded around the entrance to the east wing of City Hall that led to the courtroom. The building was two blocks from the Capitol Building. Among the faces were Amelia Bloomer and Madame X, who did not know each other.

Inside, the empty courtroom was dingy, small, with high ceilings, and tall arched windows. It had two barrel stoves. A wooden Yankee clock with a brass pendulum ticked loudly. It showed 10:00. The doors were opened to the courtroom and there was a mad rush to get in. A few young fellows even squeezed in through windows. They stood on tiptoe in the back to get a view of the proceedings. At the door, Amelia Bloomer and Madame X tried to enter but were stopped by a court officer.

"Sorry," he said. "No ladies allowed."

"What's wrong?" Bloomer asked.

"The case is very scandalous," he said.

"Yes, indeed," said Madame X.

"Not considered decent for the ladies," the court officer said.

"That's outrageous." said Amelia Bloomer.

Madame X let out a laugh. She leaned close to the officer and whispered. "Clarence, I'll remember what you said when you come to my place Friday night."

The officer blushed, looked uncomfortable. "I'm sorry. I have my orders." The two women walked away.

Inside, Judge Thomas Hartley Crawford, white hair and spectacles, entered, and sat on a high bench. He had a bad cold, pulled out a handkerchief and blew his nose. To Judge Crawford's right was the witness box and the jury panel. To his left, near a window, was the prisoner's dock, a three foot square enclosure with a waist-high railing.

Mister Sickles, Dan's father, and Mr. Bagioli, both looking quite stricken, sat together in the audience near the front. At the entrance, John Ward, the N.Y. Times reporter, pushed his way past several people and tried to slip in the door but the Court Officer barred his way. "Sorry. All filled up in there."

Ward pulled out a card and showed it to the officer. "New York Times." The officer waved him by but stopped other people trying to push their way in. Ward squeezed into the only empty space on a long wooden bench and nodded to the other reporters. It was stiflingly hot. Some were mopping their sweaty brows.

Ward reached out to the man next to him. "John Ward, New York Times."

"Bill Wiggins, Associated Press." Wiggins, upset, pointed to four reporters crowded around a table. "Only the reporters from Washington were given a table. I don't know how we're expected to take notes." The other bench mates nodded, reached over and shook his hand.

"Tim King, San Francisco Examiner."

"Gene Fairfield, Philadelphia Bulletin."

"Tom Swain, Galesburg Citizen."

Ward, surprised, asked, "Galesburg?"

"Galesburg, Illinois," Swain explained.

The big time reporters looked at each other, impressed that the case had drawn even this small town paper.

Out on the street, Dan Sickles walked from the jailhouse house to City Hall—two blocks away. He was dressed impeccably: black frock coat, gray striped trousers, choker collar, broad black bow tie, and a top hat. Two police officers walked along with him on either side. A crowd of men, young and old, ran alongside, shouting, trying to get near him, but the officers shooed them away.

It was 10:30 a.m. There was a buzz of excitement as Dan was led inside. He entered the prisoner's dock and was seated. He looked around, nodded to several friends. Judge Crawford rapped the gavel down hard, and there was silence.

Ward, sitting on the crowded bench, scribbled notes for his story and looked over at the chief prosecutor. "Robert Ould has replaced Mister Key as the U.S. Attorney for the District of Columbia. He must now prosecute the slayer of his former chief."

Sitting next to Ould, shuffling through papers, was his assistant. Mr. Ould has a single assistant, Ward wrote, J.M. Carlisle, 30, said to be quite brilliant.

Ward now looked over at the defense table where there were eight lawyers. The defense, he wrote, has assembled a powerful legal battery. The three lead lawyers are friends of Mr. Sickles from New York, who are reportedly serving without fee or reward.

There was James T. Brady, 40s, an elegantly dressed fellow who, Ward noted, recently handled the divorce of the noted Shakespearean actor Edwin Forrest. Mister Brady has won fifty-one of fifty-two murder cases.

And John L. Graham, 50s, a tall, patrician man, a great orator, who will probably make the opening statement. And Edwin McMasters Stanton of Ohio, 50s, with long black hair and beard, and a solemn expression who specializes in cases before the Supreme Court. He is also a friend and neighbor of the defendant.

There was the florid-faced Thomas F. Meagher, a rollicking Irishman. Somewhat of a windbag. The defense group includes four Washington attorneys: Daniel Ratcliffe, Allen Magruder, Samuel Chilton, and Philip Phillips. Ratcliffe and Phillips are quite expert in jury selection.

Judge Crawford blew his nose, then tapped his gavel on the desk. "We will now begin the task of selecting the jury. I'll ask the questions, if that is agreeable." The lawyers and prosecutors nodded in assent.

The first juror, Joseph Brien, was sworn in. "Mister Brien," the Judge asked, "have you at any time formed or expressed an opinion in relation to the guilt or innocence of the accused?

"I have."

"You may retire."

Defense lawyer Phillips rose. "Is the juror's opinion founded on rumor? If he is provided with the facts, perhaps he could form a fair judgment."

Judge Crawford turned to Brien. "Would you be able, on hearing the evidence, to render an impartial verdict?"

"No, Sir," Brien replied. "My mind is biased in favor of the prisoner."
"Stand aside."

The Judge questioned Juror Howe. "Mister Howe, would you be able, on hearing the evidence, to render an impartial verdict?"

Howe shook his head. "My mind is biased in favor of the prisoner."
"Stand aside."

Day Two: April 5, 1859

Ward wrote in his notebook: After one full day, thirty jurors have been called and only five qualified.

Juror Lenney, "My sympathies are entirely with the prisoner."
"Disqualified," sighed the Judge.

Juror Garrett, "I think the prisoner was justified in what he did."
Frustrated, the judge said "Disqualified."

Juror Rupp, "I shouldn't serve on the jury because I am related to the prisoner."

"Related?" the judge asked. "In what way?"

"We are both married men." Laughter erupted in the courtroom.

The Judge rapped his gavel for silence. Wearily, he said, "You may retire."

Day Three: April 7, 1859

Ward scribbled in his notebook: Jury selection has taken three days. One hundred and sixty men were questioned before twelve were chosen. He glanced up, saw twelve men seated in the jury box, and continued: Four grocers, two farmers, a shoemaker, a tanner, merchant, coachmaker, cabinetmaker, and a dealer in gents' furnishings.

Rapping his gavel, Judge Crawford said, "Case Number 124, that of Mister. Sickles, will now be heard. Are counsel for both sides ready?" The lawyers and prosecutors looked at the judge and nodded. "The prisoner will hear the indictment," he said.

The court clerk, holding the indictment papers, looked at Dan as an artist, with a sketch pad, seated among the journalists, and made a drawing of Dan.

"Stand up, Daniel E. Sickles," the clerk said. Dan stood. "Daniel E. Sickles, look on the jurors, while the indictment is being read." Dan stood while the clerk read in a loud voice. "The jurors of the United States do present that Daniel E. Sickles, gentleman, not having the fear of God before his eyes, but being moved and seduced by the instigation of the devil, on the 27th day of February, A.D. 1859, with force and arms in and upon the body of one Philip Barton Key, in the peace of God and of the United States did kill and murder. How do you plead? Guilty, or not guilty?"

In a clear, firm tone, Dan responded, "Not guilty."

Judge Crawford looked to the jury and explained. "We will now hear the opening statement from the prosecution."

Prosecutor Ould rose and addressed the jury. He was efficient, serious, understated in his style. "May it please your honor and the gentlemen of the jury. Key's murder was done on February 27th last, in the soft gush of that Sabbath sunlight, when the echoes of the church bells were lingering in the air." Ould walked to the table and picked up the Derringer and Colt. "Mister Sickles came fully prepared for his murderous work." He rested the weapons back on the table and picked up the opera glass. "To defend himself, Mister Key had only a poor and feeble opera glass."He placed the opera glass back on the table, and picked up the Derringer once more. "Mister Sickles must have known that Mister Key was unarmed when he fired the first shot." He brandished the gun, pointing downward at an invisible victim. "And if he did not know then, he must surely have known when he stood *bravely* over his victim, seeking to scatter the brains of one who had already been mortally wounded, one whose eyes were being covered with the film of death." He rested the gun on the table, picked up a thick law book, and showed it to the jury. "This book, gentlemen of the jury, is entitled Wharton's 'Criminal Law.' It explains the majestic tradition of the law. Murder has been defined all over the civilized world as the unlawful killing of a human being with malice aforethought. We will show, with one witness after another, that the actions of Mister Sickles were nothing less than remorseless revenge. No matter what the provocation,homicide with a deadly weapon, perpetrated by one who has all the advantages on his side, is murder. Ould stared at the jury for a moment, and took his seat.

The judge looked over to the defense table. "Mister Brady?"

Very politely, Brady replied, "Your honor, we prefer to make our opening statement after the prosecution has presented its evidence." There was a murmur in the courtroom.

Judge Crawford looked at the prosecutor. "Mister Ould, you may call your first witness."

Ould, caught by surprise, was a bit rattled. He hurriedly looked through some papers."Your honor, my associate, Mister Carlisle, will examine the witnesses. We call to the stand Doctor Edward Coolidge."

During Doctor Coolidge's testimony, he said, "When I examined the deceased, I saw one wound two inches below the groin, and a second wound on the left side between the tenth and eleventh rib. The second wound made a deep groove across the left kidney, passed through the liver, and entered the right cavity of the lungs."

"Was that a mortal wound?" Carlisle asked.

"It was."

Later, Coroner Woodward took the stand and was sworn in. "Mister Woodward," Carlisle said, "please state your position."

"I am the Chief Coroner for the District of Columbia."

"On the day of Mister Key's death, did you convene a coroner's jury, and take sworn testimony from witnesses to the event?"

"I did."

"And what did you conclude?"

Woodward picked up his written report. "May I read from my report?"

"Please."

"Philip Barton Key came to his death from the effect of pistol balls fired by the hands of Daniel E. Sickles, while standing near the southeast corner of Lafayette Square."

Moments later, Coroner Woodward unfolded a bundle containing the victim's clothes. He produced a pair of gray, striped pants. "Here is where the ball entered the right thigh." The place was stiffened and stained with blood. A murmur in the courtroom. Woodward then lifted up a white vest, stained with blood on the left side. "Here is where the fatal bullet entered." Another murmur in the courtroom.

Day Four: April 8, 1859

A witness, Thomas Martin, was being examined by Ould. "After Mister Sickles shot Mister Key, I heard him say 'He has violated my bed.'"

Ould interrupted. "Never mind about that."

"Your honor," said Brady, "this is part of the narrative."

"I did not ask the witness to relate what he had heard, only what he had seen," said Ould.

Brady replied, "I have never known a District Attorney to ask a witness what he had seen, and not what he had heard. The witness already testified to hearing the report of a pistol, did he not?"

"The statement is allowed," said Judge Crawford.

Day Five: April 9, 1859

The courtroom was packed. Ward, the N.Y. Times reporter sat at the crowded desk scribbling notes for his story. "The prosecution rested after calling twenty-eight witnesses. Nine of them actually saw the shooting."

Judge Crawford entered, took his seat, and rapped the gavel. "We will now hear from the defense."

Defense attorney John Graham rose to address the jury. He made eye contact with the jurors and was courtly in his manner. When he spoke, he was eloquent, theatrical. "It has been a few weeks since the body of a human being was found in the throes of death in one of the streets of your city. Had he observed the solemn precept, 'Remember the Sabbath day to keep it holy,' he might still be among the living. That body proved to be the body of a confirmed and habitual adulterer."

Ould rose angrily. "Your honor, I object."

"We will recess briefly," said Judge Crawford.

Minutes later inside the judge's chamber, Judge Crawford was seated at his desk while the prosecutors and defense lawyers stood around him. "The victim is not on trial here," said Ould. "We are supposed to be trying his killer."

"Motive is important, your honor," said Graham. "We will show that Mister Sickles actedbecause he witnessed his wife's adultery with Mister Key."

"Witnessed?" Carlisle asked. "He only heard about it. Adultery is a misdemeanor under District law. Mr. Sickles had recourse to legal redress. Your honor himself has presided over such a case in the past."

The gruff Mister Stanton intervened. "Was this not a case tried under Maryland law?"

"Yes," said Carlisle.

Stanton continued, "And was not the punishment a fine of one hundred pounds of tobacco?"

"Yes," said Carlisle.

In a mocking tone, Stanton continued, "So the only satisfaction an injured husband could have is a chew of tobacco?"

Judge Crawford allowed a flicker of a smile.

"Your honor," Brady said, "when the husband first learned of the adultery, it's the same as though it took place before his eyes. Such knowledge places the deceased in *flagrante delicto* at the time of his death."

Judge Crawford pondered his answer as the lawyers remained silent. "According to witnesses," the judge said, "the prisoner declared the deceased had dishonored his house, or violated his bed."

Ould protested. "But your honor—"

"Testimony to show the existence of an adulterous relation between the deceased and the wife of the accused is admissible," the judge said. The defense attorneys were quietly jubilant. Key and Teresa were now on trial for adultery.

Minutes later, John Graham resumed his statement to the jury. "We will show you that Mister Sickles used all his influence to secure his friend, Mister Key, an elevated position at the bar of this court. Mr. Sickles is compelled often and for considerable periods to be away from his family. For nearly one year, Mister Key visits the house but sinks to the lowest depths of baseness in betraying his friend."

Day Six: April 11, 1859

Graham was still addressing the jury. His voice now turned gentle, almost affectionate. "As for Mrs. Sickles, she is young enough to be his daughter."

While Graham spoke, Teresa sat in a chair at the Bagioli home in New York City, staring out the parlor window. On the floor next to her, little Laura played with a doll.

"Reasoning from her years, and from our knowledge of the mental structure of women," Graham continued, "it is not too much to suppose that she was susceptible to flattery. The night before his wife confessed her guilt, he had passed the night without sleeping, sobbing and sighing. Then he saw his adulterous friend prowling outside his home, waving a handkerchief, seeking to seduce his wife. Dan Sickles was driven by an irresistible impulse. He was *temporarily insane*."

Ould stood, his jaw tight, "Your honor, I object."

There was an uproar in the courtroom as the exhausted Graham sank into his seat. Judge Crawford rapped his gavel for order. "We shall recess until this afternoon."

Judge Crawford sat at his desk in his chambers as the prosecutors and defense attorneys gathered around him. "Temporary insanity?" said Ould. "Your honor, they are trying to make new law. A person is either mad, or sane."

Judge Crawford looked to Brady, who said, "Madness has been recognized as a defense in Roman Times. The Jewish Talmud also cites imbecility as a legitimate defense. King Edward affirmed the concept in England in the fourteenth century."

"But your honor—" Ould said.

Brady continued, "A quarter century ago, a deranged housepainter tried to assassinate President Andrew Jackson. Mister Key's own father was the District Attorney for Washington at the time. He allowed the man to plead insanity."

"I recall the case," the judge said.

"But your honor," Ould said. "That man was sent to an insane asylum. He remains there to this day. No one has ever entered a plea that someone is *temporarily* insane."

"Why not let a jury decide?" Stanton asked.

Judge Crawford pondered for a moment. "You may suggest this theory."

Ould tried to object. "But—"

The judge turned to Ould. "And you, sir, are free to argue that no such theory has ever been propounded in a courtroom before."

Again, the defense attorneys look pleased.

Day Seven April 12, 1859

In the courtroom, Mister Beekman was seated among the spectators. Reporter Ward scribbled in his notebook: Graham is speaking for the third day ... a true marathon.

Standing in front of the jury, Graham continued, "It has been well said, 'Frailty, thy name is woman.' It is the husband's duty and right to protect her against frailty, as much as against the violence of the robber." As Graham spoke, Ward glanced at the faces of the all-male jury. He was clearly arousing sympathy among these God-fearing people. "In Leviticus it is clear: 'The adulterer and the adulteress shall surely be put to death,'" Graham said. "In Deuteronomy, it says: 'They shall both of them die.' It is Christian to punish adultery with death. In Judea, in times of the Old Testament, the adulterer was put to death by stoning. The entire community took part in the execution." Graham paused, raised his arms dramatically, as though on stage. "Shakespeare's Othello, when he learns of his wife Desdemona's inconstancy, the Moor cries out, 'But alas! To make me a fixed figure for the time of scorn!'" Graham gazed into the eyes of the male jurors. He walked over towards the defendant. *Cuckold!* Who would live to have that word written on his back? What man is made of flint, to walk in the presence of his fellow men and feel that some person was secretly smirking, because of his wife's inconstancy? Mister Key deflowered the wife of his friend. It may be tragic to shed human blood. But there is no tragedy about slaying the adulterer."

Some spectators burst into applause as Judge Crawford rapped for silence. Graham collapsed in his chair and mopped his brow with a handkerchief. Judge Crawford looked over to Brady, the lead defense counsel. "Mister Brady, how many witnesses for the defense do you plan to call?"

Phillips handed Brady a list, which he then scanned. "Forty-three to be exact, your honor."

Later, Robert Walker was on the witness stand. "After the event, at around three in the afternoon, I went to visit Mister Sickles at his home. He took me by the hand and said, 'A thousand thanks for coming to see me.'"

"And then?" Brady asked.

"He threw himself upon the sofa and broke into an agony of unearthly sounds, something like a scream, interrupted by violent sobbing. I feared that if he continued he would become permanently insane."

Dan began to sob and broke down. His father and two of the lawyers rushed over and comforted him. Walker and some others in the courtroom were visibly moved.

A while later, Dan was quiet but still looked emotionally fragile. On the stand was Francis Mohun. Brady asked, "Did you see Mister Sickles in the afternoon, on the 27th of February last?"

"Yes sir. I was standing in front of my house on the avenue. Mister Sickles looked to me in a very excited condition. The next day, when I heard of the occurrence, I told a friend that I thought he was crazy or insane."

"Objection," said Ould. "The witness is not a medical doctor."

"I will allow it," the judge said. "You may cross examine the witness."

Ould approached Mohun. "You recollected this the next day?"

"Yes."

"If you had not heard of this occurrence would his appearance have made that impression on you?"

"It might not, but—"

"Thank you."

"But his wild appearance—"

"Thank you!" Ould said. "That is all."

Brady held up a few sheets of paper. "Your honor, we propose to read into evidence this statement, written by Mrs. Sickles to her husband."

Carlisle rose. "Objection, your honor!"

Brady continued, "This confession, your honor, explains how Mister Sickles' mind was affected so severely." Brady handed the confession to Judge Crawford, who read it over, then looked up.

"It is inadmissible on many grounds, your honor," Carlisle said. "First, it is hearsay—"

Brady interrupted. "It accounts for the defendant's state of mind. It instilled madness and led him to commit the act."

Day Eight: April 13, 1859

The lawyers were crowded around the judge at his desk.

"Your honor," said Carlisle, "the crime was committed eighteen hours after the defendant read it. Eighteen hours. That is surely sufficient time for a man to cool down."

Brady said, "Mrs. Sickles' confession proves beyond any doubt the crime of adultery—"

Carlisle interrupted, "If the defense offers evidence of adultery with the prisoner's wife, shouldn't we be allowed to reveal the previous history of the accused?"

"I object, your honor," Brady said.

"The defendant's prior conduct is not relevant," said Judge Crawford.

"Then, your honor," said Carlisle, "please consider that it is long established that a spouse cannot testify about the actions of a spouse."

"This time, I agree with the prosecution," the judge said. "The written confession by Mrs. Sickles is inadmissible." Ould and Carlisle look relieved.

Day Nine: April 14, 1859

Teresa Sickles walked hand in hand with Laura along a street in lower Manhattan. They passed a news vendor who is stood next to a pile of New York City daily papers. He waved one copy and shouted, "Extra! Extra! Sensational confession of adulterous wife! Read all about it!" As customers walked by, stopped, and bought a copy, Teresa—shocked, troubled—hurried away with Laura.

Judge Crawford sat at his desk looking at the front page of the newspaper. The headline screamed out: SICKLES WIFE CONFESSES! He was troubled. The prosecutors and lawyers stood nearby. Ould also had a copy of the newspaper, and he pointed to the front page headline.

"Your honor, this is outrageous," Ould said. "You excluded this confession; now it appears word for word in practically every newspaper in the nation? How can we have a fair trial?"

Judge Crawford looked at Brady, who feigned a mournful expression. "None of your associates gave a copy of the confession to the press?"

"No, your honor. I have no idea how they obtained it."

Judge Crawford shrugged. "I don't like it, but I see no remedy at hand."

Carlisle, the prosecutor tried to counter with his own tactic." Your honor, since this very damaging confession has been made public, isn't it only fair to examine the morals of the accused?"

Brady, upset, said, "That is totally—"

Judge Crawford raised his hand, for silence. He looked to Carlisle. "I'm listening."

Carlisle said, "While active in New York politics, and we have eyewitnesses, Mister Sickles spent a good deal of his free time with a woman named Fanny White who ran a bordello on Mercer Street.

"Your honor," said Brady.

"A bordello, your honor," Carlisle continued. "And, after his election to the State Assembly—"

"This is irrelevant," said Brady.

Carlisle continued, "He brought Fanny White to Albany and audaciously escorted her on a tour of the Assembly chamber."

"Whether or not this allegation is true, Mr. Carlisle is bringing up an incident of years ago, before Mister Sickles was married," said Brady.

Judge Crawford looked at Carlisle, who picked up a small file of papers. "More recently," said Carlisle, "a friend in Baltimore has traced Dan Sickles' activities there, with a lady not his wife."

"Your honor!"

"In early January," Carlisle continued, "he signed a register at the front desk of Barnum's City Hotel in Baltimore and went up to his room. Later, a woman entered the hotel, signed the register as Mrs. Sickles and was directed to the same room. But it was not Teresa Sickles. The proprietor of the hotel says he is ready to appear in court with the signed register—"

Brady interrupted, "Mister Sickles' moral character is not on trial here."

"On Sunday, January 16," Carlisle continued, "Mister Sickles left the hotel and went to the railroad station where he met a woman arriving from Philadelphia. The two returned to the hotel. The woman stayed overnight in his room where they had adulterous intercourse."

Judge Crawford rose, stared out the window for a moment, and turned. "This is all very interesting, but—"

Carlisle protested, "Why is only the adultery of Mrs. Sickles to be condemned? Is it not relevant that Dan Sickles was also an adulterer?"

Judge Crawford thought for another moment.

Carlisle continued, "Surely such a man cannot claim insanity because his familiar plaything has turned and wounded him!"

"We are interested in the state of mind of the accused, that's all," the judge said. Carlisle, disappointed, shook his head. The defense attorneys exchanged satisfied glances.

Day Thirteen: April 18, 1859

A middle-aged woman, was on the stand. Brady asked, "Your name please?"

"Nancy Brown. My husband, Thomas, is the gardener for President Buchanan."

"Did you ever meet the deceased, Mister Key?"

"I saw him on the Wednesday before he was shot."

"Where?"

"He was going into the house on Fifteenth Street, next to where I live."

"Mrs. Brown, when is the first time you saw Mister Key?"

"A few months ago, in October, he rode up on his horse and asked me about the vacant house at Number 383."

"And?"

"I told him the owner was Mister John Gray, a black man."

"And then?"

"He came by a week after that and tied his horse to my tree. I asked him whether he did not know that was against the law." There was laughter in the courtroom.

Ould rose. "That is not evidence."

"I asked him not to tie his horse there again," Mrs. Brown said.

"That's not evidence," Ould said. "Stop, Mrs. Brown." More laughter.

"I was only telling you what happened. He said I won't tie it there anymore. Then he thanked me and said he was renting the place for a House member, or a Senator, can't recall which. I never spoke to him anymore."

Brady asked, "How often before that Wednesday did you see him go into that house?"

"Three or four times before. We would laugh when he came."

"Why is that?"

"He would go down to the yard and get wood to make a fire. Then he would tie a white string to the upstairs shutters so that when the wind blows it would swing. Every time I saw that string, a young lady, a girl really, would arrive and enter by the back way. It was always the same young woman. That string was a signal."

"Did you know who she was?" Brady asked.

"One of my neighbors told me she was Mrs. Sickles."

"Did anyone else go in there? House members? Senators?"

"I never saw anyone but them."

"How often did you see the string tied outside the window?"

"Three or four times. If I had looked oftener, I might have seen it oftener." More laughter.

Day Fourteen: April 19, 1859

John Cooney, the Sickles family coachman, was on the stand. "Mister Sickles usually went away before twelve. Mrs. Sickles would go out in the carriage alone, usually twelve or one o'clock, and remain out till four or five."

"Did she see anyone in particular?" Brady asked.

"Mister Key always joined Mrs. Sickles in the street. I could hardly mention a day he did not meet us."

"Did Mister Key ever come into the Sickles home?"

"When Mr. Sickles was away in Albany. Sometimes he remained until very late. They always stayed in the study, with the door shut."

"Did anything particular occur to which your attention was called?" Brady asked.

"Yes," Cooney replied.

"Please relate it to the jury."

"I was going to bed about one o'clock; I went to the head of the hall stairs and met Bridget Duffy. I stood and talked a while with her. Then we thought we heard the doorbell ring. Mister Key and Mrs. Sickles came to the hall door and looked out; there was nobody there. I heard them locking the study door."

"Do you have any idea what they were doing in there?" Brady asked.

"There was a sofa in that room," Cooney replied. "With the door locked, I figured they wasn't at no good work." This provoked laughter from the jury and others in the courtroom. The judge rapped his gavel for order.

Day Seventeen: April 23, 1859.

Wooldridge took a seat in the witness chair and was examined by defense lawyer Brady. "Mr. Wooldridge, you are employed in the House of Representatives?"

"I'm a clerk in the map department," Wooldridge replied.

"And you are a good friend of the defendant, Mister Sickles?"

"Yes."

"He confided very personal matters to you."

"Yes."

"You have testified that you had a conversation with Mister Key early in February concerning his attentions towards Mrs. Sickles."

"I told him that I had witnessed certain conduct towards her which might be viewed as over attentive."

"And his reply?"

"He seemed a bit annoyed. He said he had a 'great friendship' with Mrs. Sickles … that his feeling for her were only paternal." Beekman, seated in the courtroom, snickered.

"And you said?"

"I told him his feelings might be misinterpreted. This could place him in difficulty, or danger."

"And what did he say?"

Wooldridge patted the left breast of his coat. "He laid his hand on his coat, like this, and said, 'I'm prepared for any emergency.'"

Ould rose. "We object, your honor. The suggestion is being made that Mister Key always walked around armed with a weapon."

Brady responded. "This evidence shows that Mister Key was prepared to resist the doom which rightly belongs to the adulterer."

Carlisle rose. "Your honor, really. Are we saying that every man who commits adultery is to be treated as a wild beast and slain on sight? There is no evidence to show that the deceased was armed the day Mister Sickles shot and killed him."

"The prosecution is correct," said Judge Crawford. "The evidence is not admissible."

Later, Carlisle cross-examined Wooldridge for the prosecution. He showed him the letter to Mr. Wooldridge. "On Friday, February 25, Mister Sickles showed you this letter with information of his wife's adulterous affair, is that correct?"

"Yes."

"And you claim he was greatly agitated?"

"Yes, he put his hands to his head and sobbed."

"When was this?"

"About one o'clock."

His voice drenched in sarcasm, Carlisle asked, "Are you aware of the fact that that very same afternoon, after sobbing in your presence, Mister Sickles delivered a speech in the House of Representatives?"

"No. I am not."

"So he was not too grief-stricken to undertake a speech in the House of Representatives."

Brady rose and asked, "Is that a question or a statement?"

Carlisle continued, "Are you aware that that evening Mister Sickles sat down and revised and corrected his speech?"

"No."

Carlisle stared at him, waiting for more. Wooldridge appeared uncomfortable. "Actually, his grief was not so great that Friday as it was the next day, Saturday."

"I was asking you about Friday and his reading the letter. You testified that he placed his hands to his head, and sobbed."

"The scenes I've described took place Saturday, after he learned that Mrs. Sickles was the person in the house on Fifteenth Street. If I said differently, it was a mistake."

"I see," Carlisle said. "A mistake. One wonders how reliable is your memory of the entire affair concerning this friend of yours."

Brady rose. "Objection, your honor."

Carlisle turned, walked away. "I am done with this witness."

Lively fiddle music could be heard coming from within the National Hotel that night.

The jurors sat in a parlor, as one of the jurors, the grocer, played a fiddle. Outside, Ward, the N.Y. Times reporter observed, and jotted down a note: The length of this case has wearied everyone, including the jury. One of them, Henry M. Knight, a grocer, entertains them with his fiddle during their long evenings of seclusion.

Dan rose from his bed in jail, went to a table, and picked up pen and paper. He wrote to his wife, "My dear Teresa. I've been giving a great deal of thought to past events ..."

Outside on a Washington street, Ward, the reporter, took a night time stroll. He reached a corner, looked to his right, and saw the street with the houses of ill fame.

Ward entered the ornate parlor of the brothel and looked around. He was a New Yorker and it was his first visit here. It was early, there were no customers, just a few young ladies lounging about, chatting. They eyed him up and down and smiled. He walked towards the back of the room to the small bar. He ordered a drink from the bartender and paid him.

Madame X approached, smiling. "You're one of the newspaper reporters, aren't you?"

"You've been following the trial?"

"From a distance. I tried a few times to enter the courtroom, but was turned away." She smiled. "They were afraid I might become corrupted by such goings on."

"Do you know someone connected with the case?"

She paused before her reply. "A lawyer friend of mine once told me he never talks about his customers."

"They call it attorney-client privilege."

"Yes, that's it. For example, if you ever became my *client*, it would be our secret."

Ward sipped his drink. He liked this lady. "You're obviously a good judge of human nature. Male human nature especially."

"In your profession and mine," she said, "we see plenty of it."

"Speaking hypothetically, without referring to any specific person, or revealing any confidences, why would a man kill another man over a woman?"

She shrugged.

"Could a man's love for her be so powerful?"

Madame X pondered for a moment. "Not love. Pride."

"Pride?"

"Yes," she said. "And you know what The Holy Bible says about pride, don't you?"

"I'm afraid you've got me there," Ward said.

"Leviticus 16:18. 'Pride goeth before destruction.'"

Ward smiled. He was impressed. "You're a surprising lady."

"One of my best customers, a few years ago, was a preacher. We would talk for hours. He said, 'Pride is one of the seven cardinal sins.'"

"Is that so?"

"Yes," Madame X responded. "I don't recall the other six." They laughed. She smiled at him, put her hand on his. "So," she asked, "would you like to go in?"

"Thank you," Ward said. "Some other time. I have a great deal of work remaining tonight.

Madame X shrugged. As Ward turned to leave, the door opened, and in walked two of the lead defense attorneys, Brady and Graham. The lawyers and journalist looked at each other and were somewhat uncomfortable. Graham laughed nervously. Two young ladies rose from their sofas, went over to Brady and Graham, took them by the arm, and guided them to the bar.

Madame X smiled at Graham. "Hello, dear, so nice to see you again." She gave a knowing wink to Ward.

Ward nodded to them. "Gentlemen."

"Mister Ward," said Graham.

Brady asked, "Out for a little evening's relaxation?"

Ward emptied his whiskey glass and put it back on the bar. "I was just leaving."

"See you in court tomorrow," said Graham. Ward nodded, and left. Brady and Graham sidled up to the bar and were served drinks, as Madame X and the two young ladies fussed over them.

Day Eighteen: April 24, 1859

A rainstorm, the worst gale in two decades, swept through the city. From inside the crowded courtroom, the rain could be seen and heard pelting against the windows. Ward, with a conspiratorial smile, nodded to the two defense attorneys, Graham and Brady, whom he had seen in the brothel last night. They nodded back.

Judge Crawford spoke. "We will now hear the summation for the defense. Mister Graham?"

Graham stood and approached the jury. "Here, in the capitol of this nation of thirty millions of people, a man of mature age, the head of a family, a member of the learned profession, a high officer of Government, and who for years at this Bar had demanded judgment against other men for offenses against the law, has himself been slain. Why? Because he took advantage of the hospitality of a friend." Minutes later, Graham, perspiring, had the jury in the palm of his hand. The jurors watched him with rapt attention. "This was a man living in a constant state of adultery with the prisoner's wife, a man who was daily calling her from the husband's house, drawing her from the side of her child, and dragging her, day by day, through the streets in order that he may gratify his lust."

As Graham continued, Teresa, pensive, walked with little Laura in a New York City park.

"Teresa's immoral behavior," Graham said, "has destroyed her marriage. Her daughter Laura will never enjoy the companionship of a sister, or a brother. Alone, she must journey through life, bowed down with a mother's shame. The wretched mother, the ruined wife, has not yet plunged into the horrible filth of common prostitution, which is already yawning before her."

Last night in the brothel, Graham sat on a sofa, his face smeared with lipstick, his eyes glazed. He drank from a whiskey glass while one of the prostitutes hugged him and mussed his hair. A gold wedding band was visible on one of his fingers.

Now, in the courtroom, he continued, "The death of Key was a cheap sacrifice to save one mother from the horrible fate which hung over this prisoner's wife and the mother of his child." Graham's voice turned stentorian, ragged with fierce emotion. "What would any husband have done in the same circumstances? Who, seeing this thing, would not hasten to save the mother of their child? Although she be lost as a wife, rescue her from the horrid adulterer and may the Lord, who watches over the home and the family, guide the bullet and direct the stroke."

Applause erupted in the courtroom. Graham mopped his brow.

Day Nineteen: April 25, 1859

One block from the courtroom, Amelia Bloomer stood on a small platform and addressed a small crowd of followers, others who were curious, and a few hecklers. "All men, good and bad, black and white, corrupt, debased, criminal, may vote and make our laws, and we hear no word against it. But, if one woman does or says aught that does not square with man's ideas of what we should do and say, then she should not have the right of self-government, and all women everywhere must on that account be kept in subjection."

A heckler yelled out, "It's where you belong."

Bloomer continued angrily. "The history of mankind is a history of repeated injuries and usurpations on the part of man toward woman."

Inside the courtroom, Ward, the Times reporter, scribbled his notes: Mister Brady has taken over the final argument for the defense.

"The whole world, your honor, has its eye on this case," said Brady. "When each of us shall have taken his chamber in the silent halls of death, the name of everyone associated with this trial will endure so long as the earth shall exist." Brady turned to the jury and resumed in a mocking tone. "It would have been well if Mister Key had attached as much importance to the dignity of a banner as did his distinguished father, when he used a white handkerchief to signal Mrs. Sickles. What was Dan Sickles to do that Sunday when he confronted Mister Key in Lafayette Square? Bid him good morning? Pass him by silently? Avert his eye?" A few of the jurors nodded agreement.

The other night, in the brothel, Brady, perspiring, naked, was in bed, having sex with a young prostitute. She stared vacantly at the ceiling, bored.

Now, in court, he continued. "When Daniel Sickles realized how he had been betrayed, every drop of his blood was burdened with a sense of shame." Brady pointed at the prisoner.

"Look, your honor, at Dan Sickles and think of Teresa, his wife, for whom I pray the merciful interposition of Heaven. That poor girl, although the mother of a child she still is a girl, and, as such, amenable to the influence of a master seducer. If, under these circumstances, Dan Sickles had done less than became a man, then despite our deep and abiding friendship in the past, I would have been willing to see him die the most ignominious death before I would venture a prayer in his behalf." Brady sank down in his chair and remained bowed, his face in his hands. The other defense lawyers reached over and shook his hand.

In New York, in the Baglioli home, Teresa sat in a chair in the parlor, holding a letter. Seated nearby was her mother. Little Laura was playing with a doll on the floor a in the next room. "Dan sent me this letter."

"What does he say?" the mother asked.

"He seems very affectionate, as though he has forgiven me."

"That's good!"

Teresa remained silent, near tears.

"What's the matter, dear?"

"I once loved him."

"It can be that way again."

"I don't know."

"If he has forgiven you, you can also forgive him. Try again."

Teresa looked down at the floor, shook her head, confused, uncertain. Her mother reached out a hand. "Your father and I are old, dear. When we are gone, who will help you and little Laura?" Her mother rose, hugged her. Teresa stared off into space, silent.

Some days later, a jailer brought a letter to Dan in his cell. He opened it and began to read.

"I cannot tell you, dear Dan," she wrote, "how much pleasure your letter gave me. I was pained at your silence. Thank you for all your kind expressions and God bless you for the mercy and prayers you offer up for me. The verses you sent me are very beautiful. I will keep them always. Yesterday, when the clock sounded, I thought, One month ago this day, at this hour, such and such things were going on in our once happy home. That fearful Saturday night! If I could have foreseen the scenes of the following day I would have braved all dangers, all things, to have prevented them. No, dear Dan, I can't say you ever denied me what was necessary, and you gave me many things I did not deserve."

In the cell, Dan was moved as he continued reading the letter from Teresa. "I shall commence a pair of slippers for you in a few days, my dear Dan. Will you wear them for me? Or would you dislike to wear again anything that I have made? Write when you can. God bless you for the two kisses you send me and with God's help and determination to be good, true and faithful to you and myself hereafter, those kisses shall never leave my lips while I am called wife and you husband. I swear by it. Teresa."

Day Twenty: April 26, 1859
Robert Ould rose and offered the final argument for the prosecution. He held the law book in his hand. "A woman's chastity lies in her own keeping. If it must be protected by the sword, the knife, and the pistol, it stands unworthy of protection. The question is not of adultery, but one of murder. The law is crystal clear on this point. If Mister Sickles had found Key and Mrs. Sickles in the act, the law says the homicide may be reduced to manslaughter. But if the husband pursues the adulterer, and slays him out of revenge, it is murder." Ould took his seat. The jurors were solemn.

The clock stood at 1:50 p.m. The judge looked to the jury as a profound silence fell over the courtroom. "It is for the jury to say what the state of Mister was. Sickles' mind," he said. "If the jury has any doubt, either in reference to the homicide or the question of Sanity, Mister Sickles should be acquitted."

The twelve jurors rose and headed through the little white door into the marshal's room to deliberate. The spectators broke up into small groups, talking in whispers. Dan, seated in the dock, chatted with his attorneys. The court officer came out and said, "The jurors say the room is cold; they want the stove lit."

Ward glanced next to him at a colleague. "We may be in for a long wait."

Rumors swept through the courtroom as the spectators speculated among themselves.

"I've heard it's ten for acquittal, two for conviction," said one spectator.

"No, they say it's eight for acquittal, four for conviction," said another.

"I heard it's six and six," said still another.

Later, the jurors were seated, talking calmly in the jurors' room. In the corner, an elderly juror, the merchant, was kneeling, praying for Divine Guidance. He rose, returned to the group. "My mind is fully made up."

In the courtroom, the clock struck 3 p.m. A knocking could be heard from inside the door to the jury room. The lounging reporters sat up.

The court officer called out, "Make room for the jurors."

"Here they come," said one spectator.

"Down in front," said another.

The judge rapped his gavel as the jurors filed out and took their seats. "Order in the court," said the judge.

The clerk said, "Daniel E. Sickles, stand up and look to the jury."Dan rose and faced them. "How say you, gentlemen?" the clerk asked. "Have you agreed upon your verdict?"

The jury foreman, the tanner, rose and spoke. "We have."

"Do you find the prisoner at the bar guilty or not guilty?"

"Not guilty."

Pandemonium broke loose in the courtroom. People were kissing, hugging, crying, shaking hands. Dan's father was sobbing. Beekman, seated in the courtroom, rose and revealed atriumphant grin. He walked out, making his way through the crowd. Dan's lawyers rushed to the jury box to thank the jurors. District Attorney Ould solemnly gathered up his papers. Carlisle remained in his seat, stunned, staring down at his papers. Dan, overcome by emotion, exited the court house and stepped down the stone stairs. People outside cheered him loudly as he waved.

Later, in the White House, President Buchanan was in his office, meeting with several visitors. An aide entered, leaned close to Buchanan and whispered something. Buchanan smiled as the aide left.

That evening, James Brady invited all the jurors to his suite at the National Hotel to join him and the other defense lawyers in a celebration party. Ward, the N.Y. Times reporter was also there. Juror John McDermott, a coach maker, told him, "I want you to tell the people of New York that the citizens of Washington are not behind those of any other part of the country in devotion to the family altar."

The jury foreman, the tanner, spoke aloud to anyone who could hear him. "I hope and believe that the great God would acquit as the jury did."

Juror Hopkins, the shoemaker, chimed in. "I would not have been satisfied with a Derringer or a revolver. I would have brought a howitzer!"

Music could be heard outside. The partygoers leaned out the window as the Marine Band was gathered on the street below, serenading the lawyers. The musicians, accompanied by a crowd of men and women, marched down Pennsylvania Avenue.

Later, Ward was walking outside the hotel and noticed a downcast Benjamin Brown French. "Sir, I'm with the New York Times. I noticed you in the courtroom. Were you a friend of Mister Key?" The man nodded, sadly. "What is your reaction to the verdict?" Ward asked.

"Sickles may have been acquitted," French said, "but the blood is on his hands and the damned spot will never out as long as he breathes mortal breath."

Ward continued walking down the street, turned the corner, and walked towards the brothel.

He entered the parlor and approached the bar. Madame X was there, smiling, arms wide open to greet him.

Three months later, three well-dressed women were sitting together in the gallery of the U.S. House of Representatives. Down below the Congressmen were clustered in small groups, chatting with each other. Except Dan Sickles, who sat alone, quietly dignified, ignored by the others.

One of the women looking down remarked jokingly, "Who is that gentleman down there, all by himself?"

"Dan Sickles of New York," replied her companion.

"What has the poor man done? Does he have smallpox?"

"He killed Philip Barton Key, the fellow who seduced his young wife. Shot him in cold blood."

"Ah yes, I recall the case."

"That was all right. Then he took his wife back."

The first woman looked at her, incredulous.

"He used to live in a fabulous mansion on Lafayette Square," said her companion. "Now he lives all by himself in a small apartment on Thirteenth Street."

"And his wife and child?"

"He says he forgave her, but he keeps them up in New York."

"A strange arrangement."

In New York, Teresa wrote to her husband, while little Laura played nearby. "Please come home, dear Dan. It's so lonely for us to have you so much away. Laura sends you much love and many kisses. Dear, dear Dan, write soon."

A year later there was a knock at the door of Dan's apartment in Washington. Dan opened, and was surprised to see Teresa. She looked pale, sickly.

"What are you doing in Washington?"

Teresa stared at him intently. "Where is Laura?" he asked.

"I left her with Alice Pendleton."

"What do you want?"

"May I come in?" He led her over to a chair and sat opposite her.

"What is it?" Dan asked.

She gazed into his eyes. He looked away. "Dan, you're always here in Washington. You're never home."

"I'm kept busy here all the time."

"Ours is no marriage."

"What do you mean?"

"You keep me bound."

"Bound?"

"I am not free. But we don't live as man and wife."

"What do you want from me?" he asked.

"In your letters you say that any object you have loved remains dear to you." He remained silent as she continued. "Do I now stand upon a footing with other women you have loved?"

She waited for his reply. He remained silent. She continued, "You think I didn't know about the others? You think I'm stupid?" She looked him in the eye. "I have long felt like asking you what your love affairs have been, love of the heart, or love of their superior qualities such as you have often informed me I did not possess."

"You're speaking nonsense," Dan said.

"If my good conduct did not keep you true to me during the first years we were married, can I suppose for a moment the last year has? Ask your own heart who sinned first, and then tell me, if you will." Dan stared at her, not responding. "I loved you, Dan, but you never really loved me. You owned me, that's all." Through her tears, she continued. "The only man who really loved me, who cared what I thought and felt, was Barton Key. And you killed him."

Dan remained stolid, silent. "What would you have done," she asked, "if I had taken a pistol and killed your mistresses, or aimed it at you?"

Shocked, Dan got up and raised his hand to hit her. Teresa did not flinch. She stared at him, tears in her eyes. Dan walked away from her, to the window, and stared out, silently. Teresa waited for a moment, turned, and let herself out. Dan gazed out the window and watched Teresa walk away, down the street.

Three years later, July 2, 1863. The sound of cannons and rifles filled the air. On the battlefield of Gettysburg, Dan commanded Union troops of the Third Corps, defending against a Confederate attack. Wounded Union soldiers lay on the ground; more than a third of Dan's twelve thousand men were killed, wounded or missing.

Dan crouched against a tree to rest. He pulled out a letter from his pocket and read. It was from his daughter Laura, now nine years old. "Many thanks, my darling Papa, for your affectionate letters. How very fine your soldiers and horses must appear. Will you let us all come to see you one of these days? Oh how happy we shall be if you can come to us! Accept an affectionate embrace and 10,000 kisses dear good Papa, from your Laura."

An artillery shell exploded nearby, throwing Dan into the air and shattering his right leg.

Later, jauntily smoking a cigar, Dan was borne on a stretcher to a field hospital. Of his right leg, only a bloody stump remained.

Four years later, February 5, 1867. From the front of St. Joseph's Church in New York's Greenwich Village, one could see a man half a block away, in civilian clothing, approaching. He walked with the aid of a crutch, his pant leg pinned up. He was missing the right leg. As he came closer, one could see it was Dan, now forty-nine years old. Pinned on his lapel was the Medal of Honor. With difficulty, Dan climbed the few steps to the entrance of the church. Inside, Dan worked his way down the aisle towards the altar. Seated in a rear pew was John Ward, the N.Y. Times reporter. As Dan passed he nodded to Ward. Dan walked by a few mourners seated in the pews and approached the altar. Seated in the front row, their eyes following him, were: Dan's daughter Laura, now thirteen, his parents, now advanced in years, and Teresa's parents, also elderly.

The rosewood coffin, covered with beautiful flowers, rested on a catafalque in front of the high altar, surrounded by burning tapers. A silver plaque on the coffin contained the following text: Teresa Bagioli Sickles. Age 33. Died February 1, 1867.

Dan approached the casket and looked down at Teresa, who appeared serene, beautiful. It was hard to read his expression. After a moment, he turned and made his way to the front pew. With difficulty, he sat down next to his daughter Laura, who stared straight ahead, tears in her eyes. The church organist played an anthem, "Pray for me," which was rendered with touching sweetness. The mourners sang along.

Back in the rear pew, Ward turned to a woman next to him. "Did you know the deceased, ma'am?"

"She was a neighbor." After a moment's silence, she continued. "The doctor said she died of consumption. I think it was a broken heart."

As the song continued, Dan reached his hand tentatively over towards Laura, who pulled her hand away and stared straight ahead.

At the cemetery, a small group of mourners, including the immediate family, stood around the grave as Teresa's casket was lowered into the ground. Later, the mourners stood by carriages at the cemetery. Dan reached over to put his arm around Laura, who was next to him.

"You can come live with me now," he said.

Laura backed away, retreated to her maternal grandmother's side. Through her tears, she glared at Dan, hatred in her eyes.

"I have an appointment in town," he said. "I'll be seeing you later."

Dan turned, and made his way on crutches to a waiting carriage.

Dan Sickles lived for another forty-six years, to the age of ninety-five.

Three musicians, one with a violin, another with a flute, and finally a harp, were playing a minuet. They sometimes found it difficult to compete with the chorus of croaking frogs in a nearby marsh. It was shortly before Christmas in 1793. A party was in progress at a mansion on Third Street in Philadelphia, the Nation's capital.

Mrs. Anne Bingham, the hostess, was in her thirties, low-cut gown, attractive, flirtatious. Mrs. Bingham and her husband had just returned from Paris and were celebrating with a gala reception. She whispered into the ear of a male guest, who laughed aloud, as she continued circulating among the guests.

A Negro servant stood at the entrance and, in a loud voice, announced a new arrival: "The Distinguished Minister Plenipotentiary of France, Count de Moustier." The Count—rouged cheeks, earrings, red-heeled shoes—made a grand entrance, bowing and nodding to all. Moustier and Mrs. Bingham kissed him effusively on both cheeks.

"My dear Count, I'm *so* pleased you could come," she said.

"*Mon chére* Anne," said the Count, "we meet again, on *zis* side of zee Atlantic. *Comment allez-vous?*

"After Pa-ree," she replied, "life seems *so* tiresome here in the colonies."

Moustier wagged an admonishing finger. "Zee former colonies."

"How I miss *Par-ee*," she went on. "The men. So *gallant*. And your women. They possess the happy art of pleasing both the fop and the philosopher. To make matters worse, our capital is being moved to some dismal swamp on the Potomac."

"But Anne," said Moustier, "zee beauty of zee nature in America. *Spectaculaire.* Zee past weekend, kind friends took us for a cruise on zee Chesapeake Bay.

"Cruising? I hope you didn't run into any rough trade ... er, rough seas. Or pirates."

Moustier laughed. "Dear Anne. Always so naughty."

At the entrance, the servant announced a new guest: "The honorable President of the United States. General Washington." Washington was a tall athletic man in his sixties. As the guests applauded, he raised his hands. "Thank you, thank you, ladies and gentlemen. My Martha sends her regrets. She is indisposed." He mingled with the guests, shaking hands, patting backs.

"We all do *so* adore our President." Mrs. Bingham said to Count Moustier. "He does not possess great wit, but he is so *sincere*."

Raising an eyebrow, Moustier asked, "Zis, how you say, *sincerité*, in America, it is a virtue, no?"

"Very much so."

"Your native customs, zay are *so* amusing." He leaned close to her. "You must protect me from zee *faux pas*. Tell me all zee dirt. Who is who?"

Mrs. Bingham pointed towards a cluster of guests. "The chubby little fellow over there? With the double chin? Gouverneur Morris. Very influential."

"Of which place is he Governor?"

"No, darling. That's his name. *Gouverneur*."

"Poor man," said Moustier. "He has a wooden leg. Lost in zee war?"

"A fall from a carriage while escaping from a jealous husband."

"How amusing," the Count said.

"And your sister-in-law, the Marchioness?"

"Alas, tonight she is *tres fatigue*. She remained in her room."

"Ah, *je sui désolé*," said Mrs. Bingham. I pray she has a speedy recovery."

"But she is *fascinated* with America. Especially your Indians," said the Count. "And she has procured a Negro girl. Now she wants to find a Negro boy, so zat zey may breed, and zee offspring learn zee *Francais*."

"How exciting. Perhaps my husband can assist her."

They turned as the servant announced: "The honorable Senator from New York, Aaron Burr." Burr, a short, trim man in his mid-thirties, entered, smiling and bowing to all, kissing the hands of the ladies.

"A rising star in politics," Mrs. Bingham told the count. "His late father was president of Princeton. Lives like a king. Borrows from friends, relatives, clients. His amorous intrigues are without number."

Burr approached. "Dear Mrs. Bingham."

"Mister Burr," she said, "meet Count Moustier, the new envoy from Paris." The two men bowed, shook hands. "Mister Burr is one of our most brilliant lawyers. They say he's never lost a case."

"Ah, zee law," said Moustier. "A fascinating profession."

"I derive no pleasure from its practice, monsieur," said Burr. "It is merely a means of gratifying my desire for comfort."

Mrs. Bingham smiled. "But Mister Burr, the law. Surely you—"

"The law, my dear lady, is anything which is boldly asserted and plausibly maintained."

Her smile grew wider. "Mister Burr, how can you—"

He interrupted once more. "I hold with Lord Chesterfield: 'A gentleman is free to do whatever he pleases ... so long as he does it with style.'"

Mouth open with delight, Mrs. Bingham responded, "What a scandalous idea."

Burr, in fluent French, continued, *"les grandes âmes se soucient peu des petits morceaux."*

Count Moustier laughed aloud. Mrs. Bingham looked to him. "My French is not so extensive."

Burr translated for her. "It means "great souls care little about such petty matters."

She smiled at him, shaking her head as though talking to a naughty child. "Mister Burr, I never know when to take you seriously."

"I *love* to keep people guessing," Burr replied. "Especially beautiful women." He continued, adding a dose of sarcasm, "If you'll excuse me, I must pay homage to our exalted leader." Burr bowed, and walked towards President Washington.

Watching Burr, the Count said to Mrs. Bingham, "I *like* zat gentleman."

At the door, the servant announced: "The honorable Senator from Virginia, James Monroe." Guests turned, looked towards the door. But no one appeared.

A voice still outside yelled, "Coming."

The servant repeated: "The honorable Senator from Virginia, James Monroe." Guests kept looking towards the door. Scowling, Monroe, a man in his early thirties, peeked his head into the doorway and yelled, "I'm stuck in my coat." Finally, Monroe appeared at the entrance, struggling frantically to get out of his coat, as the servant helped him.

"Absolutely no sense of wit," said Mrs. Bingham. "He'll go far."

At the door, the servant announced: "The honorable Secretary of War, General Knox, and Mrs. Knox."

Count Moustier, amazed, regarded the newly arrived couple. *"Mon dieux*, what is zat atop zee lady's head?"

"Lucy Knox's bouffant," said Mrs. Bingham. "The latest monstrosity of her hair-dresser, Antony Latour. How the Knox's survive on his government salary is beyond me. Five servants, horses, grooms, fabulous dinners. They say a quarter of his pay goes for wines and brandies."

"How amusing," said Count Moustier.

Again at the door, the servant announced: "The honorable Secretary of State, Thomas Jefferson." Jefferson, a tall, dignified, serious man, approaching his fifties, entered the room.

"You knew Mister Jefferson in Paris, did you not?" she asked Count Moustier.

"But of course."

"A slave girl was with him," she said. "To accompany his daughter, he said."

"I saw her," said Moustier. "*Tres jolie.*"

"She's given birth to a little boy, the color of *café au lait,*" said Mrs. Bingham. "The child bears a startling resemblance to guess who."

"How amusing," said Count Moustier.

Jefferson approached. Mrs. Bingham extended her hand to be kissed. Jefferson shook it gently. He spoke softly. "Mrs. Bingham."

"Mister Jefferson," said Mrs. Bingham.

Jefferson nodded to the Frenchman. "Count Moustier."

"A pleasure to see you again, Monsieur," the Count said.

"I was just telling the count how morbidly dull Philadelphia seems after Paris," said Mrs. Bingham.

Jefferson allowed a flicker of a smile. "Mrs. Bingham, your presence anywhere makes it most agreeable. But to me the simple domestic pleasures of America surpass the superficial gloss of Europe. Please excuse me. I must see the President on an urgent matter." Jefferson made a little bow and walked over towards President Washington."

Annoyed, Mrs. Bingham watched him go. "Well. When Mister Jefferson returned from France, he required an entire ship. Statues, books, Bordeaux wines, brandies, liqueurs ... he even brought a Normandy bitch, bursting with puppies. So he arrived with slaves, bitch and baggage. Now the poor dear must make do in his thirty-five room chateau, on ten thousand acres, worked by two hundred darkies, all inherited from his father and late wife. Ah, the simple pleasures of America."

The servant at the door, announced a new arrival. "The honorable Secretary of the Treasury Alexander Hamilton and Mrs. Hamilton." Hamilton, a short, slender man of thirty-six, entered with his wife Eliza, thirty-five, an attractive mother of four boys and two girls. Eliza and Mrs. Bingham kissed, like good friends. Hamilton took Mrs. Bingham's hand and kissed it with a flourish. "Mrs. Bingham, I'm sure my lovely Eliza won't mind my saying you're are as resplendent as a summer day."

"Flattery will get you everywhere, Mister Hamilton," she replied. "Please meet the new French minister, Count de Moustier."

Moustier kissed Eliza's hand. "*Enchanté madame.*"

Hamilton shook Moustier's hand and addressed him in flawless French, "*Enchanté de faire votre connaissance.*"

Surprised, Moustier replied, "*Enchanté, monsieur.* You speak my language quite well."

"In the West Indies, where I was born," said Hamilton, "many people speak several languages."

"Ah, so you are an *étranger*, like myself," Moustier said.

"In a manner of speaking."

Mrs. Bingham interrupted. "Mister Hamilton is too modest. He is a national hero. In the battle of Yorktown he led a bayonet charge of four hundred men against Cornwallis' troops."

"I only did so, Mrs. Bingham, because I heard it rumored that a lovely lady such as yourself was in distress." They all laughed.

"Mister Hamilton, once, at your home, you sang a lovely song for us. Would you favor us with an encore?"

"I'm not a gifted singer," Hamilton said.

"Please," said Mrs. Bingham. "Was it not a martial tune?"

Eliza explained, "His men sang it on their way to fight Cornwallis. But it's best when accompanied by a drum."

Burr overheard her. "I can accompany you, Colonel." He picked up two pieces of silverware and began a solemn martial drum beat on a table top.

Mrs. Bingham gently pleaded, "Please. For our guest from Paris."

Hamilton shrugged. "If you insist." He began to sing, in a clear voice:

"T'was in the merry month of May,
when bees from flower to flower did hum.
Soldiers through the town marched gay,
The village flew to the sound of the drum.
The clergyman sat in his study within,
Devising new ways to battle with sin:
A knock was heard at the parsonage door,
And the Sergeant's sword clanged on the floor.
We're going to war, and when we die,
We'll want a man of God nearby,
So bring your Bible and follow the drum."

The guests, including Burr, applauded and Hamilton bowed. Someone, in a loud whisper, was heard to say, "He struts about like a nobleman, but he's just the bastard brat of a Scotch peddler." Hamilton, apparently the only one to hear this insult, looked around, stifling his anger.

President Washington approached, smiling broadly. "Dear Mrs. Bingham. My compliments. You've gathered together so many splendid people, including my entire cabinet. Just like a big happy family." Jefferson and Hamilton glared at each other.

A few days later there was a meeting of the President's Cabinet. Washington and Knox, a portly man in his forties, sat at a table, chatting amiably. Next to them sat Jefferson, silent, brooding, drumming his fingers impatiently on the table.

The Negro servant entered, and asked Knox: "Another brandy, General?"

"Why not?"

The servant looked to Jefferson, who shook his head "no." The servant then poured more brandy for Knox.

Just then, Hamilton hurried in with a thick stack of papers under his arm and took his seat. "Mister President ... gentlemen. Forgive me. I was detained on urgent matters of the budget." Washington nodded and said, "What is the first order of business?"

"Since Mister Hamilton has mentioned the budget," said Jefferson, "I wish to voice my concern, my *grave* concern, over the unbridled growth of the federal government."

Washington turned to his Treasury Secretary. "Colonel Hamilton, can you enlighten us? How many are now in our employ?"

Hamilton flipped through his papers. "At latest count, sir, the federal government has three hundred and fifty employees."

"And the cost?" Washington asked.

"For two point two million dollars, sir, we can pay the nation's bills for a year. That includes the Congress and staff, plus the civilian and military."

Jefferson asked, "And what is the cost of just the Congress?"

Hamilton glanced at papers again. "Roughly three hundred thousand per year."

"In that case," said Jefferson, "Since Mister Hamilton's Treasury Department seems to have swallowed up the government, we could send the Congress home and save the three hundred thousand."

"Now, now, Mister Jefferson," said Washington.

"The growth of Treasury is out of all proportion to the need," Jefferson said. "They have an assistant, a controller, a treasurer, an auditor, a register, and thirty clerks. In the State Department we manage with four clerks, a messenger and an office keeper."

Washington turned to Knox. "General Knox, how many are you in the War Department?"

"I have three clerks, General."

Jefferson went on, "I've not counted the scores of customs officers scattered throughout the states, all under Mister Hamilton's direction."

The President looked to Hamilton, who explained patiently, "We require more people, Mister President, in order to collect revenues—"

Jefferson interrupted, "The Federalists are building a monstrous bureaucracy."

Hamilton, now annoyed, replied, "And you, sir, and your so-called Republicans, seem blind to the fact that without a strong central government—"

Washington interrupted them, "Gentlemen! Please! We're neither Federalists nor Republicans. We are all Americans."

Jefferson persisted, "The Constitution calls for a limited federal government. All other powers belong to the states."

Struggling to control his temper, Hamilton replied, "America is a nation of three million. If it's fragmented into small states, the European powers could invade our frontiers. The states themselves might even war against each other."

"That's an alarmist view," Jefferson said.

"History offers us clear lessons," Hamilton continued. "All too often, the private passions of leaders—"

Jefferson interrupted, "You have a low opinion of human nature."

"I'm a realist, Sir. Men are ambitious, vindictive, rapacious."

Washington broke in, "What remedy do you suggest, Colonel Hamilton?"

"The treasury is nearly empty. We depend upon small grants, alms, from the states." After a brief pause. "The United States must have the power to levy direct taxes."

Jefferson smiled. "So it really *is* all about power."

"Here we finally agree," Hamilton replied. "The greatest obstacle to a strong America is the interest of a certain class of men in every state. They resist all change which threatens to reduce *their* power."

Washington turned to his Secretary of War. "General Knox. What do you say?"

"Well, sir, I—"

Jefferson interrupted, "I don't oppose taxes in principle. But creating a vast machinery to hound our citizens questions their honor."

"When it comes to paying taxes," replied Hamilton, "I hold with David Hume: 'every man ought to be supposed a knave.' If all is based on trust, only a conscientious few will pay."

Jefferson broke in, "And why should so much trust be granted to your Department of Treasury?"

Hamilton shot back, "Simply because I differ from your Republicans, I'm accused of lacking in scruples."

Jefferson directed a withering look at him. "That, sir, is because we are trying to remove the veil of mystery with which you clothe your operations."

"Mystery?"

"Yes. *Mystery*, which allows a few speculators to enrich themselves with privileged information. Mister Church, your brother-in-law, for example."

Hamilton rose angrily. "Sir!"

Washington loudly slammed his hand down on the desk, causing the others to jump, startled. The President quickly regained his composure, and smiled benignly. "Colonel Hamilton," he said, "you promised to deliver your report on manufactures today."

"Yes, sir. With your permission I hope to present it to the Congress next week."

"Can you summarize for us?"

"Let me say first," Hamilton began, "that the cultivation of the earth has a strong claim over every other kind of industry—"

Jefferson interrupted: "Those who labor in the earth are the chosen people of God..."

Hamilton continued, "But manufactures must also be encouraged..."

"While we have land to labor," Jefferson said, "let us never wish to see our citizens at a work-bench. I say leave that to Europe."

Hamilton replied, "In England, cotton is now spun by machines, which are put in motion by water. These machines run night and day. They are the cause of the immense progress which has been made in Great Britain—"

Jefferson interrupted once more, "Progress? It's clear that you've never been to London, sir. The level of misery among the common people is shocking. The mobs of great cities live in vermin-ridden hovels. They're no better than slaves."

Washington glanced at the report and set it aside. "I shall study this tonight. Any other business, Colonel Hamilton?"

"Yes, sir. The disturbed state of Europe is inclining its citizens to emigrate. We could assist those who lack the means. They might be of value to our country."

Jefferson shook his head. "Immigrants bring with them Old World customs that are not compatible with democracy."

Hamilton raised an eyebrow. "You forget, sir, that I myself am an immigrant."

"Yes, and I wonder whether your rosy views of the British monarchy aren't the result."

Hamilton rose angrily. Before he could utter a word, President Washington slammed his hand down hard on the table, which paralyzed the others. Hamilton sat back down. Washington regained his composure and smiled, revealing his yellowing wood dentures.

Directing himself to the President, Jefferson said, "Sir, as you know, the post of Ambassador to France remains vacant. Several leading persons in New York State have recommended Aaron Burr—"

Now Hamilton interrupted, "Questions have been raised about Senator Burr's qualifications."

Jefferson plodded on, "Burr has a mastery of the French language. He's a man of culture. He has many talents."

"His principal talent is for intrigue," Hamilton said.

Jefferson was amused. "Do I detect a certain hostility … ever since Burr whipped Mister Hamilton's father-in-law in the race for the Senate?"

"That has nothing to do with it," Hamilton responded angrily. Washington again slammed his fist down on the desk. He rose and paced about. "At every meeting you two go at it like a pair of game cocks. While you bicker, the press blames *me* for all the nation's problems." Washington picked up a copy of a newspaper. "That rascal Frenau accuses me of wanting to be king. I defy any man on earth to produce one single act of mine, one single act, which was not done on the purest motives. Frenau sends me three copies of his paper every day. Three! Does he think I'm a *distributor* for his garbage? If this bickering continues, Mrs. Washington and I shall pack our belongings and return to Mount Vernon. By God, I'd rather be back on the farm than be emperor of the world." Washington sat down and sulked.

After a long interval of silence, Hamilton said, "Sir, I apologize. The country needs you."

Jefferson chimed in, "Yes, Mister President."

Calmer now, Washington said, "On the matter of Senator Burr, I hesitate to appoint any person whose integrity is questioned." He turned to his Secretary of War. "General Knox? I asked you earlier about our state of military preparedness."

Jefferson thought to himself, *Knox is a babbling idiot! And Washington lacks the good sense to see that he's become Hamilton's tool. It's monstrous that this country should be ruled by a foreign bastard.*

"Mister President," Knox said, "we now enjoy peace, but I do believe that, as a preventive measure, it would be wise to maintain a military force."

"What do you suggest?"

"It's not a simple matter to recruit troops. In South Carolina, Mister Laurens has proposed raising two or three battalions of Negroes."

As the Negro servant entered and picked up one of the glasses, the President said, "Many blacks fought valiantly in our war for independence."

Knox continued, "The owners of the Negroes would contribute troops in proportion to the number they possess. We would compensate them, of course."

Hamilton said, "Sir, Mister Laurens says his proposal has met with strong objections."

"Objections? Of what kind?"

Hamilton paused while the servant wiped off the table and exited. "The contempt we've been taught to entertain for blacks makes us fancy many things. I've frequently heard it objected that Negroes are too *stupid* to make soldiers. But I think their faculties are probably as good as ours. In fact, their want of cultivation, joined to the habits acquired from a life of servitude, will make them sooner to become soldiers than our whites."

"Do the owners raise objections?" Washington asked.

"Those who are unwilling to part with property of so valuable a kind will furnish a thousand arguments against," Hamilton said.

The President turned to Jefferson who said, "I urge caution, Mister President."

Hamilton rose and spoke dramatically, as though to a crowd. "All men are created equal, endowed by their Creator with certain rights, including life and liberty. Mister Jefferson's own words are so magnificent that I've committed them to memory. 'Caution' is a strange word coming from a man who adores the French slogan: *Liberte, Egalite* ..."

Stung, Jefferson responded, "I don't question the bravery of the blacks. If equally cultivated for a few generations, they might well become the white man's equal."

Hamilton smiled, "A generous concession."

"I support abolition of the slave trade," Jefferson said. "But many in our southern states do not. We lack the power to trample on their wishes."

"If we don't make use of the Negroes," Hamilton said, "a future enemy probably will. If we grant them their freedom with their swords, this will secure their fidelity."

"And when the hostilities end," Jefferson said, "the planters will find thousands of free, armed Negroes in their midst. In my home state of Virginia there are ten blacks for every eleven whites. Deep rooted prejudices entertained by the whites, recollections by the blacks of the injuries they have sustained, these could produce convulsions which could end in the extermination of one or the other race."

"And your solution, Mister Jefferson?" Washington asked.

Jefferson thought for a moment. "The blacks, men and women alike, should be educated at public expense. They should be freed, with tools and capital, and sent to Africa, or the West Indies, or beyond the Mississippi, to establish a state of their own."

Washington sighed. "No man living wishes more than I to see the freedom of these unhappy people. But it can only be done through the law, by degrees, slowly and surely."

Jefferson continued, "I look to the next generation, not ours, to deal with these questions."

"If we don't resolve this southern business," said Hamilton, shaking his head, "I fear it will become a very grave one."

* * *

Alone in his study, seated at a desk piled high with papers, Hamilton scribbled notes with a quill pen. On a shelf behind him, in a red velvet case, were a pair a gleaming silver dueling pistols.

His servant entered. "Sir, three gentlemen here to see you."

"Yes?"

"The Speaker of the House, Mr. Muhlenberg, Senator Monroe, and Representative Venable." The three men entered. They appeared solemn, uneasy. Hamilton rose from his desk and greeted them, shaking hands.

"Gentlemen, may I offer you some refreshments?"

"No thank you," said Muhlenberg. "We shan't take up too much of your precious time."

Hamilton nodded to the servant, who left. "I always have time for you. How can I be of assistance?" They all sat down.

Venable asked him, "Do you know a Mister James Reynolds?"

Hamilton hesitated, "I … yes … I've made his acquaintance."

Muhlenberg asked, "And a Mister Jacob Clingman?"

Hamilton searched his memory, "Clingman … Clingman … I …"

Muhlenberg reminded him, "He was once in my employ in The House."

"Ah, yes," Hamilton said. "I believe I have met him."

In a casual tone, Venable said, "Mister Reynolds and Mister Clingman have been arrested. Theft of government funds."

Muhlenberg added, "They obtained from the Treasury Department, *your department*, a secret list of individuals."

"A list," Hamilton said.

Muhlenberg went on, "A list of veterans of the Continental Army to whom the government owed money."

Monroe explained, "They then obtained their signatures, a power of attorney, in order to collect the funds for them."

Muhlenberg added, "If a veteran was owed fifty dollars by the government, they told him only ten was due him, and they pocketed the remainder."

Hamilton commented calmly, "Quite a handsome commission, I'd say."

"They did this in dozens of cases and amassed a small fortune," Venable said.

"So greedy were they," Monroe added, "that they tried to collect all of one veteran's funds. They said he'd signed the claim over to them prior to his death."

"But the corpse came to life and denounced them," said Muhlenberg.

"Mister Clingman has agreed to repay the money," Monroe said. "He's also identified the person in the Treasury Department who gave him the list; a fellow named William Duer."

"I see," Hamilton said.

"Mister Reynolds has retained Aaron Burr as his legal counsel," Venable said.

Hamilton muttered to himself, "That man is everywhere."

"Excuse me?" Venable asked.

"A very able counselor, Burr," said Hamilton.

Monroe looked at Hamilton, "Mister Clingman and Mister Reynolds claim they have it in their power to hang a high government official." After a pause. "More precisely, the Secretary of Treasury."

Hamilton leaped up from his chair. "What have those lying scoundrels said?"

Muhlenberg said, "We've been informed of a connection between yourself and Mister Reynolds. It concerns improper speculation in government securities."

Outraged, Hamilton said, "Sir!"

Venable sought to calm him. "You've misunderstood us. We don't take these facts for established."

And Muhlenberg added, "But, unsought by us, this information has been provided."

"We thought it our duty to pursue it," Monroe said.

Muhlenberg added, "We had contemplated laying the matter before the President."

"The President," exclaimed Hamilton.

"But, before doing so," Monroe said, "we decided to form a committee of inquiry."

Muhlenberg smiled at Hamilton. "We thought it only right to afford you an opportunity to explain."

"How *decent* of you," Hamilton said.

"We're influenced solely by a sense of public duty and by no motive of personal ill will," Monroe said.

Forcing a smile, Hamilton replied, "How could I think otherwise?"

Monroe held up several sheets of paper. "Mister Reynolds claims that you maintained a correspondence with him. Are these letters yours, sir?"

Hamilton looked them over. "That appears to be my hand."

"Well, sir?" said Monroe.

After a moment's hesitation, Hamilton reached into a desk drawer. "I have a few letters of my own." He pulled out a thick stack of letters and placed them on his desk. "Last August, Mrs. Hamilton and the children were away in Albany, escaping from the summer heat."

***

Hamilton sat alone at his desk, writing with a quill pen, when the servant entered.

"Sir, a Mrs. Maria Reynolds wishes to speak to you."

Maria Reynolds, in her early thirties, attractive, shapely, well-dressed entered. She appeared troubled. The servant exited.

"Sir, I am the sister of Mrs. G. Livingston of New York and wife to James Reynolds."

"And how may I be of service, Mrs. Reynolds?"

"This is very difficult to confess."

"I assure you, you can speak openly."

"My husband, for a long time, has treated me very cruelly. Now he's run off with another woman."

"How unfortunate."

"And I," she said.

"Yes?"

"I'm destitute," she said, and broke into tears.

Hamilton pulled out a handkerchief. "My dear lady, how can I be of assistance?"

"I wish to return to my friends in New York, but I have not the means."

"But how can I—?"

She interrupted, "Knowing that you are a citizen of New York, I took the liberty of calling upon you, and appealing to your humanity." She began to cry again. She leaned against his shoulder. He gently embraced her, trying to comfort her.

"My dear lady."

"There was something odd in the story," he told the visiting Congressmen. "Yet there was a simplicity in the manner of relating it, which gave an impression of its truth."

"At this instant I'm unable to assist you," he told Maria. "But later in the day, perhaps, I might call upon you?"

"Yes, please. I reside not far distant, at 154 Vine."

"That evening," he said, "I put thirty dollars in my pocket, and went to her home, a large town house near the corner of Fifth. I inquired for Mrs. Reynolds and was shown up the stairs."

Maria took Hamilton by the hand.

"She conducted me into a bedroom. I delivered the money to her. Some conversation ensued. It became quickly apparent that other than pecuniary consolation would not be unacceptable."

They embraced, and kissed, passionately.

"My God," said Venable.

"It required a harder heart than mine to refuse it to a beauty in distress," Hamilton said. "I had frequent meetings with Mrs. Reynolds, many of them at my house, when Mrs. Hamilton and the children were visiting her father in Albany. The intercourse with Mrs. Reynolds continued for at least the next year and a half."

Shocked, Venable asked, "That long?"

"I was not completely the dupe of illusion," said Hamilton, "but my vanity admitted the possibility of a sincere fondness on the part of Mrs. Reynolds. At one point she said that her husband was demanding a reconciliation. I advised her to accept."

Muhlenberg interrupted, "And that was the end of the intercourse?"

"No," Hamilton replied. "Mrs. Reynolds employed every effort to keep up my visits."

Maria spoke to Hamilton, "My husband has been engaged in some speculation—claims upon the Treasury. He can tell you about it."

"So you knew about the improper actions of which we speak." said Monroe.

"I'm coming to that, sir," Hamilton said. "I sought an interview with Mister Reynolds."

Monroe asked, "And Mister Reynolds knew nothing of your … friendship with his wife?"

"He displayed no evidence of knowing," Hamilton replied.

"What did he tell you?" Monroe asked.

"Mister Reynolds confessed that he had obtained a list of claims from Mister Duer, a clerk in my New York office, who was deeply in debt at the time."

"You knew about the lists," Venable exclaimed.

"Yes."

"Didn't you appoint Mister Duer to his post?" Monroe asked.

"Yes."

The three visitors looked at Hamilton, waiting for an explanation.

"Mister Duer resigned from his office," Hamilton said. "And, since he was in debtor's prison, I believed the matter to be resolved."

"You referred to Mister Duer as a clerk," Monroe said. "Wasn't he in fact an Assistant Secretary of the Treasury?"

"Yes."

Monroe pressed onward. "Isn't Mister Duer, in fact, a cousin of yours?"

"Not exactly. He is married to Eliza's cousin."

"I see," Monroe said. "A cousin through marriage. And isn't he also a friend of your brother-in-law, Mister Church?"

"Yes, but—"

Muhlenberg interrupted, "And why did you continue to protect Mister Reynolds?"

"I wanted to maintain his friendship."

"He asked you for employment, didn't he?" Monroe asked.

"Yes. But I told him, truthfully, that there was no vacancy in my office."

"And his reaction?" Muhlenberg asked.

"He complained quite angrily."

Venable asked, "How did you respond?"

"The situation with the wife inclined me to conciliate this man."

"*Conciliate*?" said Monroe.

"It's possible I may have used vague expressions, which raised expectations."

"Expectations of employment?" said Monroe.

"Yes," Hamilton conceded, "but the more I learned of him, the more inadmissible his employment became. I vowed to break off with Mrs. Reynolds. But upon arriving home from Mrs. Bingham's ball, it was the evening of December 15 last, I found two letters. The first one bore a woman's hand."

Hamilton handed the letter to Muhlenberg, who began to read aloud, "Dear Sir …"

"Mister has rote to you this morning," wrote Maria Reynolds.

"God," said Muhlenberg. "Her spelling, R-o-t-e for 'wrote?"

Venable smiled. "I'm sure she had other compensating attributes." He was pleased with his little joke, but Monroe glared at him and the smile faded from his face.

"He has sworn," Maria went on, "that if he does not see or hear from you to day he will write Mrs. Hamilton."

"Blackmail," exclaimed Venable.

"Oh my God, I wish I had never been born to give you so much unhappiness. Do not write to him, no, not a line, but come here soon. Maria."

Hamilton handed another letter to Venable. "I opened the second letter, it was from a very irate James Reynolds, the husband of Maria."

"Sir! I am very sorry to find out that I have been so cruelly treated by a person that I took to be my best friend, instead of that my greatest Enimy."

"He can't spell either," said Venable. 'E-n-i-m-y'"?

"Whenever I came into the house," the husband continued, "I found Mrs. Reynolds weeping. She always told me she had been reading, and she could not help crying when she read anything that was affecting. But seeing her repeatedly in that situation gave me some suspicion. I discovered a letter directed to you, which I copied. The evening after, I see her give the letter to a Black Man in Market Street, and I followed him to your door. When I showed her the copy, she fell on her knees and asked forgiveness. She told me how she called on you for the lone of some money. You took advantage of a poor Broken harted woman. You have acted the part of the most Cruelest man in existence. She says there is no other man that she Cares for in this world. I am robbed of all happiness. I am determined to leave her and take my daughter with me. There is no person that knowes anything as yet. Reflect one moment. That you should know such a thing of your wife. Would not you have satisfaction? Yes. And so will I before one day passes. I am yours, James Reynolds."

Muhlenberg shook his head, "I believe we've heard enough."

But Hamilton persisted, "I wish to erase every shadow of doubt respecting the propriety of my official conduct."

"I'd like to hear more," Venable said. Monroe glared at him.

"I sent Mister Reynolds a note," Hamilton continued, "asking him to call upon me at my office."

"Sir," Hamilton told him, "if I've done any injury to you, which entitles you to satisfaction, it lays with you to name it."

"Give me a thousand dollars," Reynolds said. "I'll take my daughter with me and go where my friend shant hear from me."

"A thousand dollars," exclaimed Venable.

"I was short of personal funds and sought assistance from a friend. A week later I gave Mister Reynolds six hundred dollars." He handed over a receipt to Muhlenberg. "On January third, I gave him the balance of four hundred. Here are receipts marked *in full of all demands*." He handed over another receipt.

"So," said Monroe, "So you don't deny your involvement with Reynolds?"

"No. But during all this time I was also engaged in conducting the nation's urgent business: administering the Treasury Department, overseeing the Customs, launching the Bank of the United States, and drafting my Report on Manufactures."

"What a busy little bee," Monroe said.

Hamilton ignored the remark. "On January seventeenth I received a letter from Mister Reynolds." He handed the letter to Muhlenberg.

"Sir," wrote Reynolds, "I suppose you will be surprised in my writing to you .It's Mrs. R's wish to see you."

"My God," said Venable.

"I find that when you have been with her," Reynolds continued, "she is Cheerful and Kind, but when you have not, she is Quite the Reverse. For my own happiness and hers, I haven't the least objections to your calling, as a friend to both of us, of course."

"This man has no shame," said Muhlenberg.

Hamilton continued, "I didn't accept the invitation, until ..." He handed another letter to Venable. It was from Maria Reynolds.

"I have kept to my bed these days and now rise from my pillow, which your neglect has filled with the sharpest thorns! My heart is ready to burst with Greef."

"G-r-e-e-f," said Venable.

"I can neither eat nor sleep. I have been on the point of doing the most horrid acts. I only wish to see you once more. For God sake, do not deny me this last request."

"Two days later," said Hamilton, "I received still another letter." He gave it to Venable.

"Really, sir," said Muhlenberg. "I think we've heard quite enough."

"I want you to know the entire story," Hamilton said.

"I thought you had been told to stay away from our house," Maria continued. "Yesterday, with tears in my Eyes, I begged Mister once more to permit your visits."

"Upon my honor!" her husband exclaimed. "It's his fault, not mine!"

"Maria continued, "If my dear friend has the least esteeme for the unhappy Maria, whose greatest fault is loving him, he will come as soon as he shall get this. Till that time my breast will be the seat of pain and woe."

"Sir, really," Muhlenberg said.

"I resisted still," said Hamilton. "But a week later I received another letter from her."

"My heart is ready to burst. My tears, which once could flow with ease, are now denied me. Could I only weep."

"Alas," said Hamilton. "I resumed our relationship."

"My God," said Venable. "And then what happened?"

"I became suspicious that perhaps the lady and her husband might be working together."

"You mean to say," said Muhlenberg, "that Reynolds was prostituting his wife?"

Hamilton nodded. "He demanded two payments of a hundred dollars for furnishing a small boarding house that they were about to set up, or pretended to set up."

"And you kept on giving, and seeing her?" Venable asked.

"Mrs. Reynolds more than once told me that her husband threatened to inform Mrs. Hamilton."

"What a scoundrel," said Venable.

The three visitors rose to leave. Monroe said, "We would like to borrow these letters, and have copies made in order to possess a complete record of our inquiry."

Hamilton gave the letters to Monroe. "I trust that these won't fall into the wrong hands."

"You have our solemn word," Monroe said.

* * *

A few years later, Hamilton, gripping a newspaper in his hand, angrily entered Monroe's office. With him were his old friends and colleagues, Venable and Muhlenberg. Hamilton threw the newspaper down upon the desk.

Monroe, startled, asked, "What is this?

"A piece of trash by a scoundrel named Callender," said Hamilton, furious. Monroe picked up the paper, looked it over.

"Callender?" Muhlenberg asked.

"James Callender," said Hamilton. "He fled from England after being charged with sedition. He called the English Constitution 'a conspiracy of the rich against the poor.' He came to America with his hand out to the highest bidder. I'm told that Jefferson has crossed his palm. Look what he says here about me."

Callender, a scruffy, shabbily dressed man, head bent to one side, waved a sheaf of letters and smirked. "So many letters could not refer exclusively to wenching. These were probably forged by Hamilton and Mr. Reynolds, to cover up a more heinous scandal ... embezzling money from the Treasury.

"Five years ago," said Hamilton, "when I showed you the letters, you gentlemen said you were satisfied."

"I assure you, sir—" said Monroe.

"And now," Hamilton interrupted, "just when my name is being mentioned as a possible successor to President Washington ... who betrayed me to that wretch Callender?"

"After returning the originals to you, I sealed up the copies and sent them to a respectable character in Virginia," Monroe said.

"This so-called respectable character ... would his name by any chance be Thomas Jefferson?"

"I did show these materials to Mister Jefferson," Monroe conceded. "But I'm confident that—"

"Then how do you explain Mister Callender getting his grimy clutches on the letters?"

Muhlenberg intervened. "The Clerk of the House, a Mister Beckley, was entrusted with copying them."

"Beckley! The fellow who was dismissed earlier this year?" Hamilton glared at Monroe. "He's a sworn enemy of Federalists. I entrusted these letters to you!"

"Upon my honor," Monroe said, "I knew nothing of this until I arrived home from Europe. I still believe that the packet of papers remains sealed up with my friend in Virginia."

Hamilton's patience was exhausted. "What you say is totally false."

Monroe stood up angrily. "You're a scoundrel!"

Staring him down, Hamilton replied, "And I say your motives towards me are malignant, and dishonorable."

"Sir!" said Monroe.

"I'll meet you like a gentleman," said Hamilton.

"I'm ready," Monroe replied. "Get your pistols."

Venable and Muhlenberg jumped between them. "Gentlemen," said Venable. "Gentlemen! Why don't we meet again in a few days?"

Hamilton glared at Monroe. "I demand an explanation. I'll have Major Jackson see your seconds to settle a time and a place."

"I'll talk, sir, with a pistol, if required," Monroe responded. "But I believe that powder and ball ill serve the truth." Muhlenberg guided Monroe and Hamilton together and they reluctantly shook hands.

A few nights later, Hamilton was in his study working at his desk when the servant looked in. "Mister Aaron Burr to see you, sir."

Aaron Burr entered. "Good evening Colonel Hamilton."

Hamilton felt uneasy in his presence, but strove to be polite. "Colonel Burr."

"Mister Monroe has asked me to represent him." When Hamilton did not reply, he continued. "I thought I might be helpful, since I'm acquainted with all of the key figures in this matter."

"All?"

"Yourself of course. Mister Monroe. And Maria Reynolds."

"You know her, too?"

"I was her attorney in the divorce proceedings against James Reynolds. I thought you knew."

"No. Actually, I had heard you represented Mister Reynolds in the criminal case against him."

"That also." After a pause, "A very attractive woman, Mrs. Reynolds … very attractive." Hamilton did not respond.

"Mister Monroe insists that he had no hand in Callender's publication," Burr said. "He would prefer to settle this matter amicably." When Hamilton did not respond, Burr continued, "But if an interview is required, he asks for three months to settle his affairs. His preferred place is along the Susquehanna."

"The Susquehanna," Hamilton said. "I see."

Burr removed a sheet of paper from his briefcase. "Mister Monroe adds that if you prefer to vindicate yourself in print, you are free to make the most of the original agreement from five years ago. I've prepared a clean draft. May I read it to you?"

"Please."

"Declaration of Messrs. Monroe, Muhlenberg, and Venable, concerning the Affair of J. Reynolds. They regret the trouble which they had occasioned to Mister Hamilton. There was nothing in the transaction which ought to affect Mister Hamilton's character as a public officer or lessen the public confidence in his integrity." Burr handed the paper to Hamilton.

"May I release this to the press?" he asked.

"Most certainly."

"Please tell Mister Monroe that I shall write to him, accepting his statement."

"Excellent," Burr responded. After a pause, "I may add, sir, that after examining the evidence, I told Mister Monroe it is also my belief that you're innocent of the charges."

"Thank you, I appreciate your intervention in this matter."

As Burr turned to leave he noticed the dueling pistols on the shelf. He stopped and ran his fingers over them. "These look familiar."

Hamilton replied, "They're the very same pair that you and my brother-in-law used when you met that morning in New Jersey."

Burr asked, casually, "And how is Mister Church these days?"

"Fine. He's away in England on matters of business."

"Please give him my regards when next you see him. Good day." Burr turned to leave.

Hamilton called after him. "Colonel."

"Yes?"

"I've been so distracted of late, I should have offered my condolences immediately upon your arrival. It was thoughtless of me."

"Thank you. Mrs. Burr is in a better place. The cancer caused her great suffering for several years."

"You have a daughter do you not?"

"I named Theodosia after her mother. She is much afflicted, but she bears the blow with more firmness than could be expected." They shook hands and Burr departed.

That evening, Burr sat in his study, writing to his daughter.

"My dearest Theo,

It was with great pain and reluctance that I made this journey without you. Your letters are my greatest consolation. But, for your sake, it is necessary that I should also peruse them with an eye of criticism. You wrote, for example, 'it was what she had long wished for, and was at a loss how to procure it.' Don't you see that this sentence would have been perfect, and more elegant, without the last 'it'? Mr. Leslie will explain to you why. Your translation of the comedy into French, if not finished, must go on; and if finished, something similar must be taken up. Some English or French history, perhaps. I hope you will ride on horseback daily if the weather should permit. My dear Theodosia, remember that occupation will expel the fiend ennui!"

Some days later, Theodosia replied, "Dearest Father: Your image, kind and indulgent, is my guardian angel. From how many follies, how many faults, does it preserve me?"

"My dearest Theo," he answered, "To return to the subject of manners, when I was about your age, and studying at Princeton, I was active in a literary club and wrote a number of essays. One of them, it was absolutely brilliant, was on the topic of 'The Passions.' Part of it read as follows: 'Do we not behold men of the most sprightly genius, who by giving reins to their passions, are lost to society, and are reduced to the lowest ebb of misery and despair.'"

"My dearest father," Theodosia replied, "The longer I live, the more frequently the truth of your advice evinces itself. You appear to me so superior, so elevated above all other men."

"That's why I say to you," he continued, "receive with calmness every reproof, whether made kindly or unkindly. If it has been groundless and unjust, bear it with composure. You will always feel much better, much happier, for having borne with serenity the spleen of anyone, than if you had returned spleen for spleen."

"I had rather not live than not be your daughter," she answered. "*Adieu.* I kiss you from my heart. Theodosia."

"Please pardon such grave comments," he wrote to her. "The happiness of my life depends on your exertions; for what else, for whom else do I live? Adieu, affectionately adieu."

***

In the Hamilton living room, Eliza, in the late stages of pregnancy, sat on a sofa and held a newspaper. She had been crying. She stared at the newspaper: "It came this morning from an anonymous 'friend'."

Hamilton rushed to her side. "My darling, can you ever—"

"That summer," she said, "five years ago, I was with my father and the children, in Albany. When the children and I felt unwell, in your letters, you urged us to remain in Albany, not to rush home to Philadelphia. You wanted to be with her, didn't you?" Hamilton looked away, ashamed, as she continued, "You've injured me deeply."

"Eliza—"

"Very deeply."

"What can I do to …?"

After a moment, she broke the silence: "I shall never forget this *error* of yours. Never!"

"Eliza, there is something else."

"Some-*one* else?"

"No," he said. "That I swear. But, rumors may be whispered about my origins."

Matter-of-factly, Eliza said, "You mean, that you are the child of an unmarried woman?"

Hamilton was amazed. "How … when did you hear that?"

"Soon after our engagement was announced."

"Sixteen years ago?"

"I received a letter," she explained, "from another 'anonymous friend.' This friend, it appeared to be a woman's hand, assured me that she only wished to *protect* me. She said that you were born to an unmarried woman of an undistinguished family on a Godforsaken island of the West Indies. Your father, she said, was a shiftless peddler, an immigrant from Scotland."

"You knew? All this time?"

Eliza continued, "Your mother died at an early age and your father vanished, leaving you to fend for yourself. A clergyman helped you to come to America to pursue your studies."

"You never let on."

"I've peeked at your account books," Eliza said. "You've sent drafts of money to a Mister Hamilton in the West Indies. I presume it is your father."

"My God, Eliza."

"I wish you would invite him here," she said, "so that he could know his grandchildren."

"I have," he responded. "But there is always an impediment. Eliza, when we met, I saw your background. The Schuylers, the Livingstons, the Clintons … the best families of New York. I feared that if you, if they, knew of my origins, our marriage would never be allowed."

"My father also knew," Eliza said. "Over the years, we both received anonymous notes."

"And didn't this perturb you?" he asked.

"Of course. But when I saw how you struggled to overcome these disadvantages—"

"Eliza, my dearest—"

"We've been married for fifteen years," she said. "We have six children together. I *know* you."

"Eliza—"

"You are so fond of quoting epigrams from Mister Pope that I've committed several to memory. One, I recall, says, 'To err is human ... to forgive divine.'"

Hamilton knelt at her feet, near tears. "I'm much more in debt to you than I can ever pay." They embraced.

"What shall you do now?" she asked.

"That rascal Callender has accused me of fabricating the story of the affair in order to cover up speculation with the husband. Dear Eliza, I've deceived you, for which I beg your forgiveness, but I have never stolen a penny."

"I believe you."

"So much sacrifice, and for what? I'm going to resign from the government. I'll return to private practice."

Eliza pointed to the newspaper. "And what will you do about this?"

"I face a terrible choice," Hamilton said. "If I tell the truth, I will humiliate you and our children. But, as a gentleman, I must tell the truth, mustn't I?"

Fighting tears, Eliza responded, "Yes, you must."

Some days later, a pamphlet authored by Hamilton was made public: "This contains the full text of all the letters, proving my innocence of speculation. My real crime is an amorous connection with Reynolds' wife."

In a tavern somewhere, Callender held aloft the pamphlet with a triumphant grin and scribbled notes for a pamphlet of his own. "Mister Hamilton says, 'I am not a speculator, I'm only an adulterer. I haven't broken the eighth commandment; it's only the seventh which I have violated.'"

"I owe to my friends an apology," Hamilton continued.

Callender went on, "Mister Hamilton, by his own account, rambled for eighteen months in this scene of pollution and squandered more than twelve hundred dollars to conceal the intrigue from his loving spouse."

"This confession is not made without a blush," Hamilton wrote. "I can never cease to condemn myself for the pain which it may inflict in a bosom entitled to all my gratitude, fidelity and love."

Callender wrote, "An eminent politician, who wishes to remain anonymous, told me, and I quote: 'Mister Hamilton obviously suffers from a superabundance of secretions, and he can't find whores enough to draw them off!'"

"I was a poorer man when I left office as Secretary of Treasury than when I went into it," Hamilton wrote.

"Mister Hamilton can fornicate with every female in New York and Philadelphia," wrote Callender, "but he'll surely rise again, for purity of character is not necessary for public office."

"Here I stand, self-tarnished, alone," Hamilton concluded.

While Callender crowed to himself, the sales of my pamphlet are booming! Positively booming.

* * *

On December 12, 1799, George Washington, now retired to his beloved Mount Vernon, as was his custom, rode out on horseback to inspect his farms. There was a cold sleeting rain. Five hours later he returned with snow hanging from his hair. The next morning, he awoke with a sore throat and had difficulty breathing. Doctors came and molasses, vinegar and butter were mixed together, but he couldn't swallow a drop. Poultices were applied. They bled him. He grew weaker.

Three days later, the former President lay in bed, propped up with pillows. A Negro servant stood nearby. General Knox entered and approached the bedside. "General. I came as quickly as I could."

"I find I am going," said Washington. "My breath cannot continue long. I had hoped to reach the new century."

Knox sought to reassure him. "En route here I passed through the new federal city. Several buildings are already completed. In the spring you must come see it."

"The Lord's been generous," Washington said. I'm sixty-seven. I've outlived my father by eighteen years. All my brothers are gone." After a pause, he looked to Knox. "And the next elections?"

"Mister Jefferson will surely mount a strong challenge to President Adams. Many believe he'll win."

Washington shook his head with frustration. "If only party disputes would subside. We must learn to live peaceably together ... farmers ... businessmen—"

"You've set a fine example, General," Knox said.

"If this country can steer clear of European politics, stand firm on its bottom, be wise and temperate, it bids fair to be one of the greatest and happiest nations in the world."

"General, don't exert yourself so much. You must rest. I'll be just outside with Mrs. Washington."

Knox left, and Washington remained silent in bed. He waved weakly at his servant. "Christopher, you've been standing there for hours. You must be tired."

"That's all right, Sir," the servant replied.

"Sit, please," he said.

"I'm just fine, Sir."

Washington tried to move in bed. The servant came over and assisted him. "I hope I'm not being too much trouble."

"No, Sir. I'm pleased to help you."

"It is a debt we must pay to each other. I hope when you want aid of this kind, you will find it."

"Yes, sir."

Washington sighed. "Tis well." He felt his own pulse. His hand fell from his wrist. He was dead. The servant reached over to him, then called out, "Mrs. Washington!"

* * *

Sometime later, Jefferson and Monroe were meeting to discuss the upcoming presidential campaign.

"All of the south is behind you," Monroe said. "But, at best, that gives us a tie with Adams. Without a northern state—"

"New England is solidly in the Federalist camp," Jefferson said."

"Pennsylvania and New Jersey are debatable," said Monroe. "But New York has a goodly number of Republicans and independents. With New York, you can win. Why not offer the vice presidency to Aaron Burr? The New Yorkers elected him to the Senate. He also has admirers in the south."

Jefferson was doubtful. "Burr tries to be of both parties, and of neither."

"Precisely," said Monroe. "He'll split the Federalist vote and swing New York to our side. Hamilton will have apoplexy."

Still unconvinced, Jefferson said, "Burr is like a crooked gun. You never know where he's aiming."

But Monroe reassured him, "Burr can do nothing as vice president. If you run for a second term, you can heave him over the side."

Shortly after election day, a downcast group of Federalists met in New York. Hamilton led the discussion. "Gentlemen, now that the Republicans have won, we Federalists must try to minimize the disaster. As you know, the Constitution provides that the man with the most electoral votes becomes President. The runner-up is Vice President."

A man in the group interjected,"But Jefferson and Burr each received seventy-three votes."

"Yes," said Hamilton. "And the deadlock must now be resolved by the House of Representatives."

"Excellent," said another man. "Since we command a majority in the House, we can block Jefferson from the Presidency."

Hamilton looked around the room. "So you all favor Burr, then?"

"You know him well, don't you?" said the first man.

"I've often been co-counsel with Burr," Hamilton said. "I've also opposed him in some trials. He argues a case quite compellingly."

A third man interrupted, "Won't Burr be more sympathetic to our cause than Jefferson?"

Hamilton shook his head. "If there's a man in the world I ought to hate, it's Jefferson. He's a fanatic in politics."

"He'll wreck the country's trade," said one man.

"Jefferson is an atheist," Hamilton continued.

"In my district," said another, "I've heard of housewives who are burying their bibles for fear Jefferson will confiscate them."

"He's a contemptible hypocrite," said Hamilton. "And with Burr, I've always been personally well. However ..."

"Why do you hesitate?" one man asked.

"Jefferson at least has *some* pretensions to character," Hamilton said. "Burr stands for *nothing*. He listens only to his ambition. He is unprincipled, dangerous."

Some weeks later, Vice President Aaron Burr wrote from Washington to his beloved daughter Theodosia, now a married woman and a mother.

"*Ma chère enfante*, how go things in South Carolina? My greetings to Joseph. Please tell dear little Aaron that his Gamps has a wonderful gift when next we meet. Our new federal capital is delightful. To be a perfect city, all it lacks are houses, places of amusement, scholarly men, amiable women, and a few other such trifles. Whenever guests come for dinner, I reserve a chair, and a place setting for you, my dear Theodosia. As you've no doubt heard, after thirty-six ballots in the House of Representatives Mister Jefferson has won the presidency. Thanks in part to Hamilton's meddling. Our esteemed President rarely deigns to consult me, or even to greet me. I now understand what John Adams said when he called the vice presidency 'the most insignificant job that ever the mind of man contrived or his imagination conceived.' So here I sit, pretending to listen to the dreary debates of the Senate, and thinking of you. *Adieu, chere enfante.*"

In New York, Knox entered Hamilton's study, waving a newspaper, and smiling. "Callender strikes again."

"Your usual, General?" the servant asked.

"Yes, please."

Hamilton looked up from his desk. "Isn't Callender in jail for sedition?"

"President Jefferson has pardoned him," said Knox.

"What has that drunken dog said about me now?"

"Rest easy," said Knox. "The dog is now biting the hand that fed him."

"Jefferson?"

The servant entered with a glass of brandy, placed it in front of Knox, and left. Knox took a sip, and smiled. "Now that he's out of jail, it seems that Callender has switched to our side. It's right here in *The Richmond Recorder*." He handed the newspaper to Hamilton and continued, "He admits that Jefferson was subsidizing him while he wrote those vicious things about you. Jefferson even sent him money while he was in jail. They were working on a book together, all about foreign affairs."

"Can that be true?" Hamilton asked.

"He says so right here."

Callender, scruffier than ever, and a bit drunk, wrote to Jefferson from prison. "Dear Mister Jefferson, thank you! I'm held here in a den of wretchedness and horror. One day when I'm free I hope to have enough money to live near you at Monticello."

Knox continued, "They say Callender was off in taverns when his wife was dying, her body covered with maggots. His four children are in someone else's care."

"I'd like to come up the James River and find fifty acres of clear land and a hearty Virginia female that knows how to fatten pigs and boil hominy, and hold her tongue and then adieu to the rascally society of mankind."

"When Callender was released," Knox went on, "Jefferson became alarmed by the venom in his writing."

"President John Adams is a hideous hermaphrodite who has neither the force and firmness of a man, nor the gentleness and sensibility of a woman. He is a repulsive pedant, a gross hypocrite." Callender, in a drunken stupor, fought off invisible hands clutching at him. "You would dare arrest me? What about the First Amendment? Is it a crime to doubt the capacity of the President?

"Jefferson wanted to keep the wretch at a distance," Knox said. "He stopped sending him money."

"Mister Jefferson of late has treated me with coolness and indifference."

"That's when he turned on Jefferson."

"It is well known that the man, whom it delighteth the people to honor, for many years has kept as his concubine one of his slaves."

Jefferson, holding up a newspaper, grumbled, "Nothing can now be believed which is seen in that polluted vehicle called a newspaper."

"Her name is Sally," wrote Callender.

Jefferson shook his head, "I pity my fellow-citizens who read the newspapers and live and die in the belief that they have known something of what has been passing in the world."

"The name of Sally's eldest son," Callender went on, "is Tom, as in 'Tom Jefferson'. The boy is ten or twelve. His features are said to bear a striking though darker resemblance to those of the President himself. By this wench, Sally, our President has had several children."

Callender held up a book. "I've obtained a copy of a book written by President Jefferson. It is entitled, 'Notes on the State of Virginia.' Here, our President writes, 'The Negroes secrete less by the kidneys, and more by the glands of the skin, which gives them a very disagreeable odor.' Obviously, Mister Jefferson has overcome this disagreeable odor by dousing his beloved Sally with plenty of French perfume!" He laughed gleefully.

Jefferson droned on, "The man who never looks into a newspaper is better informed, and near nearer the truth, than he who reads them."

"I'm told," Callender continued, "that on numerous occasions Mister Jefferson, before the eyes of his two daughters, sent to his kitchen, or perhaps to his pigsty, for this mahogany colored charmer. If there's any doubt, I'm prepared to meet the President in a court of justice with a dozen witnesses as to the black wench and her mulatto litter!

"Someone has even come up with a song to the tune of *Yankee Doodle Dandy*," Knox told Hamilton. "It's printed here." He recited it aloud:

"Of all the damsels on the green,
On mountain or in valley,
A lass so luscious ne'er was seen,
as Monticello Sally.
When pressed by loads of state affairs,
I seek to sport and dally,
the sweetest solace of my cares
is in the lap of Sally!"

Knox smiled, but Hamilton smiled wanly.

A few months later, Hamilton was again at his desk in the study when his nineteen year old son entered. "Hello, father."

"Yes, Philip?"

Philip walked slowly over towards the pistols, and ran his fingers over them.

"Your Uncle John bought those Wogdens in London," said Hamilton. "Very handsome, aren't they?"

"He used them once in a duel, didn't he?"

"Some years ago John became embroiled in a dispute with Mister Burr over a big land transaction. When John accused Burr of bribe payments, Burr called him out. I served as John's second."

"Was anyone hurt?"

With some amusement, Hamilton recalled, "John put a ball right through Burr's jacket! Burr fired, hit nothing at all. Then John stepped forward, apologized, they shook hands, and that was that, thank God."

Philip remained silent. He stared at the pistols.

"Is something the matter, Philip?"

"Several nights ago, my friend Price and I attended the theatre. In the box next to us was Captain Eacker."

"George Eacker? The Jefferson fanatic?"

"The same," Philip said. "Do you recall the speeches he made when Mister Jefferson won the presidency? How he ridiculed the Federalists? How he accused you of wanting to send the army to suppress the Republicans?"

"Poppycock."

"Before the curtain rose," Philip said, "Price and I looked in on his box. We told him what we thought of his orations."

Hamilton regarded his son with concern. "Looked in?"

"We pushed our way in."

"My God. Was he there with Mrs. Eacker?"

"We were a bit loud," Philip admitted. "People in other boxes turned their heads. Captain Eacker pretended to ignore us, but at intermission he asked us out into the lobby."

"I won't be insulted by a set of damned rascals!" Eacker said.

"Who do you mean, sir?" Philip replied.

"I mean the two of you."

"Damned rascals, you say?"

"I live at 50 Wall Street," said Eacker, "and will expect to hear from you forthwith."

"Price sent Eacker a challenge to a duel that very night," Philip said. Noticing Hamilton's alarm, he reassured him. "It's all right, father. Price and Eacker met two days ago. They blazed away, three or four shots in all. The seconds intervened. No one was hurt."

"Thank God," Hamilton said. "But what about you?"

Trying to sound casual, Philip continued, "John Lawrence urged Captain Eacker to take back the words 'damned rascals.' If he would, then I would apologize for my rudeness at the theatre."

"Seems reasonable."

"But Captain Eacker has refused to retract his words." After a pause. "I sent him my challenge for Sunday afternoon."

Hamilton rose from his desk. "Philip, I forbid you to do this."

"Father, when faced with such an insult, what choice remains for a gentleman?"

"The days of chivalry are past," Hamilton said. "In the present times, the courts can be used to prove one's innocence, or the malice of an accuser. The *worst* method you can take is to run a man through the heart, or shoot him through the head." Hamilton reached out, gripped his son's shoulders. "Philip, you are my precious first born. I was hoping, now that you've finished at Columbia, that you could join me in my practice."

"This I must do first, father."

"You're absolutely convinced? It's a question of honor?"

"Yes, father."

"And where will the interview take place?"

"Across the Hudson, at Weehawken..."

Hamilton thought for a moment. "Since you and Price provoked this incident, the honorable thing will be to ... reserve your fire until after Captain Eacker has shot. Then discharge your pistol in the air. That should satisfy everyone."

"Yes, father..."

Solemnly, Hamilton handed the pistols to his son.

* * *

Two men stood facing each other on the New Jersey shore of the Hudson. They took aim for a long while. Finally, a pistol shot was heard, and one man fell to the ground.

Writhing in pain, bloody from a gunshot wound in his side, Philip lay in bed at the Hamilton home. Hamilton and Eliza sat on the bed, overcome with grief, as friends and relatives stood around, silently weeping.

Philip reached out weakly towards Hamilton. "Father, I waited for him to fire first." His hand fell to his side. Eliza wept and embraced her dead son.

Hamilton stared at the wall. "The brightest hope of my family has been taken from me. But it was the will of heaven. He's now out of the reach of the seductions and calamities of a world full of folly, full of danger, full of evil."

On December 8, 1801, Burr wrote again to his beloved daughter.

"My Dearest Theodosia,

Greetings to you and Joseph and little Gamps. Your letter is pretty and lively. You're learned from the newspapers, which you never read, of the death of Philip Hamilton. Shot in a duel with Eacker, the lawyer. Some dispute at a theatre, arising, it's said, out of politics. I wish you would acquire the habit of reading newspapers; not to become a partisan in politics, God forbid, but they do furnish the standing topics of conversation. I have had a most interesting encounter with Celeste, a very amiable member of your sex. She may be forty-one. She is good tempered and cheerful; rather comely. Celeste was, a few months past, engaged to another. That other is suspended. When I brought up the prospect of matrimony *avec moi*, Celeste announced her intention never to marry. I told her that I certainly understood. She thanked me for respecting her wishes. However, as I was making my departure, she asked me to visit her again. Ah, women!

Adieu chere enfante."

Smiling as she read the letter, Theodosia took pen in hand and replied.

"My dearest Papa,

I see you still have much to learn about the nuances of courtship! I think that Celeste meant, from the beginning, to say that awful word *yes*! But, not choosing to say it immediately, she told you that you had furnished her with arguments against matrimony. In French that means, 'please, sir, persuade me out of them again.' But you took it as a plump refusal, and retreated. She invited you back. What more could she do? *Adieu*, silly boy.

Your Theodosia."

Three years later, on March 1, 1804, in another letter to his daughter and confidante, Burr wrote:

"My dearest Theodosia, the Republicans have again nominated Mister Jefferson. The ungrateful fellow no longer needs me to carry New York. So he's discarding me in favor of, guess who, Governor George Clinton. Clinton's nephew, De Witt, as you know, is Mayor of New York. My God, there are Clintons everywhere! Old George, now ending his seventh term in Albany, sees the Vice Presidency, quite correctly, as a "respectable retirement." Since he will likely replace me here in Washington, I thought it only fair to run for his job in Albany. Some Federalists are backing me, but Hamilton is intriguing for any candidate who has a chance against yours truly. Wish me luck! God bless thee and me, my dear Theodosia."

In Albany, a group of Federalists were meeting, gearing up for the next gubernatorial elections. "I say we should have one of our own run," said one man.

"Why not Vice President Burr?" said another. "Jefferson and the Republicans have treated him shabbily. His sympathies will lie with us."

A third man turned to Hamilton. "What do you say, General Hamilton?"

"I'm aware that some of our fellow Federalists, particularly those from New England, feel bitterly towards Mister Jefferson," Hamilton said. "They've gone so far as to suggest that the New England states secede and form a separate nation. They want New York to join them."

"Who's told you this?" one man asked.

"I was approached by Senator Pickering of Massachusetts. He contends that the five New England states, if joined by New York and New Jersey, would make a formidable nation."

"And your reply?" the man asked.

"I violently oppose any dismemberment of the Union," Hamilton said.

Another man asked, "But aren't you concerned, sir, that with the Louisiana Purchase, Mister Jefferson will depend more on the West and South? That would leave the Northeastern states to poverty and disgrace."

Hamilton shook his head in the negative. "Even more disgrace would befall us if the Union is dismembered."

"And how does this concern Mister Burr?" someone asked.

"These secessionists," Hamilton said, "have made overtures to Mister Burr."

"Do we know his reply?"

"Mister Burr is unprincipled, both as a public and private man," Hamilton said. "If he becomes Governor, who knows? He could use it as a stepping stone to the presidency. Or, he might try to dismember the Union. I don't like Clinton, but he's a man of property, and, as far as I know, his private life is unblemished. I oppose Mister Burr. I would rather see a Republican Governor, and our party broken to pieces."

One man whispered to a friend next to him, "He'd rather see a Republican win? Mister Hamilton's gone quite insane."

The friend replied, "Hamilton is unfit to lead the Federalists."

Another man raised his hand. "General Hamilton?"

"Yes?"

"You have referred to Mister Burr's private conduct. Could this have anything to do with certain rumors concerning him and his daughter?"

"What rumors?"

"It has been whispered that Mister Burr has an extreme love for his daughter," the man said. "An unnatural love bordering on the *indecent*."

Hamilton remained silent. But the man persisted, "Is there any truth to these rumors?"

Hamilton thought for a moment, then spoke, "As a lawyer, I respect facts. I have no direct evidence of such rumors." He smiled, and added, "However, from what I do know of Mister Burr, nothing would surprise me."

There was nervous laughter in the crowd. As the men continued talking, one fellow in the rear rose from his seat and left.

One month later, on April 21, 1804, Burr wrote to his daughter:

"Dearest Theo.

The affair of Celeste is becoming serious. Things are not gone to extremities; but there is danger. Poor Gampy. The New York election is lost by a great majority. Ah, just as well. Of all the earthly things, I most want to see your son. Does he yet know his letters? If not, surely you must want skills, for, most certainly he can't want genius.

Adieu, my dear child."

On June 18, 1804, Hamilton was seated at his desk in the study, engaged in paperwork, when the servant entered, and read from the calling card, "A Mister William Peter Van Ness, Esquire." Van Ness, with a very solemn expression, entered. Hamilton, rising, extended his hand. Mr. Van Ness, to what do I owe the pleasure?"

"A letter for you, sir. From Vice President Burr."

"Thank you." Hamilton held the letter in his hand. There was an awkward silence.

"Vice President Burr has asked me to await your reply."

Hamilton opened the letter, which also contained a newspaper clipping.

"Sir,

I send for your perusal a letter by a Charles D. Cooper. It was published in the Albany press on April 24. I quote: 'General Hamilton has declared that he looks upon Mr. Burr to be a dangerous man who ought not to be trusted with the reins of government.' The letter goes on, and I quote: 'Really sir, I could detail to you a still more despicable opinion, which General Hamilton has expressed of Mr. Burr.'

You must perceive, sir, the necessity of a prompt acknowledgement, or denial, of the assertions of Mister Cooper. I have the honor to be your obedient servant, A. Burr."

Hamilton stared at the letter and enclosed newspaper clipping, while Van Ness waited. Finally, he spoke, "An immediate reply is expected?"

"Yes, sir."

"Tell him I shall reply promptly, but I need a little time."

Two days later, Van Ness delivered a letter to Burr.

Sir,

In his letter, Dr. Cooper implies that he considers this opinion of you, which he attributes to me, to be 'despicable,' and that I had used others 'still more despicable.' However, he does not mention to whom, when, or where. How can I be expected to recall what I may have said of a political opponent in the course of fifteen years? I stand ready to avow or disavow any precise opinion which I may be charged with having declared of any Gentleman. I trust you will see the matter in the same light. If not, I can only regret the circumstance, and must abide the consequence. I have the honor to be, Sir, your most obedient servant.

Alexander Hamilton.

Holding Hamilton's letter, Burr angrily paced back and forth, and told Van Ness, "For years now, Hamilton has accused me of almost every imaginable crime."

"And you have never challenged his insults?"

"He has a peculiar manner of saying offensive things in such a way that cannot well be taken hold of. On two different occasions, he understood that he had gone too far. He came forward and made apologies. I've never mentioned these incidents to anyone. But *this*, in the newspaper, for all to read. I cannot let it pass."

"Perhaps he'll again apologize," said Van Ness.

But Burr remained angry. "Four years ago, who spoke against me when I tied Jefferson for the Presidency? Hamilton. And now, who spread lies to block me from being Governor? Hamilton. He has never forgiven me for taking the Senate seat from his father-in-law twelve years ago. The man is obsessed with me."

My darling daughter, to return to the subject of manners, do we not behold men of the most sprightly genius, who by giving reins to their passions, are lost to society, and are reduced to the lowest ebb of misery and despair?

Burr, momentarily rattled by the thought, quickly recovered. Van Ness tried to calm him. "But you've ignored even more vicious lies written by journalists."

"Scribblers of no consequence," said Burr. "But a gentleman must adhere to the laws of honor."

He took up his pen and replied to Hamilton.

"Sir,

I find nothing in your reply of that sincerity and delicacy which you profess to value. The question is not one of syntax, or grammatical accuracy. The question is whether you uttered expressions derogatory to my honor."

Later that day, having read Burr's reply, Hamilton was also offended and said to Van Ness, "Tell Colonel Burr that his letter contains rude and offensive expressions and seems to close the door to all further reply."

Trying to play the role of peacemaker, Van Ness replied, "Perhaps you might take time to deliberate, and reply to it."

"No," said Hamilton. "It's not possible to give any other answer."

Van Ness tried again, "Couldn't you simply state that you have no recollection of using the terms that could so be interpreted by Dr. Cooper in his letter? This might open a door for accommodation."

"No," said Hamilton. "Unless Colonel Burr takes back this letter and writes one that would allow a different reply."

"I'm afraid, sir, that seems most unlikely."

"Then Colonel Burr must pursue such a course as he deems most proper."

A few nights later, the servant entered Hamilton's study. "General Knox to see you, sir."

"Henry," said Hamilton, "if you could serve as my second on this matter, please deliver this to Colonel Burr."

Hamilton gave the note to Knox, who unfolded it and read it aloud. "Sir, your letter makes unwarranted demands, it contains rude and improper expressions." Knox stopped, looked questioningly at Hamilton.

"It's what I want to say to him."

"*Rude* is a rather harsh word."

Hamilton took back the note, grabbed a pen, crossed it out, and wrote in another. "There. I've replaced *rude* with *indecorous*. Does that suit you?"

Knox shook his head. "This is still practically an invitation to—"

Hamilton snapped back "It's what I want to say to him."

"Let me consult with Van Ness," Knox said.

That evening, Knox and Van Ness visited Hamilton. Van Ness, looking somewhat relieved, held up a letter and said, "We believe this will satisfy Colonel Burr."

He gave it to Knox, who read it aloud. ""Sir: The conversation to which Dr. Cooper alluded turned wholly on political topics, and the results that might be expected in the event of Colonel Burr's election as

Governor. General Hamilton did not attribute to Colonel Burr any dishonorable conduct, nor relate to his private character."

"Fine," said Hamilton.

Van Ness broke into a smile. "Excellent. Please sign it, and I'll deliver it to Colonel Burr."

Hamilton signed, and gave Ness another letter. "Hand him this also."

"But this is your earlier note," said Knox. "It will only provoke him."

Hamilton insisted, "Give him both letters."

Later that evening, Van Ness delivered both letters to Burr. He pointed to the first one, saying, "In this note, I think he adopts a conciliatory tone."

But Burr was not appeased. Still furious, he exclaimed, "Hamilton clearly feels a malevolence towards me. These things must have an end."

My darling daughter, receive with calmness every reproof, whether made kindly or unkindly. If it has been groundless and unjust, bear it with composure. You will always feel much better, much happier, for having borne with serenity the spleen of anyone, than if you had returned spleen for spleen.

Burr, pen in trembling hand, wrote another letter to Hamilton. "Sir, no denial will be satisfactory, unless it is *general.* It must exclude the idea that rumors derogatory to Colonel Burr's honor, at any time or place, have originated with General Hamilton."

"Sir," Hamilton replied the next day, "I cannot consent to be questioned generally. You must specify the rumors."

And the following day Van Ness appeared once more at Hamilton's home, still another letter in his hand. "Colonel Burr and I have drafted this for your signature."

Hamilton took the letter from Burr and read it. "The language I may have employed in the warmth of political discourse has been represented in a manner entirely foreign from my sentiments or wishes." He tore up the draft and handed it back to Van Ness.

Downcast, Van Ness said, "Colonel Burr predicted you would do that." He handed Hamilton another letter. He also sent you this."

Hamilton accepted the second letter. "Sir, you have invited the course I am about to pursue, and now by your silence impose it upon me."

Two nights later, Hamilton and Knox sat in the study, and the servant brought Knox his usual brandy. Knox sipped from it and said, "Do you know what Mister Franklin, may he rest in peace, thought of dueling? He once said to me, 'How can such miserable worms as we are entertain so much pride as to suppose that every offense against our imagined honor merits death?'"

"A wise man," said Hamilton, as he continued to look through some papers.

"Mister Franklin told me this story," Knox continued. "A gentleman in a coffee house desired another to sit further from him. 'Why so?' 'Because, Sir, you smell.' 'That, Sir, is an affront, and you must fight me.' 'I will fight you, if you insist, but I don't see how that will mend the matter. If you kill me, I shall smell too. And, if I kill you, you will smell, if it is possible, more than you do at present.'"

Knox laughed so hard at his own joke that he choked on his brandy. Hamilton smiled wanly, but did not respond.

"Was General Washington a man of honor?" Knox asked him.

"Of course."

Sipping again at his brandy, Knox recalled, "Many years ago, the general fell into a political argument with a fellow named Payne. Payne hit him with a club, and knocked him down."

"And what did he do?" Hamilton asked.

"The general repaired to a tavern and wrote a note asking Payne to meet him there. Payne believed the general was issuing a challenge. He went to the tavern, expecting to see a pair of pistols. Instead, there was a decanter of wine and glasses on the table. The general apologized for quarreling, and they shook hands." Hamilton remained silent as Knox sipped again at the brandy, and observed, "That's the kind of man our president was, may he rest in peace. He was big enough to acknowledge an error."

"My religious and moral principles oppose the shedding of blood," Hamilton said.

"Well then?"

"I can't deny that my comments about Colonel Burr have been extremely severe," Hamilton admitted. "I may even have been influenced by falsehoods."

"Can't you tell him that?" Knox asked.

"But there are difficulties in backing out."

Knox, frustrated, remarked, "You've always said human beings act out of self-interest. But where is the self-interest here?" Hamilton did not respond, and Knox pressed him further. "Isn't it in *your* self-interest to find some reasonable accommodation? Think of your wife. Your family."

"Eliza and the children are extremely dear to me."

"Haven't you yourself persuaded friends not to engage in duels?"

"More than once," Hamilton responded. And then, after a pause, "I haven't censured Burr on light grounds. The general disavowal that he requires is out of my power. It's a question of honor."

"Honor?" said Knox. "No, it's not honor. It's *madness*."

"You don't understand."

Knox pleaded with his old friend, "Help me then."

"One day, I was trying a case with Burr. We went to a nearby tavern for lunch and I began to discuss politics. Do you know what he said?"

Holding a glass of wine, Burr remarked, smiling, "The purpose of politics is fun, honor and profit."

"Fun, honor and profit!" said Hamilton.

"He was joking," said Knox. "Burr is a man with a keen sense of humor."

"Oh yes. I laughed," said Hamilton. "But then I thought to myself, this man is destitute of any fixed principles."

"You make too much of it," Knox said.

"Imagine if *I* had said such a thing." Hamilton said. "But, since Burr is a member of the regenerating tribe."

"A member of what?" Knox asked.

"The regenerating tribe. Burr, Washington, Jefferson ... the well-born, the sons of the 'good' families. How many times have I heard, until I want to vomit, 'Burr's grandfather was the great theologian Jonathan Edwards? Burr's father was the president of Princeton'"

"But is it his fault that?"

Hamilton interrupted him, "For those born at the top of the heap, everything is forgiven. They move through life ... no, they *glide* through life with such nonchalance. Burr was handed the vice presidency on a silver platter. The stepping stone to the highest position in the land. I served General Washington faithfully for two decades. I advised him on the most critical matters of the nation. I was the President's right hand. Yet the most innocent error causes me to be condemned. Doors of opportunity shut in my face. After so many years of sacrifice, I remain a stranger here. This American world was not made for me."

"That's nonsense," said Knox. "You—"

Again, Hamilton interrupted, "When I directed the Treasury Department, I never touched a penny that was not mine. But they never let up. 'He's not one of us. He's just the bastard brat of a Scotch peddler. The bastard thief. The son of a whore'"

"What has this to do with Burr?" Knox asked.

"Burr was born with all the advantages denied me," Hamilton replied. "Yet he takes nothing seriously."

"You're mistaken," said Knox. "He's taken this matter *very* seriously. Enough to risk his life and yours. I've never seen Burr like this. The letter that appeared in the Albany paper, which started all this, the writer refers to 'even more despicable things' about Burr. What could he have meant?"

"I don't know," Hamilton said.

"But surely you must have said *something* which prompted the remark."

"Someone brought up a rumor about Burr, that he had an unnatural love for his daughter, a love bordering on the indecent."

"That's monstrous," Knox said.

"I said that I had no personal knowledge of this."

"And?"

"I commented, flippantly, that Burr's sense of propriety was such that nothing would surprise me."

Knox stared at him in disbelief. "My God, man."

"It never occurred to me that anyone would take that seriously," Hamilton said.

Knox asked, "Do you suppose this comment of yours has gotten back to Burr?"

"There were many people at the meeting."

"You must make it clear to Burr that you oppose him only on political grounds."

"I have already done so," Hamilton said.

"Three years ago," Knox said, "your boy Philip fell in Weehawken … all for a question of honor. I saw the life bleeding out of his side, in the bed over there. Have you forgotten Philip? Have you forgotten Eliza's tears?" Hamilton remained silent as Knox continued. "And your poor daughter Angelica? Driven to madness by Philip's death, sitting at the piano, playing the same tune over and over. What will happen if you die? Think of all your children."

Hamilton shook his head. "I cannot decline Burr's call. I cannot."

"For God's sake, man, why not?"

"On past occasions," Hamilton said, "I've questioned Colonel Burr's integrity. If now I were to deny it, those who heard my references to him, would question my own integrity. I would become a laughingstock. It would be *humiliating*. I simply couldn't stand it."

The next day, Knox met with Van Ness. "General Hamilton sincerely wishes to avoid extremities, if it can be done with propriety."

"Colonel Burr is running out of patience," said Van Ness.

"The slanders circulating against Colonel Burr might be *specified*. That is all General Hamilton asks."

"The Colonel is adamant," said Van Ness. "He demands a general denial."

After a moment of silence, Knox asked, "On what date does Colonel Burr desire the interview?"

"At the earliest time convenient," Van Ness replied.

"General Hamilton says it is not proper, in the midst of Circuit Court, to withdraw his services from clients who have confided important interests to him. He requires a short delay."

"In that case," said Van Ness, "may I suggest Monday, July eleventh, at seven a.m.?"

"Agreed."

Van Ness asked him, "Would Doctor Hosack be satisfactory as the attending physician for both parties?"

"Yes. And the place?"

"The usual ledge on the New Jersey shore. At Weehawken."

That evening, Hamilton sat at his desk, pen in hand. The servant entered. "Will you be dining alone this evening, sir?'

"Yes. Mrs. Hamilton is staying up at the Grange with the children for the next few days."

"Plenty of peace and quiet for you, sir," the servant said.

"Yes. Thank you."

The servant exited, and Hamilton wrote a letter to his wife. "July 4, 1804. This letter, my dear Eliza, will not be delivered to you, unless I shall first have terminated my earthly career, to begin, as I humbly hope, a happy immortality."

That same day, Aaron Burr wrote to his daughter: "July 4, 1804. My darling Theodosia. I have written out my will, which is in the hands of Mister Van Ness. Please take charge of my private letters and burn all that could injure any person, particularly the letters of my female correspondents."

Hamilton continued to Eliza, "If it had been possible for me to avoid the interview, my love for you and my precious children would have been alone a decisive motive. But it was not possible, without sacrifices which would have rendered me unworthy of your esteem."

And Burr continued to Theo, "There are six blue boxes which contain enough information, if it be deemed worthwhile, for someone to write a sketch of my life. I believe that my estate will just about cover my debts, and no more. I mean, if I should die this year."

Hamilton went on, "The scruples of a Christian have determined me to expose my own life rather than subject myself to the guilt of taking the life of another. This much increases my hazards. But you had rather I should die innocent than live guilty."

Burr continued, "I am indebted to you, my dearest Theodosia, for a very great portion of the happiness which I have enjoyed in this life. With a little more perseverance, and industry, you will obtain all that my vanity had fondly imagined. Let your son have occasion to be proud that he had a mother. *Adieu. Adieu.*"

Hamilton concluded, "With my last idea, my dearest Eliza, I shall cherish the sweet hope of meeting you in a better world. *Adieu*, best of wives, and best of women. Embrace all my darling children for me. Ever yours."

Burr began another letter to Joseph Alston, where he laid out the truth.

"July 4, 1804. My dear son-in-law Joseph, I have called out General Hamilton, and we meet on the morning of the eleventh. Van Ness will give you the particulars. If it should be my lot to fall, I commit to you all that is most dear to me, my reputation and my daughter. As a last favor, I ask you, whatever your own feelings may be, that you stimulate Theo in the cultivation of her mind. It is indispensable to her happiness and yours that she acquire a critical knowledge of Latin, English and natural philosophy. All this would be poured into your son."

That evening, a raucous crowd of war veterans met at Fraunces Tavern in Manhattan. Among them were Burr and Hamilton. General Knox addressed the group. "Gentlemen, we are gathered for the twenty-first annual Fourth of July celebration of the Society of Cincinnati. We, the veterans of the Continental Army, are here to honor our fallen heroes, including our beloved General Washington, and to celebrate our victory in the War for Independence. I salute you all."

Knox raised his glass in a toast and was answered with applause and cheers. Hamilton was engaged in conversation with one group of veterans while Burr spoke with another group. They glanced at each other from a distance.

Knox, in a boisterous mood, called out, "General Hamilton. Remember our song from Yorktown? Will you sing it for us?"

Others joined in, urging him on. "The Drum! The Drum!"

Hamilton, wineglass in hand, stepped up onto a chair, then upon a table. A man came forward with a drum and proceeded to tap out a beat. Burr sat nearby, observing in silence, staring at him, while Hamilton sang:

T'was in the merry month of May
When bees from flower to flower did hum.
Soldiers through the town marched gay,
The village flew to the sound of the drum.
The clergyman sat in his study within,
Devising new ways to battle with sin.
A knock was heard at the parsonage door,
And the Sergeant's sword clanged on the floor.
We're going to war, and when we die,
We'll want a man of God nearby,
So bring your Bible and follow the drum.
The men joined in, singing:

We're going to war and when we die,
We'll want a man of God nearby,
So bring your Bible and follow the drum...

July 11, 1804. A pink, misty dawn. The twinkling lights of New York City were visible in the distance. Burr and Van Ness, who held an umbrella, stood waiting at Weehawken, on the west bank of the Hudson River. The sunlight grew brighter. As they waited on a narrow ledge twenty feet above the water, Hamilton set off in a small boat from the foot of Horatio Street in Greenwich Village. His second, Henry Knox, and Doctor David Hosack, accompanied him. When the boat reached the Jersey shore, Doctor Hosack and the oarsman remained at a discreet distance so as not to be eyewitnesses to an illegal act. Hamilton and Knox, who also carried an umbrella and a case holding the pistols, climbed up a path toward them. Burr and Van Ness had cleared away some underbrush.

Hamilton said to Knox, "I've made up my mind not to fire at Colonel Burr the first time. I will receive his fire, and then fire in the air."

Knox looked at him incredulously. "But that is—"

Hamilton cut him off. "I'll say no more on the subject."

In a few moments, Burr, Hamilton and their seconds exchanged salutations. Van Ness and Knox measured off ten paces. After inspecting and loading the pistols, they gave the weapons to Hamilton and Burr, who took their stations.

Knox spoke loud for all to hear, "I will give the command *present!* Which means to elevate the arm, point and aim. The parties shall fire when they please. If one fires before the other, the opposite second shall say: *one, two, three, fire* and he shall then fire, or lose his shot. A snap or flash is a fire."

Hamilton raised and leveled his pistol, then lowered it. "I beg pardon for delaying you gentlemen, but the direction of the light ...," He drew from his pocket a pair of spectacles, and put them on.

Knox looked to both of them. "Gentlemen, are you prepared?" Burr and Hamilton nodded. Knox said, "Present!" They raised their weapons.

Burr fired first. Struck, Hamilton raised himself on his toes, turned a little to the left. His pistol fired in the air as he slumped to the ground.

Knox yelled out, "Doctor Hosack."

Dr. Hosack came running up the grade towards the fallen Hamilton. Knox rushed over and lifted Hamilton to a sitting position. A bloody wound was visible in his right side. Burr advanced towards Hamilton in a manner that appeared to express regret. Van Ness stopped him, opened his umbrella, to conceal Burr from sight, and escorted him away.

In a weak voice, Hamilton said to Doctor Hosack, "Take care of that pistol; it may go off and do harm. My vision is indistinct. My legs … I can't feel them. This is a mortal wound. Doctor, Please send for Mrs. Hamilton. Let the event be gradually broken to her, but give her hopes." He sank away, and appeared lifeless. Knox and Doctor Hosack lifted him up and carried him down towards the boat.

Hamilton lay on his death bed at home with a grief-stricken Eliza and Doctor Hosack at his side. The servant entered and handed a letter to Doctor Hosack. "This came for you, sir."

Hosack opened and read the letter, which was from Burr. "Mister Burr's respectful compliments. He requests Doctor Hosack to inform him of the present state of General Hamilton and of the hopes which are entertained of his recovery." Folding the letter, Doctor Hosack put it in his pocket, patted Eliza on the shoulder and left the room. Eliza wept at her husband's side.

"Remember, my Eliza," Hamilton said, "you are a Christian."

Bishop Benjamin Moore, the rector of Trinity Episcopal Church, entered. Through her tears, Eliza said, "Bishop Moore. He keeps asking for you."

Barely audible, Hamilton said, "For some time it's been the wish of my heart to unite myself to the church, to receive the Communion at your hands."

"General," the Bishop said, "dueling violates the law of God. I regret that I can only seek to comfort you as a friend."

The Bishop turned to leave. Hamilton weakly raised his arm. "Wait. Please." The Bishop turned back.

"I used every expedient to avoid the interview," said Hamilton. "But I've found for some time past that my life must be exposed to that man."

"Should it please God to restore you to health," the Bishop said, "will you never again engage in a similar action?"

"I will."

"Will you employ all your influence to discontinue this barbarous custom?"

"I will."

"Do you sincerely repent of your sins past?"

"I do."

"Have you a lively faith in God's mercy through Christ with a thankful remembrance of the death of Christ? Are you disposed to live in love and charity with all men?"

Hamilton weakly raised one hand. "I have no ill will against Colonel Burr. I forgive all that happened."

As Eliza wept, Bishop Moore solemnly prayed over the dying man. "Almighty, ever living God, Maker of mankind, who dost correct those whom thou dost love, and chastise everyone whom thou dost receive, grant that thy servant recover his bodily health, if it be thy gracious will; and that whensoever his soul shall depart from the body, it may be without spot; through Jesus Christ our Lord. Amen."

Thomas Jefferson, seated in his study, wrote to his daughter on July 17, 1804. "My dear daughter Martha, I presume the newspapers will inform of the death of General Hamilton, which took place on the 12th. It was one of several remarkable deaths lately. General Hamilton was indeed a singular character: honest, amiable, yet so bewitched and perverted by the British example as to be thoroughly convinced that corruption was essential to the government of a nation!"

Van Ness wrote to a distant friend, "The shocking catastrophe which terminated the life of Alexander Hamilton has spread gloom over our city. Some may question the soundness of his judgment, but all must be ready to do justice to the nobleness of his nature."

Knox was asked to deliver a public eulogy. First, to himself, he thought, *He was a foreigner of illegitimate birth. He was indiscreet, vain, opinionated. He was opposed to republican government.* Then, to a large crowd, he said, just as sincerely, "At Philadelphia, he helped to form that constitution which is now the bond of our union, the shield of our defense, and the source of our prosperity. He was ambitious only of glory. I declare before God, that in his most private and confidential conversations, the single objects of discussion and consideration were the freedom and happiness of the American people."

On August 2, 1804, there was an Inquest on the Death of Alexander Hamilton. John Burger, the Coroner, in his report, wrote: "We do, upon our oath, say that Aaron Burr, Vice President of the United States, not having the fear of God before his eyes, but being moved and seduced by the instigation of the Devil, on the eleventh day of July, willfully and of his malice aforethought, did make an assault, with a certain pistol, against Alexander Hamilton. And so the jurors upon their oath do say that Vice President Aaron Burr feloniously did kill and murder."

A few days later, on August 10, 1804, Burr wrote to his beloved daughter:

"Darling Theodosia,

There are two ways of telling a story. One, by beginning with the oldest event, is the mode commonly used by philosophers and historians. The other is by commencing with the most recent incident. This is the mode universally practiced by lovers, and, generally, by poets. I could even quote Homer and Virgil as authorities. This arrangement, I may add, seems more congenial with the temper and feelings of the fair sex. Thus, you see, most ladies turn first to the last chapter of a novel or romance. In defense of this practice, I will tell you that a subject now in dispute is which state, New Jersey or New York, shall have the honor of hanging the vice president. You shall have due notice of the time and place. Wherever it may be, you may rely on a great concourse of company, much gayety, and many rare sights, such as the lion, the elephant …"

"Dear Father," Theodosia wrote back. "There are a thousand vague reports about you."

Burr went on, "You will find the newspapers filled with all manner of nonsense and lies."

"My mind is anxious—impatiently anxious—in regard to your future destiny," Theodosia wrote.

"My dear creature," her father wrote, "I absent myself from home, into a sort of exile, merely to give a little time for passions to subside."

She worried, "What will occupy you? How will this terminate?"

"Don't let me have the idea you are dissatisfied with me a moment. I can't just now endure it."

"My brain is dizzy," wrote Theodosia, "my poor little heart cries out. When shall we meet?"

"I regret sorely that we shan't see each other for a time," her father replied, "but somehow and somewhere, we surely will. I am heading for points south, but am now in Philadelphia, trying once more to win Celeste's hand. However, I fear nothing can be done to convince her. If any male friend of yours should be dying of ennui, recommend that he engage in a duel and a courtship at the same time."

* * *

The years passed, and people followed their separate destinies. Mrs. Anne Bingham had been the toast of Philadelphia, until the smallpox epidemic swept through the city. When they lowered her into the grave, she was just thirty-seven. Count Moustier tarried a few years in America, then sailed home to France and enjoyed a long and fascinating life. Thomas Jefferson, after two terms as President of the United States, retired to his beloved Monticello. He died at the age of eighty-eight, on July 4th. As for General Henry Knox, shortly after Hamilton's demise, he retired to Maine and died two years later, age fifty-six. Mrs. Eliza Hamilton, the widow of Alexander Hamilton, would preside over her family until the age of ninety-seven. The journalist James Callender was forty-two when they found him face down in three feet of water, drowned while drunk, or murdered. James Monroe became the fifth President of the United States and his two terms were characterized as "an era of good feeling." But Burr recalled, "Monroe was once my client. He was dull, stupid, and hypocritical. He had no opinion on any subject. He called himself a lawyer, but he was far below mediocrity. He never tried a case worth more than a hundred dollars." Afterwards, Monroe retired to his Virginia home and died at the age of seventy-three.

As for Aaron Burr, the murder charges were eventually dropped. He returned to Washington where he served out his term and presided over the Senate. But the bullet that killed Hamilton also destroyed Burr's political career; the former Vice President of the United States left public life altogether, settling for the relative obscurity of the profession of law.

Eight years later, Burr received a letter from his daughter in South Carolina. "July 12, 1812. My dear father, a few miserable days past, and your letters would have gladdened my soul. But there is no more joy for me. Little Aaron, your noble grandson, is gone. He expired on June 30, one month after his eleventh birthday. My head is not now sufficiently collected to say anything further."

A few days later Burr received another letter from his son-in-law, Joseph Alston. "My dear sir, one dreadful blow has destroyed us. That boy, our companion, our friend, he who was to have transmitted down the mingled blood of Theodosia and myself, who was to have redeemed all your glory, that boy is taken from us, is dead. My own hand surrendered him to the grave."

Another letter arrived from Theodosia. "I have been rereading your letter, dearest father. I am not insensible to your affection, though I can offer nothing in return but the love of a broken, deadened heart."

And still another from Joseph Alston. "My present wish is that Theodosia should join you. I part with her reluctantly, but my command here as brigadier-general detains me. Yours with respect and regard, Joseph Alston."

Theodosia wrote again to her father. "Oh, my guardian angel, I wish to see you, so that we may mourn together. I will leave as soon as possible. When I do go, I think of going by water. God bless you, my beloved father."

Not long afterwards, Burr received an alarming letter from his son-in-law. "My dear sir, Wretched, heart-rending forebodings distract my mind. Tomorrow will be three weeks since I took Theodosia to Georgetown harbor where she boarded a privateer bound for New York. The vessel normally ensures a passage of no more than six days. Three weeks, and not yet one line from her. Gracious God. Is my wife, too, taken from me?"

Burr replied, "I feel severed from the human race."

And Alston, in turn, wrote, "Your letter of the 10th, my friend, is received. My boy, my wife, gone, both! She was the last tie that bound us to the species. Oh, my friend, if there be such a thing as the sublime of misery, it is for us that it has been reserved."

***

A quarter of a century later, a minister, holding a Bible stood near a gravestone, together with a group of mourners. The minister said, "Here in Princeton, on this 16th day of September 1836, we bid farewell, in his eighty-first year, to Aaron Burr, Vice President of the United States, Colonel in the Army of the Revolution, and a valued alumnus of this college. We lay him to rest at the feet of his father, mother and grandfather. I have asked one of his oldest friends, Doctor David Hosack, to say a few words."

He turned to Doctor Hosack, now an elderly gray-haired man, who appeared sad and slightly uncomfortable. Finally, he said, "Colonel Burr was a secretive man. Perhaps because of this, countless rumors have emerged over the years, and they have been perpetuated by malicious tongues. I, who knew him as well as anyone could know him, would like to offer my portrait of the man. Aaron Burr was a man of gallantry. In the course of his long life, he had many intrigues with women, some of which, not many there is good reason to believe, were carried to the point of criminality."

This comment evoked polite laughter from the mourners.

Doctor Hosack continued, "But he was not a debauchee, not a corrupter of virgin innocence, not a betrayer of tender confidences. Not every woman could attract Aaron Burr. A woman of wit, vivacity and grace, whether beautiful or not, whether the inhabitant of a mansion or a cottage, was the creature who alone could captivate him. As for *a certain event*, the tragic encounter with General Hamilton at Weehawken, thirty-two years ago, both men were my friends. I recall my last visit to Colonel Burr's room on the Staten Island shore. It was the day before he expired. A series of strokes had paralyzed his legs."

The elderly Burr sat up in bed, holding a book, when Doctor Hosack entered. "Good afternoon, Doctor."

"Lovely day," said Doctor Hosack. "Not a cloud in the sky."

Burr stretched to look out the window. "From here I can see Newark, where I was born, and the shore of Elizabethtown, where I romped as a boy." He chuckled, remembering. "One day, I must have been eight years old, I climbed up in a cherry tree. An elderly woman strolled by. She was wearing a fancy silk dress. On a whim, I began to bombard her with ripe cherries. She became quite angry and summoned my Uncle Timothy. He raised me, you know. I was just two when the smallpox took my parents."

"And what did Uncle Timothy do?"

"He commanded me to climb down. First he lectured me. Next he joined me in a prayer, and then he gave me one devil of a whipping!" Burr laughed. "A good man, Uncle Timothy."

Doctor Hosack asked him, "Would you like to revisit New Jersey? Perhaps next Sunday we could arrange for a carriage."

"I had another caller earlier today," Burr said. "A minister, from the Dutch Reformed Church. Don't recall the name. Very inquisitive."

"Ah yes?"

"First, he asked, 'Are the rumors true? That you have had several children out of wedlock?' I replied, 'Sir, when a woman does me the honor to name me as the father of her child, I trust I shall always be too gallant to show myself ungrateful.'"

"Well spoken."

"Next he asked, 'Do you believe God in his mercy will pardon you for your sins?' I replied, 'Sir, on that subject I am coy.'" Burr laughed and began to cough.

Hosack did not reply and searched about for something in his bag.

"When my time comes," Burr said, "I wish to be buried at Princeton, near my parents and my grandfather."

"Yes, of course," the doctor said. "When the time comes."

"Death doesn't frighten me, doctor," he said. "I have a morbid fear of only one thing."

"And what is that?"

"Boredom, doctor. I fear boredom."

More silence as Doctor Hosack continued searching about in his bag.

"I can't stop thinking of the past," said Burr.

"Don't we all when we reach a certain age?"

"Daydreaming," Burr said, "I recalled a walk in the woods long ago. I was observing the animals scampering about. And I thought to myself, why does all nature enjoy its being but man? Why is man alone discontented, anxious, sacrificing the present to idle expectations? Never enjoying, always hoping."

The ghost of Alexander Hamilton entered the room. A benign, invisible presence, he glided over to Burr's bedside, stood near his old nemesis, and observed.

"Colonel," Doctor Hosack asked, "that morning long ago in Weehawken—"

"Ah, yes. That fateful morning when I shot my friend Hamilton."

"All these years—"

"A true gentleman, Hamilton," said Burr.

Hamilton smiled.

Doctor Hosack said, "I've never understood—" But Burr raised his hand, as though imploring him not to persist with his question. Changing the subject, Hosack pointed to the book in Burr's hand. "What have you been reading?"

"*Tristram Shandy*. It was one of my daughter's favorite novels."

"A masterpiece," said Doctor Hosack. "Sterne is such a splendid writer."

They remained silent for a moment, and Burr said, "Do you recall the passage about Uncle Toby and the fly?"

"Yes. I do recall it."

"I adore this part," said Burr. He read aloud, "An overgrown fly had buzzed about Uncle Toby's nose and tormented him cruelly all dinnertime. He caught it at last, and cupped it in his hand."

Burr cupped his hand, holding an invisible fly. He continued reading, "I'll not hurt thee, says Uncle Toby, rising from his chair and going across the room. Go, says he, lifting up the window sash and opening his hand as he spoke, to let it escape." Burr opened his cupped hand. "Go, poor devil, get thee gone, why should I hurt thee? This world surely is wide enough to hold both thee and me."

Burr stared right through the smiling Hamilton, into space, and mused, "Perhaps if I had read Sterne more, and Voltaire less, I might have known, this world was wide enough for Hamilton and me."

The Hydrogen Thing

Early morning in a suburb of Oslo, Norway there was the chatter of birds, the sound of a man breathing heavily, and the crunch of feet on gravel.

Tor Ekland, a man in his fifties, jogged along a tranquil country lane not far from his home. Jogging several yards behind, with a grim expression, was Ernie, big, like an NFL lineman, and murder on his mind. Ernie sped up, came closer behind Ekland, who glanced back curiously, then nervously.

Victor, Ernie's accomplice, a slender little fellow, suddenly jumped out from behind a bush, and blocked Ekland's path. Grinning, Victor held a hypodermic needle. Ekland, bewildered, looked around frantically. Ernie seized Ekland, who put up a struggle, but Ernie knocked him to the ground and pinned him down.

Victor injected Ekland in the neck. Paralyzed, Ekland gasped for air, stared up desperately at Ernie who lit a cigarette and stared right back, watching him die. Victor pulled Ernie away, and they hurried off, leaving Ekland's corpse alone on the country lane.

***

An afternoon in Palo Alto, California, Melvin Berger drove his convertible on a narrow twisting highway overlooking the Pacific Ocean. He had a blissful expression as he basked in the sunlight and enjoyed the Mozart piano concerto on his CD player.

A second car drove up behind him, dangerously close. Inside, Victor was at the wheel. Beside him was Ernie, smoking a cigarette.

Berger glanced into his rearview mirror. Annoyed, he stepped harder on the gas pedal. The second car also accelerated. As they approached a sharp curve, the second car spurted forward, bumped him from behind. Panic-stricken, Berger swerved and narrowly avoided going over the cliff. Another sharp curve loomed ahead. The second car accelerated again, bumped him from behind, and Berger's car plunged down the cliff.

As Berger screamed, and the Mozart played, his convertible careened downward and exploded in a ball of fire. The second car pulled over to a small outcropping on the side of the road. Ernie and Victor got out and looked down impassively at the mangled, burning car below. Ernie dropped his cigarette to the ground, crushed it with his heel. The two men returned to their car and drove away.

***

A nightclub in Tokyo was throbbing with rock music. Toshiro Chiwaki, wearing glasses, sporting a dark blue suit, entered. He walked up to the bar, ordered a Scotch and soda.

A topless dancer, a shapely Caucasian woman with brilliant blonde hair, was doing her thing on a tiny raised stage behind the bar. Chiwaki was mesmerized; droplets of perspiration gleamed on his forehead; his glasses fogged over. The dancer looked down at him, amused. After her number, the dancer stood near him at the bar. He ordered a drink for her. Moments later, they walked upstairs and into a dimly lit room, where there was only a bed, a chair, and a small table with a lamp.

Later that night, Chiwaki lay asleep in bed next to the dancer. She rose quietly, put on her robe, and opened the door. Victor and Ernie tiptoed in. Ernie bumped against the chair, causing it to make a slight squeaking sound. Chiwaki stirred. Victor, annoyed, gave Ernie a dirty look and put a finger to his mouth. Victor handed a wad of ten-dollar bills to the dancer, who quietly left the room.

Victor removed a hypodermic needle from a small leather briefcase. He leaned over and injected Chiwaki in the neck. Chiwaki was startled awake, his eyes bulged out as he gasped for air. Victor and Ernie pinned him down as he shuddered and died. They exited the room, leaving Chiwaki's corpse on the bed.

***

A bright, sunny morning in Hoboken NJ. The New York skyline was visible a few miles eastward. Becky McLean, an attractive brunette in her twenties, dressed for an office job, carrying a briefcase, exited the terminal, and boarded the ferry bound for Manhattan.

Becky sat on a bench on the open deck of the ferry, which made its way across the Hudson River. She pulled some papers from her briefcase and read. A man sitting opposite her holding a *Wall Street Journal* stared at her. As Becky looked up, the guy flashed a flirtatious smile. Becky, all business, ignored him, returned to her reading.

Several minutes later, Becky ascended the stairs from a New York City subway station and continued up 6th Avenue. She entered the lobby of the Hilton Hotel and ascended the escalator to the second floor conference area. A few dozen people were milling about, registering at tables, chatting. A sign above the registration table said: WELCOME TO THE FUTURE! RENEWABLE ENERGY.

Becky registered, picked up materials and a nametag, which she placed on her lapel. It read: Rebecca McLean, Stevens Institute of Technology, Hoboken NJ. She entered the ballroom where the plenary session was about to begin. About 200 people were already seated.

On the stage, a speaker was holding forth with great enthusiasm. Behind him on a huge screen was the projected letter "H". "What if," the speaker asked, "there were a form of energy that could solve our pollution problems, end our dependence on foreign oil, solve our balance of payments woes, generate jobs, and could be made from unlimited, renewable resources? Well, there is."

He pointed to the screen and smiled. One by one, the letters "Y-D-R-O-G-E-N" appeared on the screen. "It's hydrogen."

As Becky took a seat in the auditorium, the speaker continued.

"And now, to kick off today's proceedings, I bring you, direct from the White House, the President of the United States."

On the screen, a projected live TV image of the President appeared. He was seated at his desk in the Oval Office, a large U.S. flag behind him. There was applause from the audience. "Good morning." And, after a slight pause, he continued. "Sorry I can't be with you today, but urgent matters are keeping me in Washington. Talking about urgent matters, America imports more than half its oil—millions of barrels every day. This dependence on foreign oil is a challenge to our security. Solar energy will help. And wind power, too."

Smiling, the President paused, leaned forward and spoke as though confiding a secret. "Wind power. We got plenty of that here in Washington!" This got a big laugh from the crowd. "Seriously folks," he continued, "we're promoting more R&D. In January, Secretary Abraham announced a hundred fifty million dollar plan to develop hydrogen fuel cells that power cars with little or no waste. They're the wave of the future. I wish you all the best." The audience applauded, and the screen went blank.

A few minutes later, Becky walked down a hotel corridor to one of the smaller meeting rooms. On an easel near the room entrance was a large sign with a printed title of the scheduled panel discussion: HYDROGEN CELL TECHNOLOGY, LATEST DEVELOPMENTS. Crossed over the title, in red hand-written magic marker, it said: CANCELED. Becky stared at the sign, and the empty room.

A man approached. He looked every inch the academic, fifty-ish, gray hair, complete with leather elbow patches on his tweed sports jacket. On his lapel was a name tag, reading: Dr. Philip Cosgrove, NYU.

"May I help you?"

"I was so looking forward to this panel," she said.

He looked at her name tag. "Stevens. Do you know Doctor Kalfus in Engineering?"

"I'm an assistant professor, in History."

He raised an eyebrow.

"I'm working on my thesis: the impact of technology on world history."

"Fascinating," said Cosgrove. "I believe a Doctor Henry Gomberg published on that topic years ago."

"Yes, it's a classic."

She looked wistfully into the empty room, then down at her program. "Oh. Doctor Cosgrove. I see you were supposed to be on the panel."

He shrugged. "The other three were all due in yesterday. Nothing. Last night I tried to reach Doctor Berger in Palo Alto. His wife told me he died in an auto accident. Car skidded off a cliff. Terrible."

***

That same morning, Michael Stern, early thirties, strolled dreamily along a garbage-strewn street in a poor neighborhood of Jersey City. He was dressed casually in a windbreaker and khaki slacks. Michael smiled and nodded at passersby, who ignored him. A young guy, disheveled, glassy-eyed, stood hunched over on a street corner, puffing on a cigarette, holding a paper bag which contained an open bottle of beer. He glared at Michael. "Fuck you lookin' at, man?"

Michael shrugged, averted his eyes, kept on walking. He stopped at a rundown apartment building. Next to the steps leading down to the basement were two hand-lettered signs. One read: "SHELTER." The other said: "JESUS CHRIST BLESS THIS HOME."

Michael entered a dreary, basement level homeless shelter. A woman in her fifties stood waiting. "You from the Record?"

Michael nodded, extended his hand. "Michael Stern."

"Valerie Cruz, Hudson County Social Welfare. Our shelter burned down last week. For now, we're housing a few of the men here." Valerie pulled open a hospital-style curtain. Behind the curtain were five cots. Two were empty. In two others, homeless men lay curled up, fast asleep. One of them was snoring loudly.

Sitting on the fifth cot was Johnny Mills, an African-American in his seventies. He was clean shaven, with close-cropped gray hair. His bloodshot eyes had a blank expression. Beneath the cot were four plastic bags, his worldly possessions.

"If you write a story for your paper," she said, "maybe we can get some funding to rebuild."

"Sure," said Michael, as he pulled out a pen and reporter's notebook from his jacket.

"I'd like you to meet Johnny Mills." Valerie leaned over, spoke to him as though to a child. "Mister Mills? This is Michael Stern. He's with a newspaper. Here to do a story about you, about all of us."

Johnny looked up, smiled, and gestured with his hand for Michael to sit beside him. Michael sat, pen poised, as Johnny gazed off into the distance. "I was born in Stalingrad in 1921." Michael began to write. "In World War Two I was a bombardier in the German air force." Michael stopped writing, stared at him. "Later I traveled through Latin America."

Valerie whispered in Michael's ear. "He's been sleeping in doorways the last few years."

Johnny pulled up a pant leg, pointed. "The burn scars on my legs are from a plane crash near Boston. Before that, I had a license for landscaping under water."

Valerie whispered to Michael. "He was a short order cook in a restaurant a few blocks from here. But a few years ago, he lost his way."

Michael, looking as though he were in pain, listened as Johnny continued. "I was born in Halifax. That's in Canada. Later I stowed away on a ship. Spent time in Prague, Geneva, and London."

Valerie shook her head sadly. "He knows all about fine wines, the good life. But *Pobrecito,* he's not playing with a full deck."

"I went to Heidelberg University. That's in Germany."

Later that morning, Michael sat at a computer terminal in the city room of *The Jersey City Record*. As he read his notes, he reached into a drawer, pulled out a Kleenex, and dried the tears from his eyes. Then he began typing.

***

Becky and Michael, sitting opposite each other in a booth, had just finished dinner at a bar in Hoboken. A soulful jazz tenor sax flowed from a jukebox in the corner.

Becky tried to get his attention, but Michael stared at his coffee cup, nodding his head to the music.

"...so the guy from Stanford died in a car crash. I don't know what happened to the guys from Oslo and Tokyo." Becky picked up her spoon and tapped it lightly against his coffee cup. "Becky to Michael ... Becky to Michael ... come in."

Michael looked up. "Sorry."

"What's the matter?"

He shook his head sadly. "This homeless guy I interviewed today. God, I hope I never end up like that."

She reached over, caressed his cheek. "C'mon, sweetie, let's go home."

Becky and Michael left the bar and strolled along Hoboken's main street. Michael slowed down as he walked past a parking meter. He looked at the meter, smiled, and said, "How you doin' buddy?"

Becky stopped. He stopped. "What?" she asked.

"I wasn't talking to you."

Becky looked around as if to say, then who. Michael pointed to the parking meter. "I read somewhere that John Steinbeck, the novelist—"

"I know who John Steinbeck is."

"I read somewhere that Steinbeck used to tip his hat to dogs and he would talk to parking meters."

Becky smiled, shook her head. That's what I love about you. You're nuts."

Michael put his arm around her, pulled her close, and wiggled his eyebrows up and down, like Groucho Marx. "You love my nuts?"

Becky laughed out loud. "No. You *are* nuts."

They continued walking, arm in arm. Becky suddenly stopped. "Oh, almost forgot. It's talent night at Rick's. Ramon is at the piano."

Michael smiled. "This I gotta see."

***

Rick's Bar was a dimly lit, friendly little place, a homage to *Casablanca*. The walls were covered with large black and white photos of Bogart and Bergman and smaller ones of Claude Rains, Paul Henreid, Peter Lorre and Sidney Greenstreet. The place was about two-thirds filled with an eclectic mix of young singles and couples.

Michael and Becky entered and headed towards the piano in the corner. Playing the piano and singing *As Time Goes By*, was Ramon Delgado, mid-forties, very smartly dressed in all black, his dark hair impeccably combed. Ramon finished the song to applause. Ramon spotted them, smiled, waved, and motioned for them to sit nearby at a small empty table.

"And now, for my final number," said Ramon, "here's a tune from The Great Depression. That's before they had Prozac." This evoked groans and giggles from patrons. Ramon played a lively tune and began to sing. As he did, he looked first to Becky, then to Michael. "The things I long for are simple and few-ooh, a cup o' caw-fee, a sandwich, and yoo-oooh."

After the song, Ramon, carrying a small paper bag, came over to their table. He held out his arms for Becky, who hugged him. "You were fabulous, Ramon."

Ramon looked at Michael, and pouted. "Don't I get a hug?" Michael smiled. This was an old game they played. Ramon whispered to Becky, loud enough for Michael to hear, "*Muchacha,* if you ever decide to leave him, let me know."

Ramon sang a few lines from an old Noel Coward tune, "Mad, about the boy, I'm simply mad about the boy." Ramon playfully jabbed Michael in the ribs. "Just kidding! *Not.*" Then, "Come up to my place for tea?"

"It's kinda late, Ramon," said Becky.

Ramon held up his paper bag, smiled. "I've got some fresh chocolate biscotti." They hesitated. "Just for a few minutes, I've got big news."

***

Becky and Michael sat at the dining room table in Ramon's tastefully furnished studio apartment. The biscotti were piled on a dish. Ramon approached with a steaming teapot and poured.

"So?" Becky asked. "What's the big news?"

"I'm making good money at the shop. Some clients, like Mrs. Felder, when she comes in for her monthly touch-up, she tells me her *tsooris,* and I tell her mine. It's wonderful." He reached over and put his hand on Michael's. "*Tsooris.* That's a Spanish word for—"

"I know, I know," said Michael, smiling, shaking his head.

"But some of those broads, so much money and all they do is bitch, bitch, bitch. The other day, this was *el colmo,* the TV shows a suicide bomb in Iraq. People are dead, bleeding. Tears are streaming down my cheeks. This *señora* in my chair, I won't mention her name, while all this tragedy is on the TV, she looks at herself in the mirror, and she says to me," Ramon imitated her and rubbed his palms over his cheeks. "'Ramon, I've never had any work done.'" Still imitating, he pursed his lips, sucking in his cheekbones and angling his face from side to side. "'Tell me honestly, could I use some?' That was it. I decided, I've had it. So …," Ramon smiled, holding back. Michael and Becky leaned in, waiting. "I've just been accepted to law school." Michael and Becky were dazed. "I've saved up, and I'm just going to work part time at the shop until I get my degree. And then—"

Becky interrupted, "Why didn't you tell us you applied?"

"I was afraid they wouldn't accept me. But they did." Ramon smiled. "I'm going to help poor immigrants. You know, get their work permits, citizenship, do something good in the world."

"That's wonderful, Ramon," said Becky. Michael chimed in, "That's great!" He reached over, gave Ramon a hug.

"Ramon," said Becky, "you haven't read our cards since I don't remember when."

Ramon walked over to a kitchen drawer, pulled out a deck of cards. He shuffled the deck, looked to Michael. "Cut." Michael cut the cards. Ramon shuffled again and laid out several cards face up. Ramon studied the cards for a couple of beats and looked impressed.

"What?" Becky asked.

"I see Michael coming into money."

"How much?" Michael asked.

"Can't tell. But it's money." Ramon pointed to the cards. "This is definitely a money card. And I see a trip. No, two trips."

***

Tap-tap-tap. Becky, at her desk, stared into a computer screen. The *tap-tap-tap* continued. Frowning, she rose and entered the small living room where Michael sat at another desk, typing on an ancient Underwood manual typewriter. To one side of the typewriter, resting on its haunches and staring intently at the machine, was Mister, a large black cat who loved the noise and movement of the Underwood. Next to Mister was a small pile of old hardcover books. Among them were *The Grapes of Wrath* and *For Whom The Bell Tolls*.

Becky petted the cat. "Hi, Mister. Michael, when are you going to donate that relic to the Smithsonian?"

Without looking up, still tap-tapping, he replied, "Hemingway wrote all his stuff by hand, then he typed on one of these."

"Sweetie, Hemingway was writing in the 1920s. If he were alive today—"

"I think he'd still use one of these."

"At the newspaper office, don't you use a computer?"

"I hate it."

"You can't cut and paste on this."

Michael pointed to a pair of scissors and a jar of rubber cement.

She came closer and leaned over him. "How about spell check?"

He put his arm around her, smiled. "You're my spell check."

Becky shook her head. "This is ridiculous. You don't have E-mail."

"Saves me lots of time, not having to answer stupid stuff."

Becky reached into her bag and pulled out a cellphone. "And these, I suppose, are useless?"

"They have payphones everywhere."

"Michael, you're not even in the 1960s. You're like frozen in the fifties."

"They tell me it was a good time then." He continued typing. *Tap-tap-tap.*

"What are you working on?"

"An idea for a screenplay."

"Another one?"

"The main character is a journalist. He meets this poor homeless guy—"

"And?"

"I dunno. That's as far as I got."

"Why such great interest in that?"

"At the paper I see all kinds of sad stuff. Murders. Suicides. People killed in car crashes. Burned out by fires. You get used to it. But today," He paused, tears welled in his eyes, "the homeless guy, he reminded me of my Dad. Those last few years of his life," he pointed to his head, "gone."

Becky patted him on the shoulder. Hugged him. "I've got a better idea. Come."

"Where?"

"Come." She reached out for his hand, pulled him out of his seat, and over to her desk near the computer. Mister, the cat, followed and jumped up next to Michael.

"What?" he asked.

"Patience, young man." She pecked away at the computer as Michael and Mister stared at the screen. "Remember last night, when you weren't listening, I told you about these three scientists who didn't show up for the conference?"

"Uh-huh."

"I did a keyword search." She pecked away, and they gazed at the screen. She pointed. "Look at this AP report. Doctor Melvin Berger, Palo Alto, California, died when his car plunged off a cliff into the ocean."

"Isn't that what the guy at the conference told you?"

She pecked away again, and they looked at the screen. "Here's the second man who couldn't make it. Reuters. Doctor Tor Ekland of Oslo, Norway, died of a heart attack, while jogging near his home."

"So?"

"Doesn't that sound strange to you?"

"What about the third guy?"

She pecked away again. "Doctor Toshiro Chiwaki of Tokyo." She looked at screen, shook her head. "Nothing on him yet."

"So?"

"Michael, use your imagination. What if evil people—"

Michael's face lit up. "Yes! There's a plot to kill all three of these guys to ... to ..."

"To stop them from releasing their research?"

A light seemed to come on in Michael's head. "Yes. What kind of research were they doing?"

"Hydrogen fuel."

"What's that?"

"It would end our need for oil."

They both thought for a moment and then something dawned on them. "The Arabs," said Michael. "If they couldn't sell oil they'd be broke."

"Texas depends on oil, too," said Becky. "And Venezuela."

Michael rose and paced about the room. "What if some Texas oil baron, or an Arab, or a Venezuelan, hired someone to kill these scientists? What if all these evil guys got together, an international plot, to kill off anyone who threatens their interest?"

"True or not," said Becky, "wouldn't it make a great movie?"

"Yeah, I think so."

She tapped him on the shoulder. "Well, get on it, Mister Hemingway."

***

Michael, holding a slip of paper, walked along Seventh Avenue in Manhattan's Garment District, a few blocks south of Times Square. Immigrant workers pushed huge racks of clothing. Smartly dressed models and executives, talking on cellphones, hurried by.

Michael approached a rundown looking office building, checked the address on the slip of paper, and entered the lobby. An elderly guard sat at a reception desk, reading *The New York Post.* In front of him was a notebook for visitors to sign in.

"Mister Bernie Schwartz?"

"Sixth floor," said the guard. "You gotta sign in."

Michael signed in and walked to the elevator. He smiled at the guard. "Nice day."

"Woke up this morning," said the guard, "opened my eyes, pinched myself. I was still alive. Any day's a nice day."

Moments later, Michael walked down the darkened hallway of the office building. He stopped at a door that read: BERMUDA SCHWARTZ AGENCY.

Michael entered a cramped reception area, barely large enough for a desk, a chair, and a bench in front of the desk. The decor was mid-1950s and the place hadn't been painted since then. A few dozen black & white photos of actors and dancers, none of whom Michael recognized, were taped to one wall.

Michael heard a man's voice coming from the inner office. This was followed by a woman's loud laughter. Not wanting to interrupt, Michael sat on the bench. More loud laughter.

The door opened and out came a tall, busty platinum blonde woman in her forties, heavy makeup, tight dress, high heels. She smiled, winked at Michael, and walked out. Michael hesitantly approached the door to the inner office. He opened it part way and peeked in.

Bernie Schwartz sat feet up at his desk in a tiny cramped office with a window overlooking mid-town, his face obscured by the copy of *Backstage*. Papers were piled high on his desk and on a credenza behind him. The walls were lined with photos of performers. Also on the desk was a nameplate: BERMUDA SCHWARTZ.

Michael gently knocked at the door. Schwartz put the paper down, revealing the tanned, wrinkled face of a man in his seventies. He wore a striped silk shirt and loud wide tie. His suit jacket hung on a wall peg in the corner.

"Yeah?" said Schwartz.

Hesitatingly, Michael asked, "Mr. Schwartz?"

"Who wants to know?"

"Michael Stern. My Uncle Morty—"

Schwartz broke into a wide grin. He rose and extended his hand. "Morty said you'd be coming by."

"I really appreciate this."

Schwartz sat down, motioned for Michael to sit, too. "I usually don't take on beginners. But your uncle and me, we went to high school together in Newark. That was way back. When Newark was Newark."

Michael nodded, smiling.

"I haven't seen Morty since our reunion, a few years ago. How is the old fart?"

"He had some problems with his prostate."

"*Oy vey!* Haven't we all?"

"But he's fine now. Spends the winters in Florida."

"Great. His younger brother was your dad, right?"

Michael's expression darkened. "He … passed away five years ago."

"Sorry." Schwartz leaned forward. "So, what can I do for you?"

Michael looked around the room, the peeling paint, the black and white photos, the pile of manuscripts. A mess. "Nice place you have."

Schwartz shrugged. "It's a shithole, but I'm comfortable."

"You're an agent, right?"

"Guilty."

The door to the office opened part way. A young Asian man peeked his head in, held up a brown paper bag, smiled widely, then said very loud, "Derry here."

This was a daily routine. Schwartz smiled, waved him in, and yelled, "Hey, it's Ho Chi Minh."

The Asian man giggled, gave him a "get outta here" wave, put the bag on the desk, and handed the check to Schwartz, who looked into the bag, then at the check. He reached into his pocket and pulled out a wad of bills. He peeled off a few and gave them to the man. "Keep the change." The Asian man nodded, waved goodbye, and was gone.

Schwartz pulled a thick pastrami on rye sandwich out of the bag. Then a bottle of cream soda. He proceeded to drink and chew.

Michael pointed to the BERMUDA SCHWARTZ nameplate on the desk. "My Uncle called you Bernie."

Schwartz, still chewing, explained. "There's a million Bernie Schwartz's out there. Bermuda's my professional name. In this business you gotta stand out."

"What kind of stuff do you handle, Mister Schwartz?"

"Didya see that lovely lady who walked outa here? Does dinner theatre all over the country. Erie PA, Bridgeport, Akron, cruise ships. She's one of my top earners."

"But you do movies, too, right?"

Schwartz pointed behind him to a stack of videotapes. "Versatile's my middle name." Michael glanced at the stack. The titles on one of the tapes said: BIG DICK TRACY, HOT HUNKS, Michael's eyes widened as he continued reading the titles on the tapes, FREDDY FUDGEPACKER, DEFLOWERING JENNIFER.

"Years back," Schwartz explained, "I had this client, Marty Scheps, out in Hollywood. That's when Hollywood was Hollywood. Marty was a real good earner. Remember those old Charlie Chan mysteries?"

Michael smiled. "I've seen 'em on AMC."

"Marty was in almost every one of them. Like sometimes Chan or his Number One Son would come into an apartment, they open a closet door, and wham! Out falls a dead body; Marty. If ya blinked, ya missed him. But it was a good day's pay. Every little bit counts. Remember that free advice."

Michael, a bit bewildered, smiled. "Mister Schwartz, I have this idea for a screenplay—"

"Idea? That's it?"

"It's about these three scientists."

"Uh-huh."

"They're working on a new invention."

"Uh-huh."

"Something that will change the world."

"Uh-huh."

"A new source of electrical energy for cars, for houses."

"Uh-huh," said Schwartz, his eyes nearly closed.

"And all three of them, in different parts of the world, are murdered."

Schwartz perked up. "Uh-huh. So how can I help?"

"I've heard that the Hollywood studios won't even look at a script if it's not submitted by an agent."

"Sure, they're scared some crazy shmuck'll sue them."

"I was wondering, when I get the script written, maybe you could—"

"Sure, sure. Sounds great. When can you get it to me?"

"I just started outlining it."

"Outlining?"

"I once took this screenwriting course, with Jeffrey Magee."

"Magoo?"

"Magee. He talks about setting up the structure first. Into three acts."

"Acts?"

"Then establishing your character's arc."

"Ark. You mean like Noah's Ark?"

Michael motioned with his hand, describing an arc. "No. It's like hard to explain."

Schwartz put down his sandwich, and leaned forward as though he was about to impart a secret. Michael leaned forward. "Lemme tell ya something, kiddo. A script is like a meal."

"A meal?"

"You're the chef."

Michael stared at him, fascinated. Schwartz held up one finger. "First ingredient." Schwartz put on a ridiculous comic expression. "You gotta make 'em laugh."

Schwartz held up two fingers, then looked as though he was on the verge of tears. "Then you gotta make 'em cry."

Schwartz held up three fingers, made a fist. He threw a punch at Michael, stopping just short of his face as Michael flinched. "Then you gotta scare the shit outa them."

Schwartz held up four fingers and began shaking imaginary salt and pepper shakers. "Then you add a little T&A."

Michael stared at him, uncomprehending.

Schwartz explained, as though to a kindergarten kid. "Tits and ass, my friend, tits and ass."

Michael was speechless as Schwartz continued. "Why the hell do people go out to the movies on a Friday night? All week long they're working their tookus off." Schwartz picked up what was left of his pastrami sandwich, waved it for emphasis. "Arks, shmarks, they wanna have a good time." He took a big bite out of the sandwich. "Free advice."

***

Becky sipped a soft drink as Michael entered the restaurant and took a seat. "How did it go?"

"Great," says Michael. "He loved the idea."

"Now what?"

The waitress came over. "Dos Equis, please," he said.

Michael now put on a sad face. "He wants to read it."

"And?"

"All I've got is a paragraph. A screenplay is around ninety pages."

The waitress brought over the beer and Michael took a sip. "If it's about these scientists and their discovery ... I don't know my ass from my elbow about science."

"Didn't you take any science in high school or college?"

Michael shrugged. "The only formula I remember is: *The angle of the dangle is equal to the mass of the ass.*"

Becky was amused, but pretended to be cross. "You are terrible." She reached over and patted his hand. "Can you get off around three tomorrow?"

***

The next afternoon Michael walked up to the Stevens Institute campus located on a hill with a sweeping view of the Hudson River and New York City. He entered a building and found his way to Becky's classroom where about half a dozen students were seated. Becky was up front, near the blackboard, leaning over a desk, reviewing her notes. She noticed Michael, smiled, and motioned for him to sit in the back. He took a seat and pulled out his notebook and pen. More students came walking in, talking, joking. In a few moments there were about twenty students seated.

Becky clapped her hands. "Okay, we've got lots of ground to cover today. I want to give you an overview of how the fuel we consume affects the way we live."

She wrote FUEL on the blackboard, then turned to face them again. "Fuel generates energy." She wrote ENERGY on the board. "Can someone think of a fuel that generates energy?"

A wisecracker in the third row raised his hand. "M&Ms?"

The students burst into laughter, but Becky surprised them. "Good. Fuel is anything that produces energy, even M&Ms."

She pointed to the word FUEL. "In ancient times the center of the home was not the TV set." The students laughed. "It was the fireplace. And what do you burn in the fireplace?"

Several students responded aloud, "Wood."

On the blackboard, Becky wrote WOOD. "People in the Stone Age used wood to cook their food, heat and light their caves and huts."

Several minutes later, Becky had written on the blackboard and explained: FUEL, ENERGY, WOOD, COAL, SOLAR, FIRST ENGINE, 1700s, FIRST BATTERY, 1700s, HYDRO, 1800s, GEO-THERMAL, 1800s.

Michael and the students scribbled furiously in their notebooks as Becky continued. Below GEOTHERMAL she wrote OIL. "By the early 1900s, we learned to refine oil to make gasoline. Soon almost everyone was driving a car."

She wrote NUCLEAR. "In the second half of the 20th century, scientists tapped into a new source of energy: nuclear power. So, what's the problem?" She looked around the room. No answer. On the board she wrote: RENEWABLE and NON-RENEWABLE, and POLLUTION.

A few hands shot up. She nodded to an African-American student who answered, "You're saying we're either gonna run out of some fuels, or the ones we use are gonna mess up the environment."

"Exactly. Wood generates only a limited amount of energy and it pollutes." She erased the word WOOD. There is enough coal for the next two hundred years. But coal pollutes the air."

She erased the word COAL and then pointed to NUCLEAR. "Nuclear waste remains dangerous for thousands of years. Storing it is expensive." She erased the word NUCLEAR and all the other words except RENEWABLE and OIL. "Oil is our most important energy source today." She paused, looked around the room. "But, there's only enough oil to last us about forty-five years." She erased OIL and, in very large letters, wrote, NO MORE OIL.

This prompted some murmurs and puzzled looks among the students. "That's right," she said. "When all of you are old fart retirees, collecting your Social Security checks, and taking your grandchildren to Disneyland, all the oil will be gone. No more oil." The students suddenly became solemn. This had gotten their attention.

"Don't look so glum. Help is on the way." She pointed to the word RENEWABLE. "On Wednesday, we'll discuss some promising sources of renewable energy."

Everyone in the class nodded. She wrote on the board HYDROGEN FUEL CELLS. "On the Internet, try Googling 'hydrogen fuel cells'. This stuff is so new there aren't any up to date textbooks." She looked around, smiled. "Who knows? Maybe one of you will make a great discovery some day. It's an exciting time to be alive."

After class, Michael and Becky were walkin across campus. Michael regarded her admiringly. "You were great."

"Preparation, Michael. It took me hours yesterday to get my notes together."

He hugged her. He asked, "How do we know there's only forty-five years of oil left?"

"Extensive surveys," she said. "Ninety percent of all the world's oil has been found."

"Amazing. Gotta get back to the office. See you tonight, teach." He gave her a kiss and hurried off.

*****

Early that evening, Michael rushed out of the corner candy store holding a lottery ticket and grinning. He walked, faster and faster, then began to run, nearly knocking over a pedestrian. Michael burst into the apartment, smiling and radiant. He waved the ticket. "Becky!"

Becky was in the kitchen, cutting veggies for a salad. Michael hugged her, stepped back and waves the ticket in front of her. "Ramon was right." Becky was smiling, speechless. Michael pointed to the ticket. "I just checked it out at the candy store."

"Are you sure?"

With a wide grin, Michael nodded yes.

"We're millionaires?"

"I got five out of six on the Pick Six." He waved the ticket. "Four thousand, eight hundred and seventy-six bucks."

Becky, kidding, asked, "That's all?" Michael looked deflated. Becky smiled, hugged him. "That's wonderful."

"Next week's your Spring break, right?" he asked.

"Right."

"I'll take a week off, too. Didn't Ramon talk about a trip?"

"Where?"

"You name it!"

She shrugged. "This was meant to be, Becky," he said. "I'm working on this screenplay, and you're writing your thesis. Why don't we go somewhere and *both* do research?"

"Great, but where?"

"Isn't there something going on somewhere?"

"Wait," she said. "On the back of the program, that thing I went to at the Hilton." Becky rushed over to a cupboard and picked up a program. "It mentions a big conference on hydrogen fuel cells, next week." She looked at the program, raised an eyebrow, surprised, and said, "In Las Vegas? They can't be serious."

*****

One week later, Becky and Michael, with their carry-on luggage, descended from a shuttle bus in front of the dazzling facade of a five-star Las Vegas hotel.

Becky looked around, skeptically, as though to ask, "What are we doing here?" Michael smiled. "We'll try it for one day," she said. "Then back home. One day. That's all."

"Okay, one day," he said, as they entered the lobby.

After checking in to their room, they approached the entrance to the exhibit hall. Above the door was a huge sign: FUEL CELL WORLD. They entered and were dazzled by a wonderland of futuristic exhibits. People from all over the world strolled among the booths, some in modern suits, others in traditional attire.

At the Casio booth, a smiling Japanese technician typed on a small laptop computer. He turned to them and explained, "Lithium battery last only five hours. Our fuel cell go twenty hours."

They approached a bus with a large sign above it: DAIMLER-CHRYSLER. Next to the bus stood a young German woman. "The European Union," she explained, "has hired us to produce these vehicles powered by fuel cells." She pointed to a large map of Europe with red dots highlighting several major cities: Amsterdam, Barcelona, Hamburg, London, Luxembourg, Madrid, Porto, Stockholm, Stuttgart. "They'll be used in nine major cities." She stepped over a few feet to a sleek passenger car. "This is our Necar 4 model." She motioned to Michael to get in. He hesitated, but she smiled and urged him.

"Start it up," the woman said.

Michael turned the key. There was a smooth low rumble. "Top speed ninety miles per hour," the woman explained. "Range of two hundred eighty miles. Zero emissions."

Two Texans, with large-brimmed hats, stood nearby. "What kinda fuel they use?" one of the Texans asked.

"Hydrogen," the woman responded.

The Texan whispered to his partner, "We don't get on top o' this soon, we're gonna be up shit's creek without a paddle."

Michael turned off the engine and got out of the car. He and Becky continued. Next to a large TOYOTA CORP sign, a smiling young Japanese woman spoke to them. "We are making hydrogen fuel cell vehicles in Tokyo."

"How much do they cost?" Becky asked.

"Seventy-four thousand, but cost is coming down," she replied. "We already have few hydrogen stations. Cars filled up in less than five minutes."

Another nearby booth said: U.S. ENERGY DEPARTMENT. A man there handed them some brochures. "If Americans are gonna drive cars that run on hydrogen," he said, "we need places to refuel. We eventually hope to convert seventy thousand stations across the USA."

They approached a booth, with a sign above it that read: HYDROGENICS. A forlorn looking young woman sat at a chair behind the table, with a small stack of brochures. She wore a black armband on her left arm.

"Hi," said Becky.

"Hello…"

Becky picked up one of the brochures and began to leaf through it.

"We were supposed to have our R&D team here," the woman said. "Weirdest thing." She pointed to her armband. "All three died the same week."

"My God. How awful," said Becky.

The woman, tears in her eyes, pointed to a small placard on the table with the names and photos of the three men. Doctor Ekland in Norway, heart attack, Doctor Berger in California, car crash, Doctor Chiwaki in Tokyo, heart attack."

Becky and Michael exchanged glances. "Doctor Chiwaki, too?" Becky asked.

"You knew him?"

"Just by reputation."

"We're still in shock," the woman said, shaking her head.

Becky and Michael continued walking. They approached a booth with a large sign: H-RON INC. "At the front of the booth, a smiling young man, handed out brochures to passersby. Seated at a table in the rear part of the booth, talking with a potential client was Doctor Cosgrove.

Becky nudged Michael and pointed. "That's the man I met at the New York conference."

Cosgrove looked up. Becky smiled and waved. He waved back, then motioned for her to wait. Cosgrove came out from behind the booth. "Hello, Miss Stevens Tech."

"Hi, Doctor Cosgrove. Rebecca McLean."

"Yes, yes, how are you?"

"And this is Michael Stern."

Cosgrove shook his hand. "A fellow historian?"

"I'm a reporter. Jersey City Record."

"Ah-ha."

"We're here to do some research," Becky explained, "for my thesis and Michael is—"

Michael interrupted. "I'm doing an article for my paper about cutting edge new technology."

"Very good," said Cosgrove.

Michael motioned to the floor of exhibits. "This is mind-boggling. But I don't get the science behind it."

Cosgrove looked at his watch. "May I invite you for a bite of lunch in the coffee shop?"

Michael, Becky and Cosgrove sat at a table near a window that looked out at the exhibit floor. They had just finished lunch and were sipping coffee. Cosgrove pulled a pen from his pocket and a sheet of blank paper from his briefcase. Becky and Michael pulled out notebooks and pens.

"I read that the first working fuel cell was produced way back in the mid-1800s," Becky said.

"Yes," said Cosgrove, "but the idea lay dormant for nearly a century. Then GE produced a fuel cell for the Gemini and Apollo space capsules. Hydrogen fuel cells still power the space shuttle."

Michael was amazed. "I didn't know that."

"I'm familiar with the history," Becky said, "but I'm not quite sure how they work."

"A fuel cell is like a battery. No moving parts, no noise." Cosgrove wrote H and O on the paper. "Electrical energy is produced by a chemical reaction between hydrogen and oxygen. He drew a rectangular shape on the paper. Then several lines through the rectangle. "Each cell is like a sandwich, with two chambers. The negative chamber is called an anode. The positive chamber is called a cathode."

Michael, getting lost already, silently mouthed anode, cathode?

Cosgrove looked at them. "Are you with me so far?" Becky nodded yes, eagerly. Michael didn't look so sure. Over the next few minutes, as Cosgrove explained and scribbled on the paper, Becky listened and nodded. Michael, brow furrowed, was concentrating hard, but didn't get it.

"So," said Cosgrove, "the electrons are forced to take an external circuit to the other side. This flow of electrons creates—" He looked to Becky expectantly.

"Electric power," she said.

"Right. When the electrons return from doing their work, lighting a house or powering a car motor, they recombine with the hydrogen protons and oxygen to make ..." He looked to Michael who shrugged. Cosgrove put down his pen, picked up his glass of water and jiggled it.

"Water," Becky said.

Cosgrove flashed a triumphant smile and took a drink. He put the glass back down. "That's it."

Michael looked perplexed. "I am totally lost."

"I got it," said Becky. She turned to Michael. "Don't worry, I'll explain it to you later."

She looked to Cosgrove, jabbed her thumb towards Michael. "He still uses a manual typewriter." Cosgrove laughed.

"What I don't get," said Michael, is ... everything runs on hydrogen, right?"

"Right," said Cosgrove.

"Where do you get the hydrogen?"

Cosgrove's face lit up. "Ah-ha." He reached across the table, shook Michael's hand. "You, sir, have asked the sixty-four billion dollar question." Cosgrove waved his arms. "Hydrogen is all around us." He picked up his water glass again, held it in front of them and shook the glass a bit. "H-two-oh. One part oxygen, two parts hydrogen." He put the glass down. "But, to separate hydrogen, so that one can use it as fuel, we need a process of..." He looked to Becky.

"Electrolysis," she replied.

"Right. Scientists all over the world, hundreds, perhaps thousands of, are working on ways to separate hydrogen. But what is the problem?" He paused, waiting for an answer. Cosgrove took out his pen again and drew a large DOLLAR SIGN on the paper."

"Cost?" Michael asked.

Cosgrove nodded. "When the day comes that someone breaks through and produces low-cost hydrogen that, my friends, will change the way we live." He took a drink of water and sat back.

"Doctor Cosgrove," Becky said, "I sense a real passion behind your work. That's wonderful, to do something you love."

Cosgrove's expression softened. "My father worked in the coal mines in Pennsylvania. When I was just five years old, he died from inhaling the fumes and dust in the mines. He was only thirty-seven." Tears welled in his eyes. "It took him two years to die. Very painful. My mother would take me to the hospital to see him."

Now, tears welled in Michael's eyes. "I lost my Dad, too."

"In college," Cosgrove continued, "I decided that I would work in a field that would produce clean energy so that children like myself would not lose their fathers. I hope someday to have a research institute named after him." He looked off dreamily into the distance. "The Clarence Cosgrove Institute." Cosgrove reached over to the paper napkin dispenser, pulled out a napkin, and wiped his eyes.

Michael reached over, grabbed a napkin, too, and wiped away the tears.

Cosgrove blew his nose in the napkin and laughed. "God, I feel as though I've just been through a therapy session." He rose from the table holding the check. "I must get back to our booth."

Michael reached into his pocket to pay the bill. "No, no," said Cosgrove, "this is on me." As they stood by the cashier at the entrance, Cosgrove paid the check. "I have some literature at the booth."

As they walked along the exhibit floor with him, Becky asked, "Doctor Cosgrove?"

"Yes?"

"Have you been over to the Hydrogenics booth, on the other side of the hall?"

"Not yet."

"Remember the panel in New York and the other three speakers didn't show up?"

"Of course."

"All three of them were on the R&D team for Hydrogenics."

"Is that so?"

"And all three died the same week."

Cosgrove stopped in his tracks, shocked. "I heard that Berger died in a car crash—"

Becky interrupted. "The other two? Heart attacks."

"My God. That's terrible."

"Very suspicious, I'd say," Becky added.

They resumed walking. "Yes," Cosgrove said. "It seems quite strange."

Michael turned to Cosgrove. "Actually, I told you a little fib."

Cosgrove seemed amused. "A fib?"

"I'm not working on an article. I'm writing a screenplay."

"Ahh."

"When Becky told me about these scientists dying I thought, what if they were murdered? Wouldn't that make a great movie?"

"Quite possibly."

"The question is: why?"

"Why?"

"The motive. For the murder."

"Ah. Yes, the motive."

"Maybe they stumbled on some big breakthrough," Michael said. "The sixty-four billion dollar question you were talking about and someone doesn't want their discovery to come out. So they are killed."

"Sounds intriguing," said Cosgrove.

"Who," Becky asked, "would profit most from killing off the three scientists?"

Two men in Arab attire, and a Latin man, in a tailored suit, walked by. They appeared upset, and spoke in low voices.

"We were thinking," Michael said, "maybe the countries that depend on oil."

"If hydrogen comes along," said Becky, "won't their economies be destroyed?"

"You mean OPEC?" Cosgrove asked. "The Arab nations, and Venezuela?"

"Right, right," said Michael.

"It's true," said Cosgrove. "Without oil, their economies would be destroyed." The two tall Texans walked by. They also spoke to each other in low, secretive tones. "Of course," he added, "oil companies right here in America also would be hurt."

"We were thinking," Michael said, "we might check out these two heart attacks in Norway and Tokyo."

"Ask the FBI," said Becky.

"Actually," Cosgrove said, "Interpol would handle things like that across borders."

"Maybe they could do an autopsy," Michael said. "Find out if they were really heart attacks, or —"

"Murder," said Becky.

"God," Michael said. "If they found out it was murder, I'd dump the screenplay idea."

"Really?" Cosgrove asked.

"With a news story like that, I could win a Pulitzer."

"Soon as we get home," Becky said, "let's contact Interpol."

"I think you're on to something," Cosgrove said. They arrived at his booth. He picked up some brochures and handed them to Becky. "These will help clarify the science."

"Doctor," Michael said, "if we need an expert to read the script, check out the science when it's done, would you give it a look?"

"I'd be delighted. So, are you two staying for the entire conference?"

Michael looked to Becky who replied, "We'll be here two nights and leave the following day."

"Then perhaps I'll see you again before you leave." They shook hands. Cosgrove stood by the booth and watched Michael and Becky walk away, hand in hand

He pulled a tiny cell phone from his breast pocket and punched in a number. "Eddie? Philip here. About the hydrogen thing, we've got a problem. " Towards the end of the conversation he said, "They're leaving day after tomorrow. We'd better have our friends here right away. Late tonight? For sure? Good." Cosgrove turned off the cell phone and put it back in his pocket.

**

A car, engine running, was parked by the front entrance of the main terminal at Las Vegas Airport. Dr. Cosgrove, in the driver's seat, waited nervously. He looked at his watch. It was around midnight. Victor and Ernie walked out of the entrance. Each pulled a carry-on suitcase. Cosgrove popped the trunk and they dropped the luggage in and entered Cosgrove's car. As the car pulled away, Ernie lit a cigarette.

Cosgrove made a face, pushed the button to roll down his window, and waved at the air in front of him. "Must you smoke?"

"It's either that or strangle somebody," Ernie said.

They drove on in silence for a few beats. Cosgrove was nervous. "I rented this Camry for you. Hope it's okay."

"It's fine," Victor said.

"Did our friend in Jersey settle the money question?"

"Yeah," Victor replied. "Plus, since it was on such short notice, he threw in a sweetener."

"Oh?"

"Shares in the company," Victor said.

"Good, good," Cosgrove said.

Ernie, in the back seat, leaned forward. "What about the fringe benefits?"

"The what?"

"The hookers," Ernie said.

"I spoke to the concierge at the hotel. He said to tell him a little about your preferences, and he'll take care of it."

"Preferences?" Victor asked.

Victor smiled. "Ernie here'll screw anything that walks."

Ernie interjected, "So long as she ain't got a wooden leg or a mustache."

Victor and Ernie broke out into raucous laughter. After a few silent moments, Cosgrove asked, "Have you decided how?"

"Needles are no good," Victor said. "There's two of 'em. They're too young to make it look like a heart attack anyways."

"Right, right." After a few more moments of silence, Cosgrove asked, "So, what's your plan?"

"We were thinkin'," Victor said, "maybe a stickup gone sour."

"Do you have everything you need?"

Victor shook his head, disgusted. "Ever since nine-eleven, the fuckin' security's unbelievable. Can't stash a piece in a suitcase and check it. I hadda Fedex it overnight. Be here in the morning."

"A stickup. You think that will work?"

"Happens in Vegas all the time," Victor said.

"You've been here before?"

Ernie was offended. "Whaddya think, we're a coupla hicks? Vic, how many times we seen Wayne Newton here? Four times? Five times?"

"Five, at least."

Ernie smiled, looked out the window. "Norway, Japan, California, Vegas … hey, we're buildin' up lotsa frequent flier miles." Ernie broke into laughter. They drove on, silently.

***

The next day, Becky and Michael walked through the lobby and up to the front desk. Cosgrove was standing off to the side of the lobby. Victor and Ernie stood behind him, partly concealed by a large potted palm. Cosgrove walked towards Becky and Michael, as Victor and Ernie observed.

"Hello," he said, smiling.

"Hi, Doctor Cosgrove," Becky replied.

"How's it going?"

"We saw so much yesterday and this morning, my head's swimming."

"This afternoon," Michael said, "we're just gonna relax, take in the sights."

"Well, enjoy," Cosgrove said. He walked away and directed a meaningful glance at Victor and Ernie. They nodded back.

Later, Michael and Becky walked through a crowded gambling casino, with dazzling lights, and the din of machine sounds and voices. Victor and Ernie followed, at a distance. Becky sat at a One-Armed Bandit, Michael behind her. She threw in two quarters, and had no luck. She shrugged, got up, and they walked away, arm in arm.

Later, Becky and Michael were seated in a darkened nightclub, sipping exotic mixed drinks through straws. An old-time comic, holding a cigarette, directed a world-weary look at the audience. "In the words of my old pal Lenny Bruce," he said, "welcome to the City That Never Sleeps, Lost Wages, Nevada". The audience laughed. Standing in the rear, Victor and Ernie, unsmiling, kept their eyes on the couple.

Still later, Michael and Becky, in a large crowd, watched a spectacular water show choreographed to music on an eight-acre manmade lake. The performers were singing and dancing to *Singing In The Rain*. Becky, despite her initial reluctance, was beginning to enjoy all the glitz and Michael was delighted.

Michael and Becky strolled through a hotel lobby. Following them at a distance were Victor and Ernie. They passed near a portly laughing man behind a registration table. He waved at them. "Hiya folks. C'mere." A banner on the wall behind him read: WORLD LAUGHTER TOUR.

The man handed out two tickets. "Here," he said, laughing. "Free tickets. Go on in for a few minutes." Becky and Michael shrugged. Michael took the tickets. They entered a large conference room filled with a couple of hundred smiling people. Curious, they sat down.

Standing at a lectern on stage was a laughing emcee. Behind him on the wall was a large banner: 8TH ANNUAL WORLD LAUGHTER CONFERENCE. The emcee addressed the crowd.

"Hi folks!"

The audience responded, "HI."

"Ho, ho, ho," said the emcee.

"HO, HO, HO," said the crowd.

"Ha, ha, ha, said the emcee.

"HA, HA, HA."

Everyone applauded. Becky and Michael were fascinated and dumbfounded. They looked at each other and smiled. Standing at the entrance, unsmiling, were Ernie and Victor.

Laughing, the emcee explained, "Seven years ago, a doctor in India gathered a group of people and urged them to laugh in public. It became so popular that there are now more than a thousand laughter clubs in India and the word has spread here." The audience applauded.

The laughing emcee continued, "We now have nearly five hundred laughter clubs in the USA, spreading from New York to California. Now it gives me great pleasure to introduce Doctor Kataria, the Guru of Giggles."

There was loud applause as a bearded, middle-aged man from India, with a turban, came out on stage and approached the lectern. He was laughing. "Laughing is good for you," he said. "It can raise the spirit and heal the body. Preschool children laugh 300 to 400 times a day. Adults laugh only seven to 15 times a day. We lose a lot of playfulness in our lives. And here, to bring some of that fun back, is Jim Millington, president of the Dearborn, Michigan Laugh Chapter!"

Up came Jim in a bright red shirt, a big red and white striped tie, and a funny hat. He said, "There are lots of good laughing styles. There's the He-He." He imitated a whistling, wheezing laugh. "There's the Ho-Ho." He let loose a loud guffaw, bubbling up from the stomach. Michael and Becky were now laughing along with the rest of the audience. Still laughing, Jim continued. "There's the Hee-Haw. A one-minute Hee-Haw is equal to ten minutes on the rowing machine and it's more fun." He let lose a loud HEE-HAW and Michael and Becky joined in. Everyone in the room was laughing. In the back, the Laughing Man looked at Ernie and Vic and, with his hands and body language, urged them to join in. They glared menacingly at him. He nervously looked away.

Later, Michael and Becky made their way through Madame Tussaud's "Celebrity Encounter," with more than a hundred lifelike wax figures standing around as though at a cocktail party. They pretended to be wax figures themselves, posing, making faces at each other like little kids, they played "hide-and-seek", hiding behind the figures, sticking their heads out. Nearby, stalking them, were the grotesquely lit faces of Victor and Ernie.

Later, Becky and Michael took the elevator to the top of the Eiffel Tower. The elevator held ten passengers. Squeezed in with them were Victor and Ernie and a married couple with two bratty little boys who kept pushing each other. One of the kids pushed the other, who fell back and elbowed Ernie in the groin area. Ernie winced, and elbowed the kid in the head. When the kid began to cry, Ernie gave him a fierce, dirty look and he shut up.

They emerged from the elevator, fifty stories up, overlooking the dazzling sights of Las Vegas. Tourists were looking down, pointing, chatting. Michael leaned over the edge, pointed down. Ernie and Victor, standing a few feet away, edged towards them, thinking about pushing them over the side. But other people walked by and got in the way. The two brats ran by and one of them stuck his tongue out at Ernie.

Michael pointed west towards the sun, which was just beginning to fall in the late afternoon sky. "Boy, look at that."

"Gorgeous," Becky said.

"Beck, let's rent a car, drive out into the desert, follow the sunset."

Becky looked at him, as though questioning his sanity. "We can use it tomorrow to drive to the airport." He put his arm around her. "C'mon." He pointed to the sun. "Solar power?"

***

A few minutes later, in a rented Ford, they drove away from the front of the hotel. They were soon heading west, away from Vegas, on a country highway, admiring the view, as the sun dipped below the horizon.

"God," Becky said. "It's beautiful."

In the rearview mirror, off in the distance, a Camry was approaching. Victor was driving, and Ernie, seated next to him, lit up a cigarette.

The Camry gained slowly on Michael and Becky's car. Suddenly, the Camry sped up and bumped the rear of their car. Michael and Becky were startled by the collision. "Hey," Michael yelled. He looked into the rearview mirror and Becky turned to look back. The Camry sped up again and bumped their car quite violently.

"Michael," Becky yelled, "let's get out of here."

Michael floored it and the speedometer needle moved up sharply. But the Camry also sped up and in a moment it was pulling up beside their car on the left. Michael glanced over, and Ernie, grinning at him, opened a side window and raised a gun.

"Holy shit," Michael yelled and slammed on the brakes. His car skidded to the shoulder of the road and made almost a complete turn, as the Camry hurtled by and then, brakes screeching, tried to slow down. Michael gunned his car and sped back towards Las Vegas with the Camry in hot pursuit and gaining. As they got closer to town there was a highway intersection with a traffic light. Michael sped towards the intersection, glancing anxiously into his rearview mirror. He saw the Camry pursuing him.

Ernie leaned out of his window, aimed and fired. There was a loud "ping" as the bullet ricocheted off the rear of the car.

Michael looked off to his right and spotted a huge truck approaching the intersection. The driver of the truck was smoking a cigar and enjoying some country music on his radio. He looked up ahead and saw two cars speeding towards the intersection.

The traffic light facing Michael turned orange, then red, but he kept going. The truck driver gave a loud warning honk-honk. Michael and Becky's car was just fifty yards from the intersection, speeding towards the red light. The truck, approaching from the right, was about the same distance.

As their car hurtled towards the intersection, Michael and Becky screamed. The truck driver, his eyes bulging with disbelief, pressed hard on the wheel, making a deafening honk-honk-honk. Michael and Becky's car just barely zipped across the intersection, beating the truck by a split second.

Then the truck rammed into the Camry. There was terrible screeching sound of metal on metal. The truck stopped about fifty yards past the intersection with the crushed Camry pushed a few yards ahead.

Michael slammed on the brakes. He was shaking with fear and pinched his cheeks. Satisfied that he was alive, he reached over and hugged Becky. "Are you okay, Beck?"

She nodded and caressed his face. "We'd better go back there."

Michael turned the car around and headed back to the crash scene. As they got out of their car, the truck driver came running towards them, furious. He yelled, "Didn't you see the fuckin' red light?"

Becky, just as angry, pointed towards the Camry. "They were trying to kill us!"

The truck driver, Michael and Becky walked towards the Camry, which was terribly mangled. The truck driver pulled a cell phone from his shirt pocket and punched in a number. "Police?"

Both men were dead. Victor was pinned behind the steering wheel. Ernie, seated on the passenger side, was slumped just outside the door, a bloody mess. Ernie's gun was on the ground next to him.

Next to the gun was a book of matches. Michael leaned over, picked up the matches. He read the cover, which said: BASILICO RESTAURANT. 832 MILLBURN AVE., MILLBURN, NJ. Michael opened the match book. A phone number was scribbled inside: 973-804-0022.

A police car, lights flashing, pulled up. Two officers got out of the car, guns drawn. As the truck driver explained what happened to one of the officers, the other one leaned into the Camry and opened the glove compartment. He pulled out some papers and said, "The car's rented to a Doctor Philip Cosgrove." Michael and Becky exchanged glances.

"Probably stolen," said the first officer.

Michael pocketed the book of matches.

Back in their hotel room, while Michael packed, Becky sat on the bed and dialed a phone number. "Operator. How can I help you?"

"I want to speak with one of the guests. Doctor Philip Cosgrove."

After a pause, the operator responded, "He checked out earlier this evening." Becky, mystified, put down the receiver.

***

Michael and Becky entered the reception area of the FBI office in Newark. They were greeted by two agents.

"Agent Ralph Fortson," he said. "My associate, special agent Joe Visotksi." They all nodded to each other. Fortson invited them into an office.

"What's this all about?" Fortson asked.

"Long story," said Michael.

Becky asked them, "Ever hear of hydrogen fuel cells?"

Forty minutes later, as agents Fortson and Visotski watched, Michael dialed a number. A woman's voice answered. "Short Hills Brokers."

"Where are you located?" Michael asked.

"Twenty-two hundred Morris Turnpike."

"Your hours?"

"Ten to six, Mondays through Fridays." Michael hung up.

Fortson looked at Michael. "Can you go this afternoon?"

Michael was hesitant. "I … guess."

Moments later, Michael was being fitted for a wire by Agent Visotski as Becky.

"You gonna be okay?"

"I'm scared shitless," he said, "but I'm fine otherwise."

"Michael, maybe you shouldn't—"

"I'll be fine. See you back here later."

Michael drove along in his beat-up Toyota and approached a suburban office building: Twenty-two hundred Morris Turnpike. Following at a short distance behind him was a cable TV van. Michael parked, and the van parked half a block away.

Inside, Michael exited the elevator, walked along the corridor, and spotted the door he was looking for: SHORT HILLS BROKERAGE. He entered and spoke to a receptionist, who showed him in to a small, nicely furnished office.

Standing near the desk was a big, beefy guy in his thirties, bulging out of an expensive suit. He held a copy of *The Daily Racing Form*. He folded it up, dropped it in the chair behind him. They looked at each other, puzzled, searching their memories.

Michael was shocked. "Eddie ... Eddie Weidel?"

Eddie, eyes wide, smiled, pointed at him. "Yeah, didn't you write for the school paper at West Side?"

"Yeah. Michael Stern." They shook hands.

"Jesus," said Eddie, "what's it been, fifteen years?"

"About that." Michael looked Eddie over. "Weren't you all state? I thought you were headed straight for the NFL."

Eddie shrugged. "Second year at Penn State, fucked up my knee."

Eddie pointed to a chair by the desk. Both of them sat down.

"So, Michael, you married?"

"Not quite."

"I'm on my third. You know me. One day I like veal, next day pasta, next day filet mignon." Eddie pointed to the credenza behind him and a framed photo of a woman. "This one may stick though. I'm slowin' down."

Michael turned pale, broke into a sweat. Eddie looked at him, concerned. "You okay?"

"Something I ate at lunch." Michael rose from his seat. "Let me go to the john. Be right back."

Michael, fully dressed, sat on a toilet seat, depressed, not sure what to do. He reached over to the toilet paper roll, tore off some paper, and wiped his forehead. He checked the wire under his shirt and returned to Eddie's office.

"You okay, man?"

"I'm fine. Thanks."

"You sure?" Eddie pointed to a desk drawer. "I got some Rolaids."

"No, I'm fine." Michael looked around. "Nice office. And Short Hills. Wow!"

"Ever hear of Willie Sutton, the gentleman bank robber from Chicago?" Michael drew a blank, but Eddie continued. "After a bunch o' bank heists, the cops arrest the dude. On the way to court a reporter asks him, 'Willie, why do you keep robbing banks?' Eddie looked at Michael. "D'ya know what Willie answered?" Michael shrugged. "Willie said, 'Why do I rob banks? 'Cause that's where the money is.'" Eddie gestured, winked. "Lotsa dough to invest here in Short Hills. I'm talkin' big dough. By the way, what kinda work do you do?"

"I'm a reporter. Jersey City Record."

"Ah, still in the same field. You write financial stuff?"

"Nah. Just general assignment."

The Cable TV van was parked on a street near the office. Inside, agents Fortson and Visotski, and an FBI technician were listening to the conversation.

"So," said Eddie, "What's up?"

"I came into some money recently."

Eddie, kidding, asked, "D'ya rob a bank?"

"Actually, I hit the lottery."

"Wow!"

"Not the big one. I've got maybe ten thousand and I want to make it grow."

"You're smart. Not like some dopes puttin' it up their nose. Believe me, I been there." Eddie looked around as though to make sure no one is listening. "Don't go spreading this around, but since you're an old high school buddy, I've got a way to make that grow real fast."

"Really?"

"There's a tech stock."

"Tech?"

"Technology. It's gonna be very hot."

"Uh-huh."

"A new kind of energy. From hydrogen."

"Uh-huh."

"Don't ask me how the fuck it works. All I know is it's gonna be a real winner."

"Uh-huh."

The receptionist looked in, knocked on the door. "Excuse me. Doctor Philip Cosgrove calling. Says it's urgent." Michael stiffened.

"Gotta take this," said Eddie. "Be a minute."

"Philip, back from Vegas? I got someone in the office right now. A client. I'll ring you back in a coupla minutes ... promise. Okay buddy."

Eddie hung up. "Sorry. Where were we?"

"You were telling me about this great tech stock."

"Right." Eddie leaned forward. "This company, H-Ron, nobody's ever heard o' them. When they announce their new discovery in a coupla weeks their stock's gonna go through the roof! From pennies a share to at least ten bucks."

"Is that right?"

"This is big time stuff."

"So if I put ten thousand in—"

"You could be lookin' at maybe half, or a million."

"Aren't there a lot of these tech companies doing the same kind of research?"

"Sure," said Eddie. "But these guys at H-Ron have the inside track."

"What if, say a few months after their announcement, another company comes along and comes up with something even better?"

Eddie was thoughtful for a second. "That could happen."

"So wouldn't the value of our shares fall?"

Then Eddie brightened. "Sure. But way before that we sell our shares and walk away with the profits."

"When is this announcement coming?"

"Coupla weeks."

"So, if I invest now, my money's okay for a coupla weeks, and then it takes off?"

"Sure," said Eddie.

"What if between now and a coupla weeks some other company beats these guys to the punch?"

Eddie was getting impatient. "Look, do you wanna get in on this or not?"

"Yes, but this is my whole savings."

"Listen, I can't go into details. But no one is gonna beat H-Ron to the punch."

"You're sure."

Eddie smiled. "Dead sure."

"I'll mail you a check tomorrow." Michael got up, shook hands with Eddie and was about to leave.

"Michael?"

"Yeah?"

"The paper where you work. You know the guys who cover financial news?"

"I see them around."

"Once you buy your shares, it wouldn't hurt to tell 'em about this stock. You know? Goose it up a little?" He winked. "Every little bit helps."

"Right, right." Michael waved, and left.

Eddie picked up the phone, and dialed. "Hey, Philip, how are ya? Guess what? I got my first investment for the hydrogen thing. An old high school buddy. Just walked in the door. Haven't seen him in fifteen years. Yeah, just like that. He's a reporter. Maybe he can squeeze in a news item for us. Name's Stern, Michael Stern." Eddie's face turned pale. "What?" He listened, with growing concern, as Cosgrove explained who Michael was. Eddie bolted up from his desk. "Holy fuckin' shit. Listen, I'll get back to you." Eddie slammed down the phone, grabbed his briefcase, and rushed out the door. The receptionist looked up, puzzled.

As Michael pulled away in his car, Eddie hurried out the front door and walked towards his Mercedes. FBI agents Fortson and Vistotski blocked his path.

"Mister Weidel?" Fortson asked. "Eddie Weidel?"

"Sorry," Eddie said. "Never heard of him."

Vistotski flashed his FBI badge. "Can you come with us please?"

Weidel tried to bull his way past them. They grabbed him and escorted him towards the van.

Michael and Becky were now in the FBI office. The two FBI agents were helping him to disconnect his wire.

"The SEC's been looking at Weidel for a while," said Visotski. "All kinds of shady deals."

"We got the phone records," said Fortson. "When you were in Vegas, Cosgrove called Weidel, and right after that Weidel called the two hitmen."

"We've got Weidel in custody," said Visotski.

"What about Doctor Cosgrove?" Becky asked.

"Wasn't in his office. Or at home," said Visotski. "But we'll find the sonofabitch."

Michael and Becky walked outside the FBI building. He sat on a bench, looking depressed. She sat next to him.

"What's the matter?"

"I feel like shit, ratting on Eddie."

"Michael, I know he's your old high school buddy, but he tried to have us killed."

"I know, but he didn't know it was us."

"Oh, so it's okay if he has someone else murdered, but not us?"

"No, I mean ... God, I don't know. It's just I remember when he was different." Becky shook her head.

***

A few days later, Michael and Becky drove up in a car to the front of the Golden Years Tower building in Jersey City. They got out of the car and entered the lobby.

"The homeless guy I interviewed a few weeks ago, I got him on a waiting list for this place. Suddenly there was an opening." As they waited in the lobby, the door opened. In walked the social worker, Valerie Cruz, arm in arm with the homeless man, Johnny Mills.

"Valerie Cruz, this is my fiancée, Becky McLean."

Becky did a double take at the word "fiancée."

"You're marrying a real nice guy, Becky."

"And this," said Michael, "is Mr. Johnny Mills." Johnny nodded.

Valerie spoke as though to a young child. "Shall we go in and check it out, "Johnny?" He nodded again. They entered an elevator to the third floor. Valerie led them along the corridor to a door, pulled out a key, and opened it. It was a sunny, cheerful studio apartment, sparsely, but adequately furnished. Valerie led Johnny around, showing him the kitchenette, the closet, the TV.

Michael told Becky, "I picked up a lot of the stuff at the Salvation Army. They have nice things there."

Valerie took Johnny by the arm. "This is your new home, Johnny."

Johnny looked around, tears in his eyes. He embraced Valerie. "It reminds me of my place in Prague." He embraced Michael. "Thank you so much. Soon I'll have you all over for dinner. Cornish hens with a fine sauvignon blanc." Now tears welled in Michael's eyes

As Becky and Michael left the building, they walked along a bit, and then she stopped. "What's this about 'fiancée?"

"After four years, isn't it about time?"

"You're proposing?"

"Yes."

She stared at him. "You're kidding."

Michael dropped to one knee. "I'm dead serious."

A man reading a newspaper walked by, looked and smiled. Becky was embarrassed. In a loud whisper she said, "Michael."

"I'll stash my typewriter in a closet," said Michael, "and buy a computer."

"Michael."

"I'll even open an email account."

"Michael. Get up!"

"And buy a cellphone. And even an iPod."

Across the street a teenage girl and a boy were watching, and laughing. The boy, imitating Michael, suddenly dropped to his knees and mimed dramatically as though he were begging. The girl pulled off his cap and slapped him in the head with it. From a window in the house nearby, an elderly woman looked out and applauded.

***

At Rick's bar that evening, someone was playing *As Times Goes By* on the piano. Michael and Becky sat at a table in a quiet corner.

She shook her head, sadly. "I don't know."

Michael reached over, took her hand. "Why?"

"I've told you."

"Just because your Mom and Dad divorced when you were a kid."

"You don't have any idea how that affected me. Your parents were together forever."

"I know, I know."

"It seems that nothing lasts."

"Beck, everything in life is a gamble. You know that."

Tears welled in her eyes, she looked at him tenderly."

"Beck," he said, "I wanna grow old with you. We can sit on a porch in rocking chairs and I'll look over at you, and ask, 'Did we eat yet?'"

Becky smiled.

"Sweetheart," he said, "without you ... you're my rock." Michael shrugged, made a funny face, and wiggled his eyebrows up and down.

Becky smiled. "Okay, when?"

"How about next month?"

Becky was startled. "What?"

"Your classes end the first week of May, right?"

"Yes."

"I can get another week off."

"What about my folks in Chicago? My sister in Chapel Hill? Your Mom in Florida? There are so many arrangements."

"Do you really wanna go through all that stuff? Mailing out invitations? And a gown? And a caterer?"

"Not really."

"Beck, let's just get married." They rose from the table and hugged.

***

That night, Michael and Becky were in bed. Michael lay on his side, eyes closed. Becky, lay face up, wide awake, smiling. She giggled. Michael, half asleep, asked, "What?"

"I'm remembering our first date."

"Uh-huh."

"We were having coffee, in that diner."

"Uh-huh."

"And after the stuff about jobs, and favorite movies, and favorite things to do ..."

"Yeah."

"... you asked me about toilet paper."

Michael stirred, turned towards her. "Did I?"

"You asked me if, when I replace my roll of toilet paper, do I do it this way," she motioned palm down, "or this way?" She motioned palm up. "And I said this way." She motioned palm down. "And you broke into this big smile and said you did it the same way."

"Oh yeah."

"What would have happened if I'd said this way?" She motioned palm up. After a moment's silence, "Would you have asked me out again?" More silence. "Would you?"

"Well," said Michael, "I don't know."

"So, you would have stopped seeing me?"

"You've gotta understand," he said. "Having done this all my life," he motioned palm down. "It would have been a tremendous adjustment, sitting on the john, day after day, year after year, having to do this," he motioned palm up. Then he reached over, hugged Becky, and kissed her on the cheek. "Isn't it great that we've got so much in common?"

***

Michael and Becky, nicely dressed, entered Rick's Bar. Ramon at the piano, smiling, began to play *"As Time Goes By."* It was a slow weekday night, and there were just a couple dozen patrons, but they all stood and applauded.

Near the piano was a gray-haired woman minister, holding a Bible. Standing next to the Minister was Valerie Cruz, the social worker. Becky looked to Michael, amazed.

"You did all this?"

Michael smiled proudly. He led her up to the Minister, who extended her hand to Becky.

"Ethel Simmons, Unitarian Church in Hoboken." Becky shook her hand. The Minister looked around. "Your witnesses?" Valerie Cruz, the social worker, was standing next to Becky. She raised her hand.

A flustered looking Bermuda Schwartz hurried in. "Sorry, the PATH train was delayed." Schwartz looked around, bewildered. "This is it?"

"This is it," said Michael. "Just in time."

Schwartz walked up to Michael. "Mr. Schwartz, this is my bride, Becky McLean."

He sized her up, "A real *shayna maidel*. An angel. Mazel tov."

"And this is our friend, Valerie Cruz, who is also a witness."

He sized her up and smiled even wider. "You look just like Dolores Del Rio, the movie star of years ago. That's when Hollywood was Hollywood."

"I've seen her on AMC," she said.

He gave her another look. "Are you married, Valerie?"

She laughed. "Boy, these New Yorkers don't waste any time."

"At my age," he said, "I can't afford to waste time."

They all got a laugh over that one. Schwartz looked at the Minister. "Maybe we can have two weddings for the price of one."

Valerie enjoyed his joking. "I like this guy."

The Minister performed the brief ceremony. Michael and Becky exchanged rings. "And now," she said, "since the groom is Jewish, I thought we'd add a little ecumenical touch." She reached over to a table, picked up a wineglass and wrapped it in a white linen towel. "To complete the ceremony, the groom will smash the glass with his feet." She put the glass down at Michael's feet, and nodded to him. Nervous, Michael stomped down on the glass; it rolled out of the towel, and across the floor. There was a collective gasp from the spectators. Ramon covered his mouth to stop from laughing. Michael, determined, ran after the glass as though it were an evasive cockroach, and stomped again, crushing the glass. Everyone smiled and applauded. Michael, looking sheepish, shrugged his shoulders. Becky looked at Michael adoringly and gave him a big kiss.

There was more applause as Ramon began to play the piano and sing "The things I LONG for are simple and FEW-ooh ... A cup o' CAW-fee, a sandwich and YOO-ooh!"

Later, as people were drinking and eating, Schwartz tapped Michael on the shoulder. "What about your screen play?"

"I'm working on it."

Becky interrupted. "Not during our honeymoon."

Schwartz took Valerie by the arm. "I love rice and beans. The black beans, especially."

"*Frijoles negros.*"

"Yeah, and those cooked bananas."

"Plantains."

"Right. Do you like potato pancakes?"

"Actually, I do. With gobs of apple sauce."

Schwartz's face lit up. "It's a match made in heaven."

***

In the living room of Becky and Michael's apartment later that night, Ramon sat on the sofa, petting Mister the cat. He yelled into the bedroom, "I'll watch Mister while you're gone, won't I Mister?" He hugged the cat.

"Thanks so much, Ramon," said Becky as she and Michael kept packing. "So where the hell are we going?"

"All I'll say now is pack a bathing suit."

"Ooh, the Bahamas?" He shook his head no.

"Puerto Rico?" He shook no again.

"Cayman Islands?" Another no.

"It's a place with energy," he said. "Lots of energy."

"Energy?" she asked.

The doorbell rang. Ramon shouted, "I'll get it."

Ramon opened the door. Doctor Cosgrove stood there, unshaven, disheveled, eyes glazed over. He was holding a handgun. He mumbled, "Is this Becky McLean's place?"

Ramon stared at the gun. "Yes."

Cosgrove mumbled again, "May I come in?"

Ramon backed away and Cosgrove entered. Ramon, voice trembling, called out, "Becky! Michael! You have ... *una visita!*"

Michael and Becky came in from the bedroom. They froze when they saw Cosgrove. He waved the gun at them, motioned for them to sit. Michael, Becky and Ramon huddled close together on the sofa. Cosgrove slumped down in a large easy chair opposite them. Mister the cat hopped up on the sofa and stared at Cosgrove.

Ramon whispered to Michael, "Who is this *loco?*"

Michael whispered back, "Bad news."

Becky said, "Doctor Cosgrove."

He interrupted. "It all was going to be so wonderful."

"Listen," said Michael.

Cosgrove glared at Becky and Michael. "Until you two fucked it up."

Ramon, indignant, said "Hey, watch your tongue."

Becky reached over to calm Ramon. "Doctor Cosgrove," she said, "we didn't mean—"

"After fifteen years of sweat and toil I've made a fantastic breakthrough."

"That's wonderful," she said.

"A cost-effective way to extract hydrogen from seawater. Or recycled water. Or even from garbage. Using solar energy. The end product? Fuel, and water. Inexhaustible. Non-polluting!" Cosgrove entered a half-dreamy state. "It was going to be called *The Cosgrove Process*. In honor of me and of my father, Clarence Cosgrove."

Michael tried to interject, "But we—"

"Then I heard these three idiots at Hydrogenics had stumbled onto something similar, perhaps better. There's no second best in this business. Who remembers the guy who almost beat Edison to the light bulb?"

Becky tried to console him. "Doctor Cosgrove ..."

Cosgrove rested the gun in his lap, stared blankly at them. "I came to apologize." Michael, Becky and Ramon stared back at him, dumbfounded. "I never meant for it to go this far. You're a nice young couple."

Michael blurted out, "We accept your apology."

"I want you to know," he said, "with Eddie Weidel it may have been greed. But with me, it wasn't greed."

"We believe you," Michael said.

Cosgrove raised the gun and waved it. They cringed. "It was immortality I wanted. Not money, you hear?"

"Yes," said Michael. "Immortality."

"Immortality. Not money." After a pause, he said, "Now, I have to do what I have to do." He raised the gun. Becky, Michael and Ramon clung to each other. He pointed the gun at his temple.

Becky yelled out, "Doctor Cosgrove, wait." He paused.

Michael asked, "Your discovery is still your discovery, right?"

"That's true."

Becky tried to calm him. "If it works—"

Offended, Cosgrove waved the gun. "Of course it works."

"Yes, of course," she said. "What I meant is, those three men are dead. You've got a clear field for your invention."

Cosgrove appeared puzzled. "That's true."

"When it's put into practice," she said, "it can change the world. Just think of the contribution you'll be making."

He shook his head. "The FBI is after me. They want to put me in jail."

"But your invention is still yours," she said.

"You think if I'm in jail, they're going to put the name 'Cosgrove' on it?"

"We can talk to them," Michael said. "Maybe part of a plea bargain."

"No, I'm a disgrace." He lifted the gun to his temple again.

"Listen," Ramon said. "Are you a Christian?"

"Yes."

"Haven't you heard of redemption?"

Cosgrove paused. Tears in his eyes. "Redemption?"

"Yes, yes. You said you're sorry. We forgive you." Ramon looked to Michael and Becky. "Don't we?" They eagerly nodded yes.

"But I can't spend the rest of my life in a jail cell. I can't." He raised the pistol to his forehead and pulled the trigger. There was a loud CLICK. Confused, he stared at the gun. Michael and Becky remained frozen in their seats.

Ramon leaped up, jumped on Cosgrove, and pinned him down. But Cosgrove kept waving the gun. Ramon, desperate, looked to Michael and Becky. *Ayuden, muchachos!*

Becky seized Cosgrove's arm. The gun fired, and shattered the head of a porcelain cat on a shelf. Mister, the cat, jumped up, hid beneath the couch, and stared out.

Michael pried the gun away from Cosgrove and sent it skittering across the floor to the opposite wall. Michael and Ramon sat on top of Cosgrove as Becky scrambled over to the telephone.

Cosgrove was crying. "God, I can't do anything right."

Ramon patted him on the shoulder. "There, there. You'll be okay."

Becky dialed the phone. "FBI?"

Michael looked admiringly at Ramon. "You were terrific."

Ramon gave him a dig in the ribs and winked. "Three years in the U.S. Marine Corps." Ramon gazed off into the distance, reminiscing. "Ah, those were the days. And nights!"

***

Michael and Becky walked through the JFK Airport terminal a few days later, each of them pulling a carry-on suitcase. He was smiling, enjoying his secret.

"Michael, where are we …?"

They approached the counter of Icelandic Airways. Michael stopped abruptly and made a dramatic wave of the arm. "Da-DAH."

Becky was intrigued. "Iceland? But—"

"I looked it up on the Internet at the office," he said.

As Michael pulled the tickets out of his pocket and gave them to the counter clerk, Becky looked at him, amazed. "You went on the Internet?" He smiled, proudly. "Michael, you're becoming a techie nerd." He nodded.

"But why Iceland?"

"You'll see."

As she approached the corridor leading to the plane, she stopped and asked, "A bathing suit? Iceland?"

"You'll see."

Becky pulled out her cell phone, and dialed. "Ramon? Is Mister okay? Great!" Becky put the phone close to Michael.

He yelled, "Hi Ramon."

Becky took the phone back. "Listen, Michael's taking me to Iceland." Becky giggled at Ramon's reply. "No, Ramon, I don't have any *cojones* to freeze off." Michael tugged at her arm, pulling her into the corridor.

***

A sunny day in Reykjavik, Iceland. Michael and Becky, wearing bathing suits, had covered themselves with heavy robes. They stood indoors looking through a picture window at The Blue Lagoon, a spectacular sight. Blue water steamed up in the air. Off in the distance, white fleecy clouds floated in a brilliant blue sky. Low dark cliffs were visible in the background. A few dozen people, in bathing suits, were wading or swimming in the water, as though they were in the tropics.

Michael took Becky by the hand. They opened and walked through a thick glass door, stepping gingerly onto a deck overlooking the lagoon. It was chilly. They were both shivering.

"Michael, I don't know if this is such a good idea."

"Trust me, sweetie. I read all about it."

"I know. On the Internet."

"Did you know that in Iceland they use hydrogen fuel cells to run the buses? And the power plants are run by—"

"Michael, I'm freezing."

Michael took off his robe and let loose a loud "WHOOP." He ran and jumped into the water. Becky slowly removed her robe, and hesitatingly approached the water. She was shivering.

"I can't do this, Michael."

Michael blew her a kiss, and waved her in. She jumped into the water. It was warm, steaming. She was amazed.

"This is wonderful."

"Natural geothermal heat," Michael said. Holding her close, Michael raised a "professorial" finger, as if to deliver a lecture. "If you're not sure what 'geothermal' is, I can explain."

Becky splashed water in his face. Holding each other's nose, they submerged in the warm water, then leapt upward, and laughed.

About the Author

Kal Wagenheim (born in Newark, N.J.in 1935) is a journalist (formerly with The New York Times and currently editor of Caribbean UPDATE monthly newsletter), author and translator of eight books, and ten plays and screenplays. His biography of Babe Ruth was a Playboy Book Club selection and was adapted for an NBC-TV film. His biography of Roberto Clemente, first published years ago, was reissued in 2010 by Markus Wiener Publishers of Princeton NJ. His novel, **"The Secret Life Of Walter Mott" was published in July 2010 by All Things That Matter Press.** His plays, "Bavarian Rage", "We Beat Whitey Ford", "Coffee With God", and "Wegotdates.com" have been produced Off-Off-Broadway. His poetry and fiction have been published in online literary magazines jersey.com and PulpLit.com. He has also taught creative writing at Columbia University (as an Adjunct Associate Professor) and the State Prison in Trenton NJ (as a volunteer).

Member: PENAmericanCenter and The Dramatists Guild of America. Film producers may access his screenplays on the website www.inktip.com. Website: www.kalwagenheim.com

www.ingramcontent.com/pod-product-compliance
Lightning Source LLC
Chambersburg PA
CBHW051653260626
47170CB00004B/1476